The Amazing CRAFTY CAT

The Amazing Crafty Cat

Charise Mericle Harper

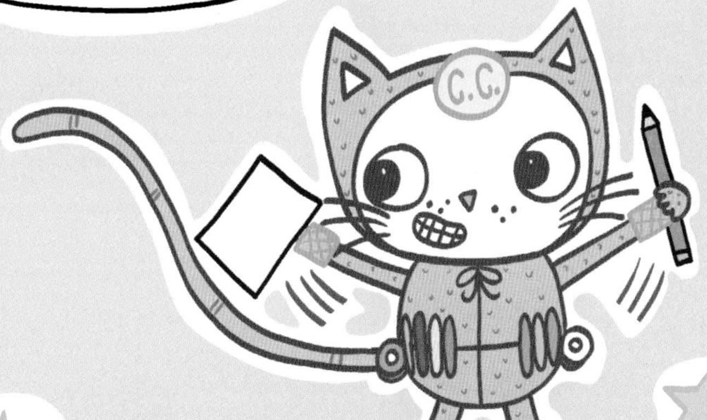
C.C.

:01
First Second
New York

First Second

Copyright © 2017 by Charise Mericle Harper
Published by First Second
First Second is an imprint of Roaring Brook Press, a division
of Holtzbrinck Publishing Holdings Limited Partnership
175 Fifth Avenue, New York, New York 10010

Library of Congress Control Number: 2016938573

ISBN: 978-1-62672-486-0

Our books may be purchased in bulk for promotional, educational,
or business use. Please contact your local bookseller or the
Macmillan Corporate and Premium Sales Department at (800) 221-7945
ext. 5442 or by e-mail at MacmillanSpecialMarkets@macmillan.com.

FIRST
EDITION

First edition 2017
Book design by Joyana McDiarmid
Printed in China by Toppan Leefung Printing Ltd.,
Dongguan City, Guangdong Province

1 3 5 7 9 10 8 6 4 2

Sketched, inked, and colored on a Cintiq
in Photoshop with a digital nib.

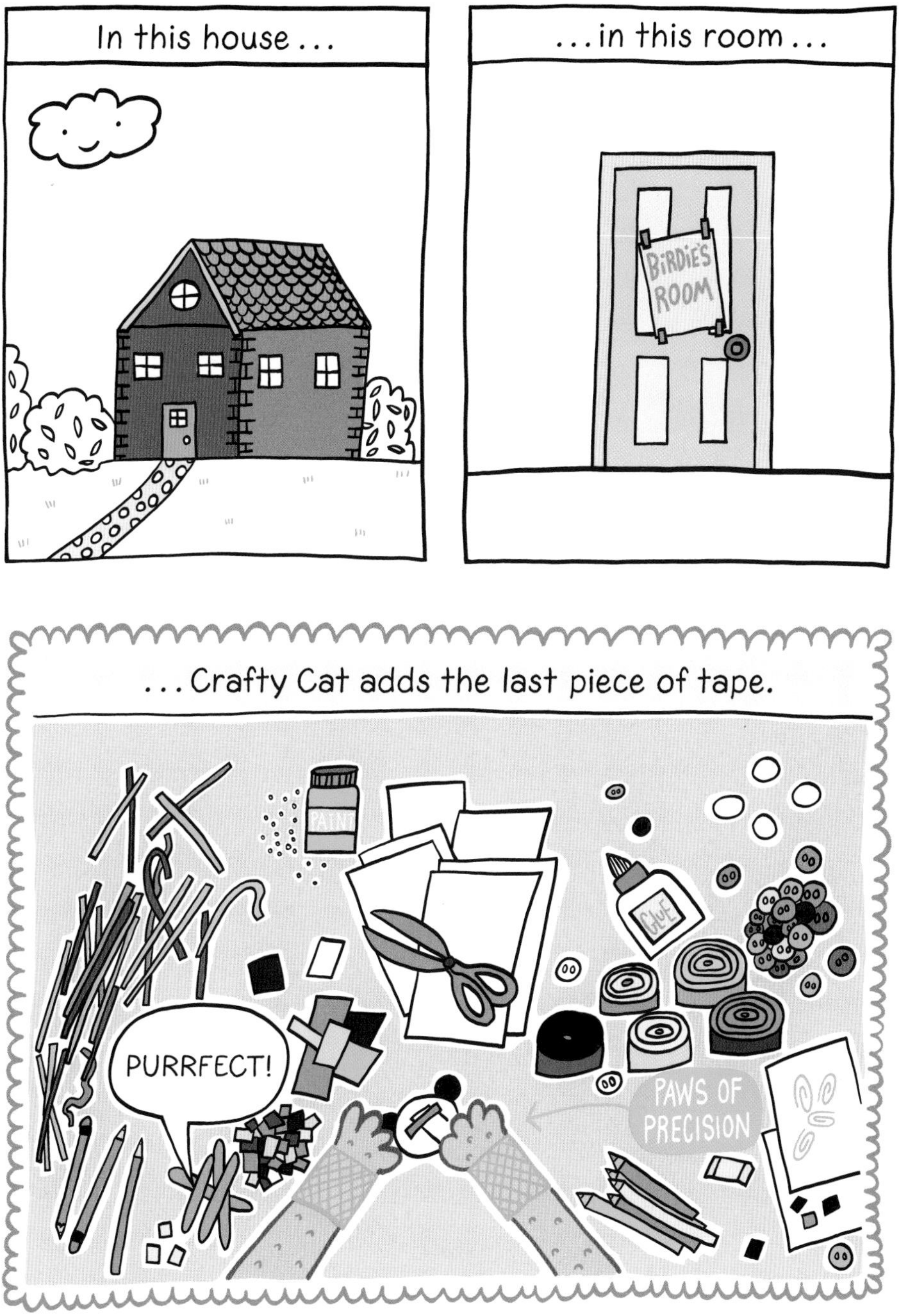
In this house...
...in this room...
BIRDIE'S ROOM
...Crafty Cat adds the last piece of tape.
PAINT
GLUE
PURRFECT!
PAWS OF PRECISION

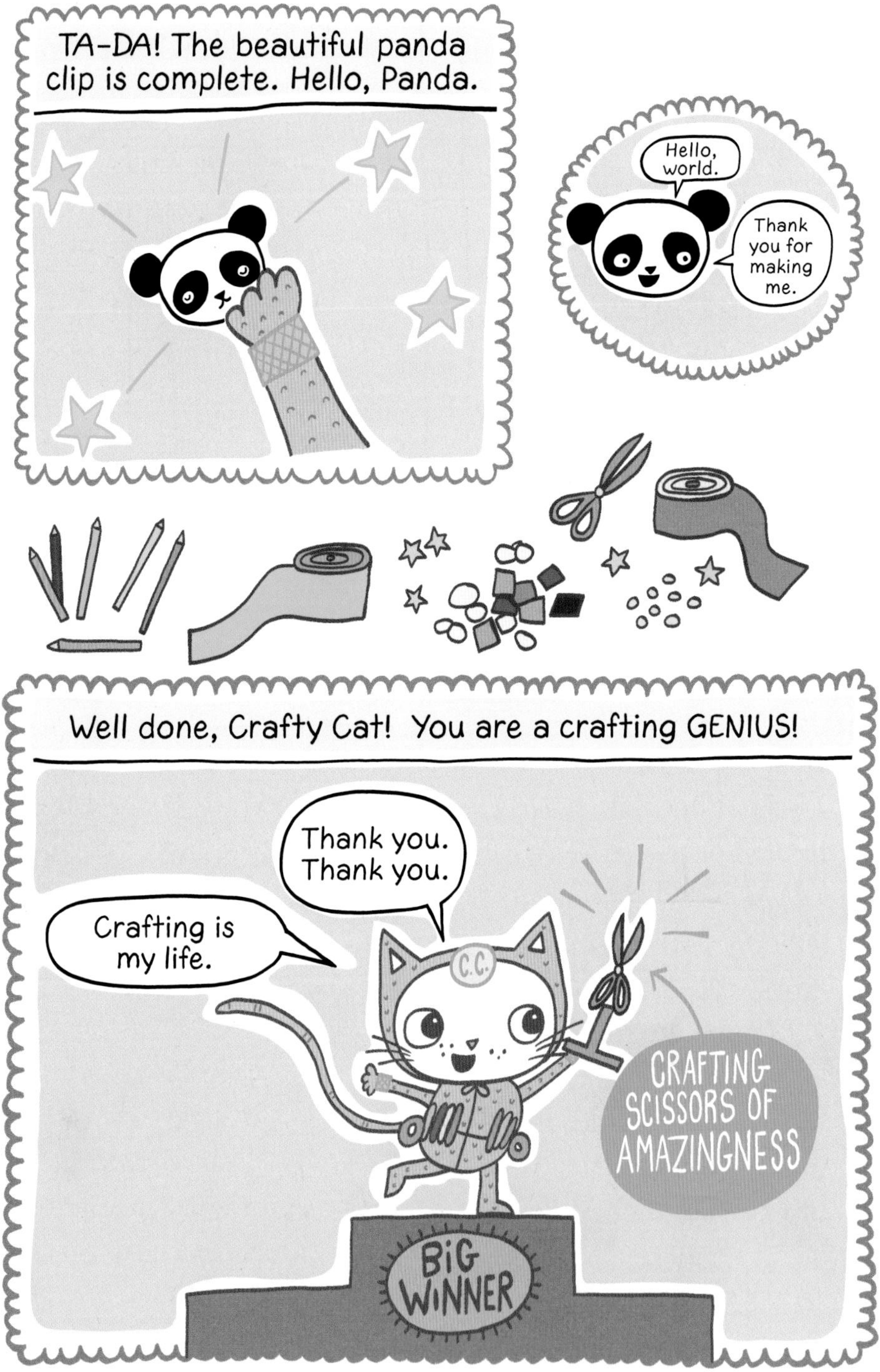
TA-DA! The beautiful panda clip is complete. Hello, Panda.
Hello, world.
Thank you for making me.
Well done, Crafty Cat! You are a crafting GENIUS!
Thank you. Thank you.
Crafting is my life.
C.C.
CRAFTING SCISSORS OF AMAZINGNESS
BIG WINNER

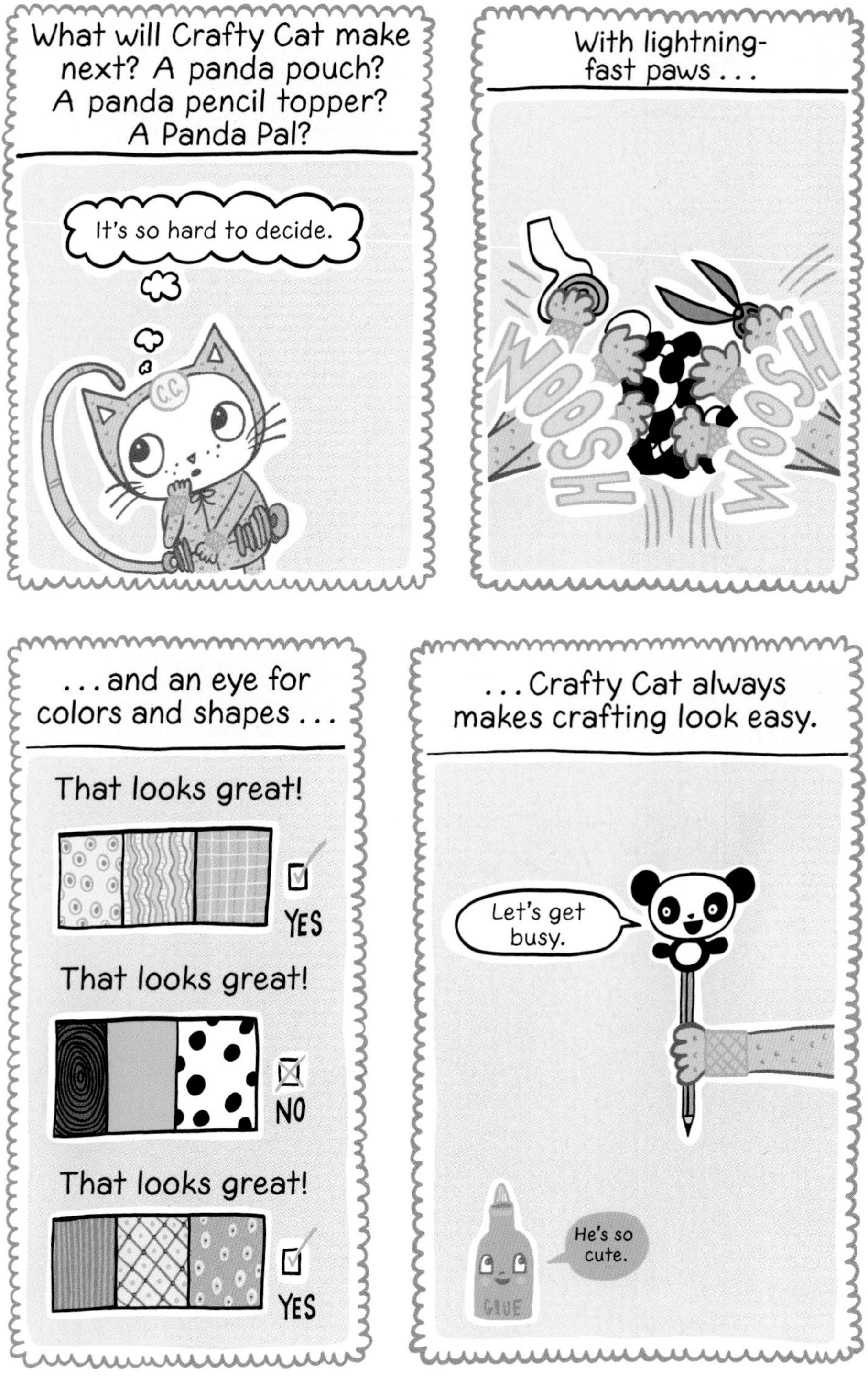
What will Crafty Cat make next? A panda pouch? A panda pencil topper? A Panda Pal?
It's so hard to decide.
C.C.
With lightning-fast paws . . .
WOOSH
WOOSH
. . . and an eye for colors and shapes . . .
That looks great!
YES
That looks great!
NO
That looks great!
YES
. . . Crafty Cat always makes crafting look easy.
Let's get busy.
He's so cute.
GLUE

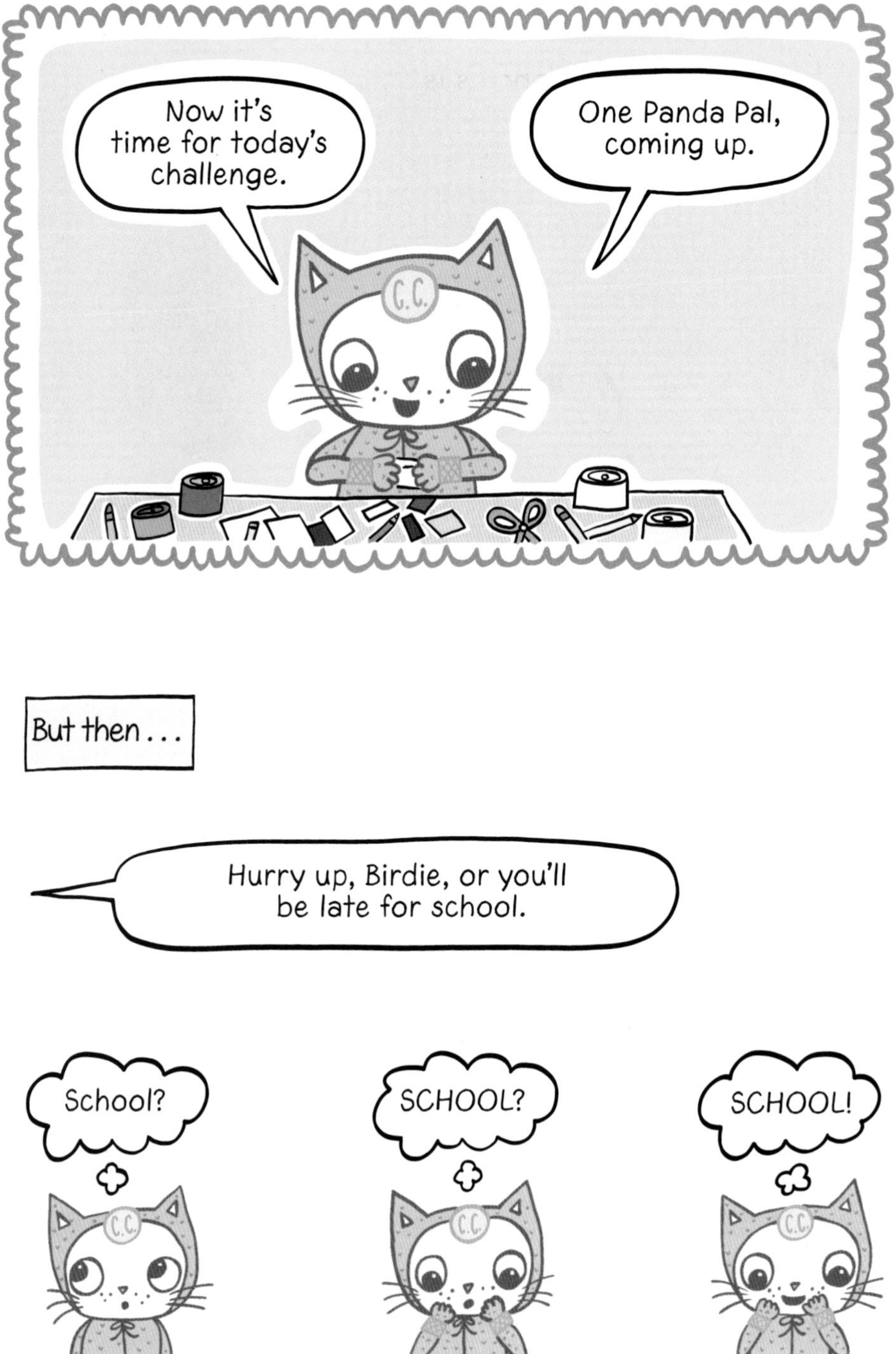
Now it's time for today's challenge.
One Panda Pal, coming up.
But then . . .
Hurry up, Birdie, or you'll be late for school.
School?
SCHOOL?
SCHOOL!

The spell is broken.
The metamorphosis is quick but backward.

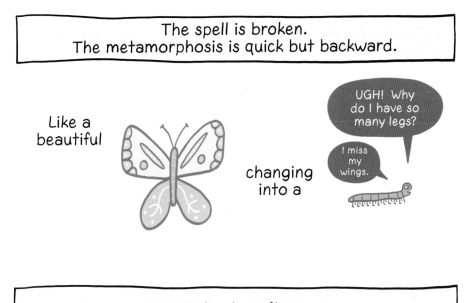

Like a beautiful

changing into a

UGH! Why do I have so many legs?

I miss my wings.

But Birdie doesn't care.
There's too much to do.
Today, she won't complain about unfinished crafts.

SCHOOL!

SCHOOL!

SCHOOL!

OUTFIT?

Panda-riffic!

CUPCAKES?

Only the best can come.

HOMEWORK?

Homework?

SUPER HEAVY

I don't want to talk about it.

Oh dear!

That does look heavy.

CUPCAKES

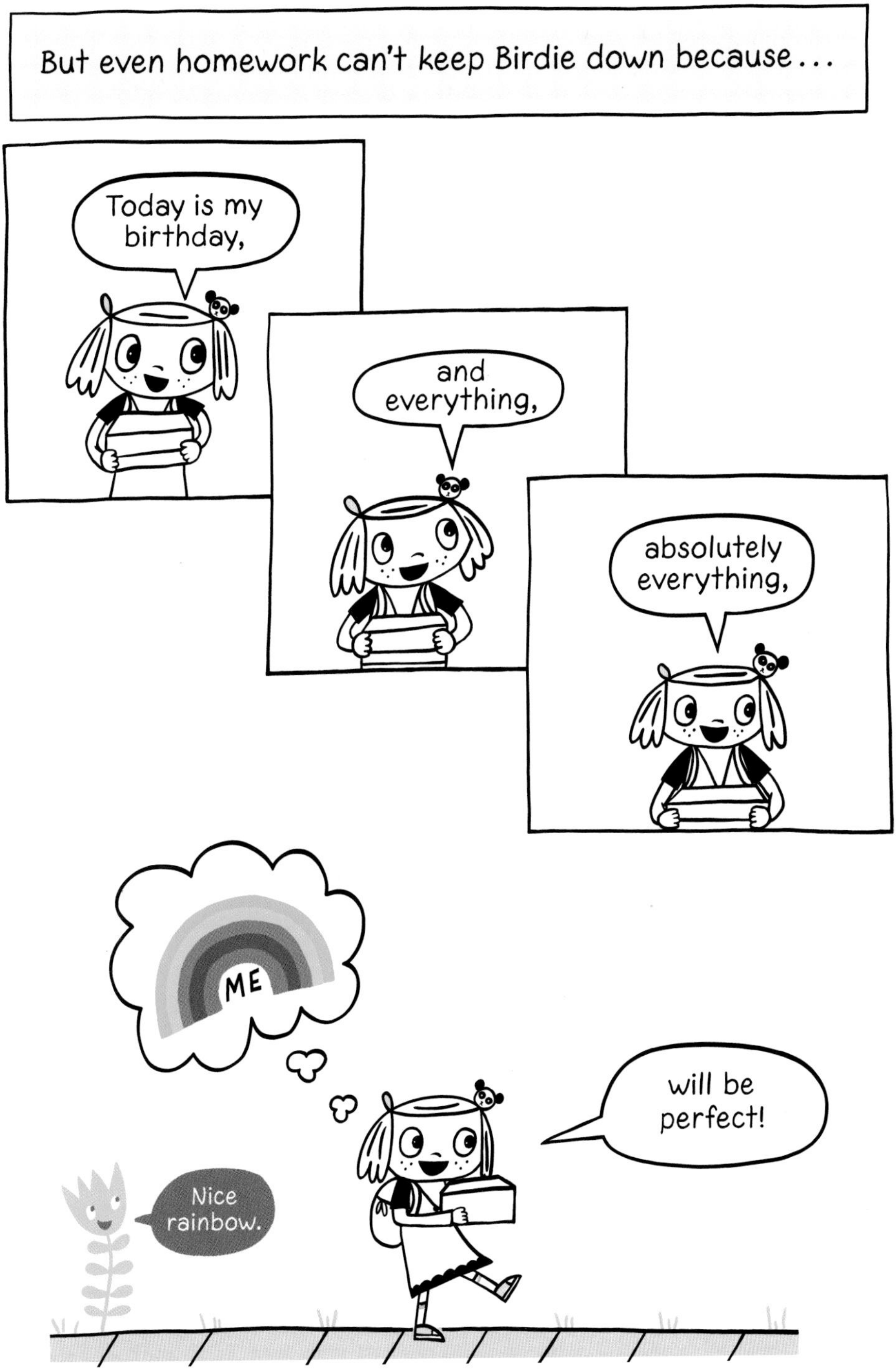
But even homework can't keep Birdie down because...
Today is my birthday,
and everything,
absolutely everything,
ME
will be perfect!
Nice rainbow.

Sometimes, imagining can be fun.

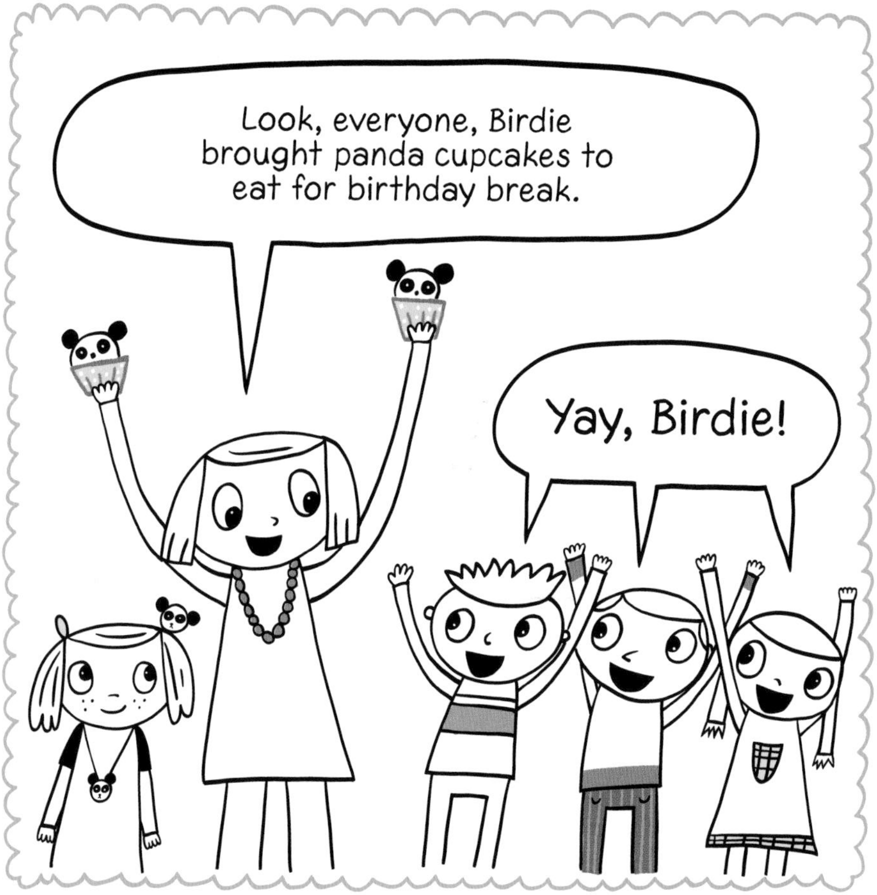
Look, everyone, Birdie brought panda cupcakes to eat for birthday break.
Yay, Birdie!

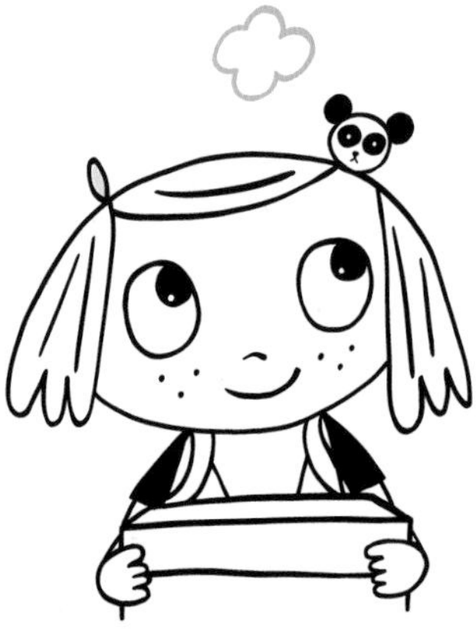

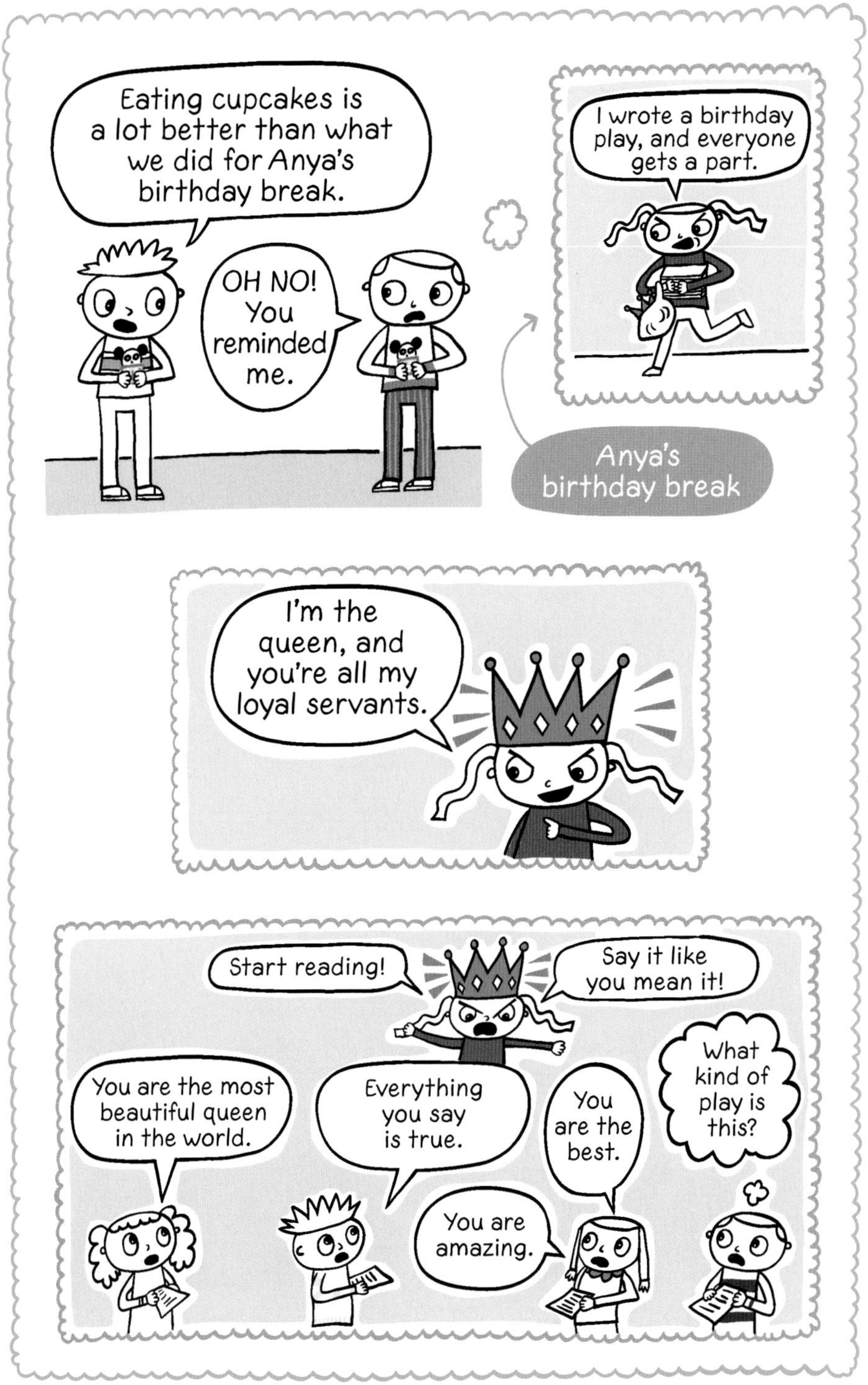

Eating cupcakes is a lot better than what we did for Anya's birthday break.
OH NO! You reminded me.
I wrote a birthday play, and everyone gets a part.
Anya's birthday break
I'm the queen, and you're all my loyal servants.
Start reading!
Say it like you mean it!
You are the most beautiful queen in the world.
Everything you say is true.
You are the best.
What kind of play is this?
You are amazing.

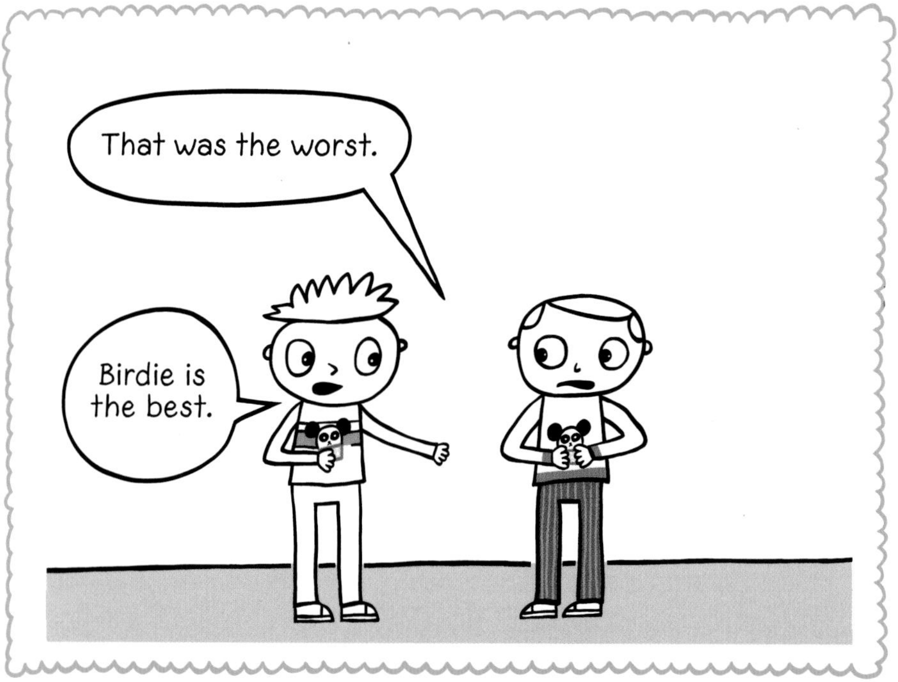
That was the worst.
Birdie is the best.

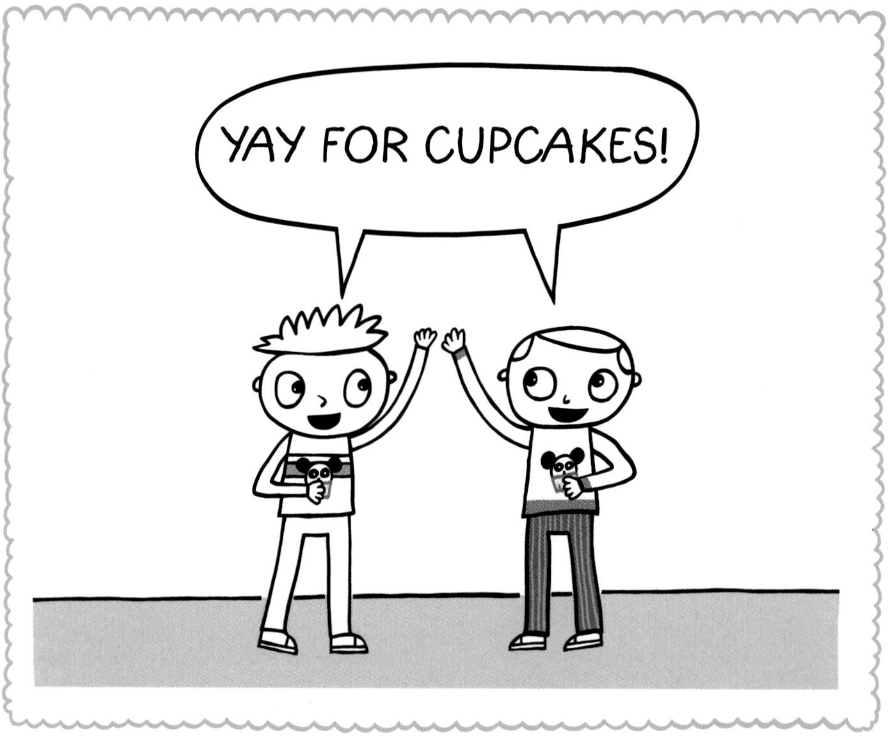
YAY FOR CUPCAKES!

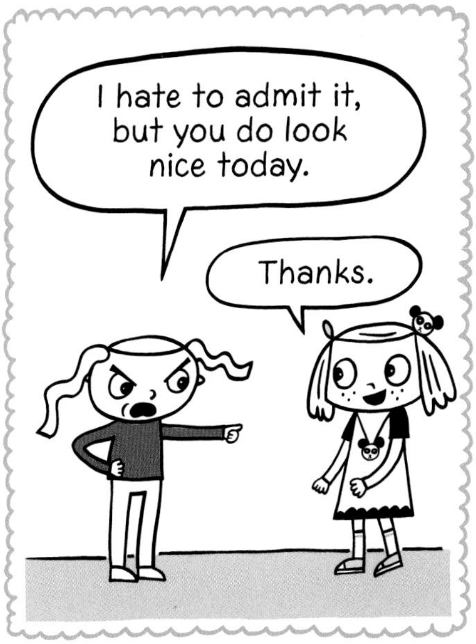
I hate to admit it, but you do look nice today.
Thanks.

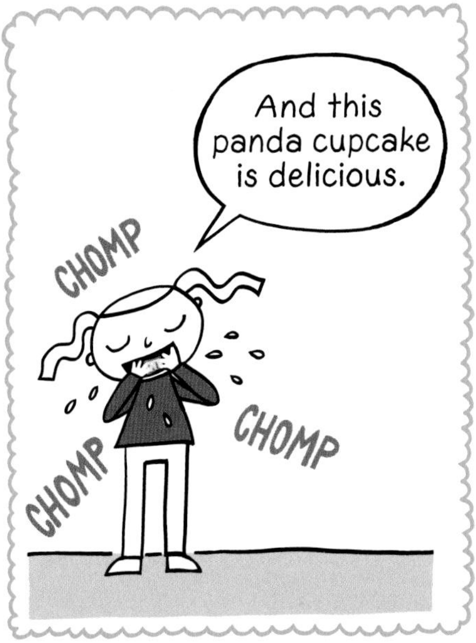
And this panda cupcake is delicious.
CHOMP
CHOMP
CHOMP

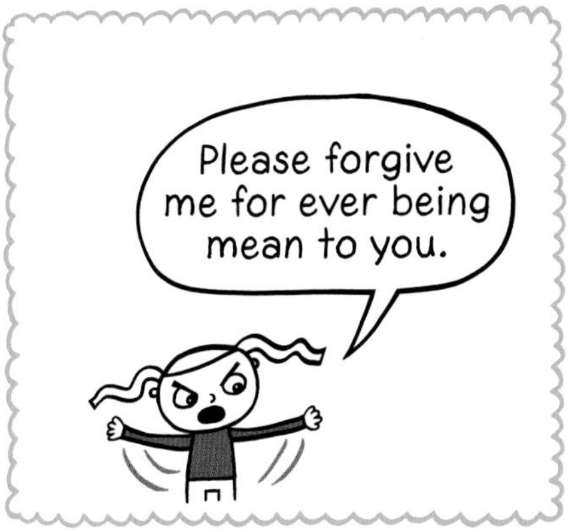
Please forgive me for ever being mean to you.

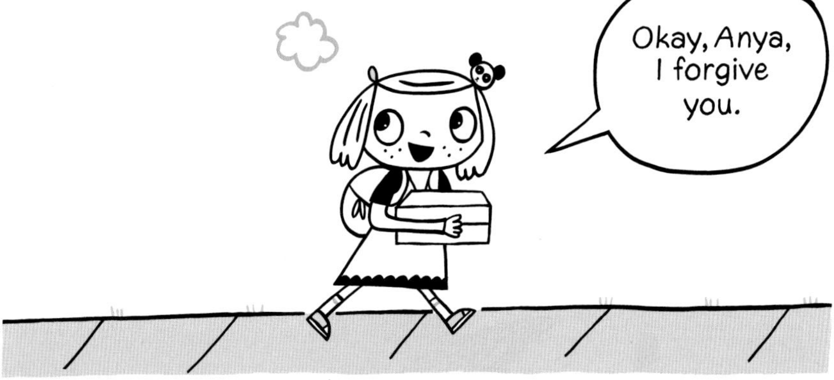
Okay, Anya, I forgive you.

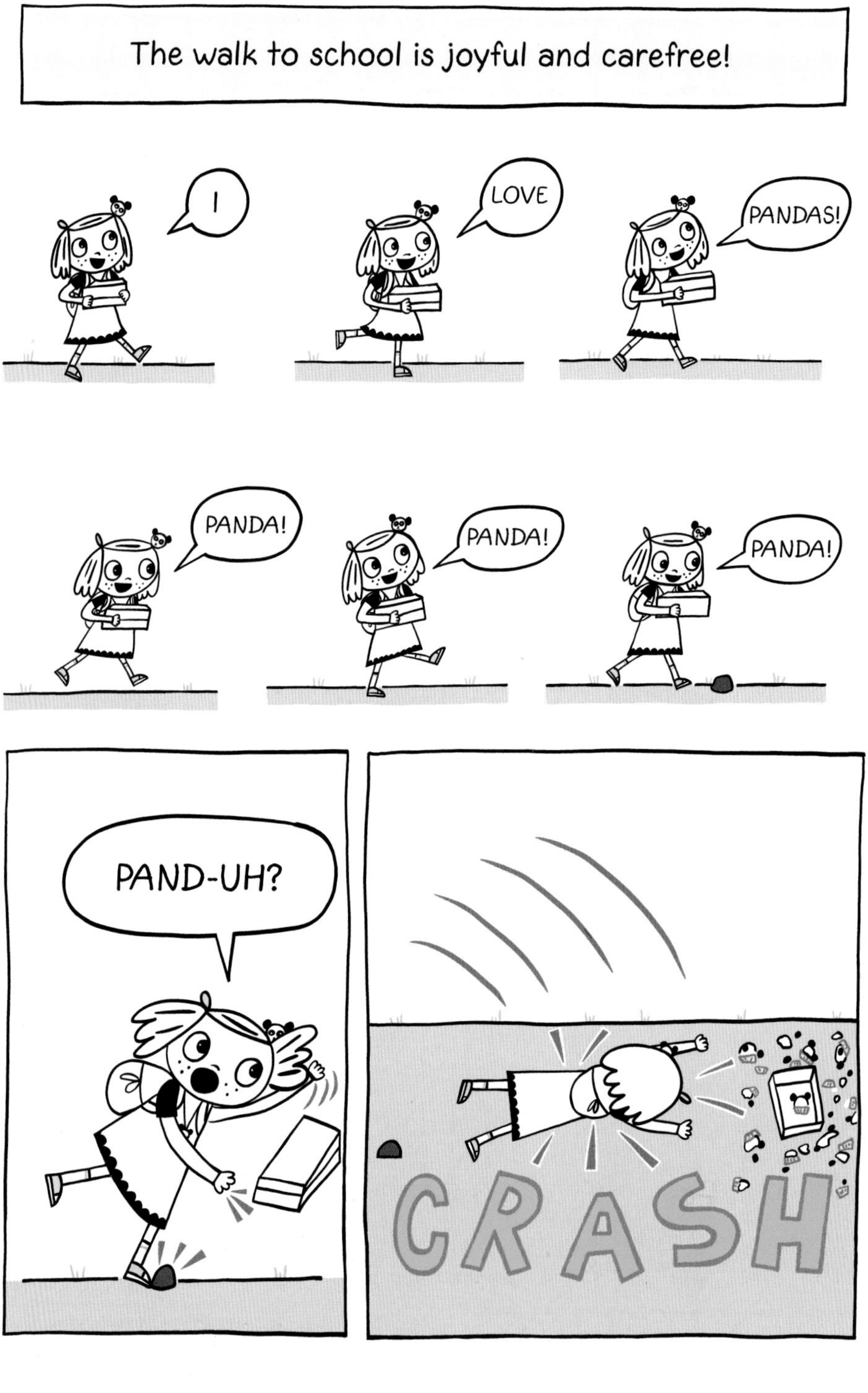

The walk to school is joyful and carefree!
I
LOVE
PANDAS!
PANDA!
PANDA!
PANDA!
PAND-UH?
CRASH

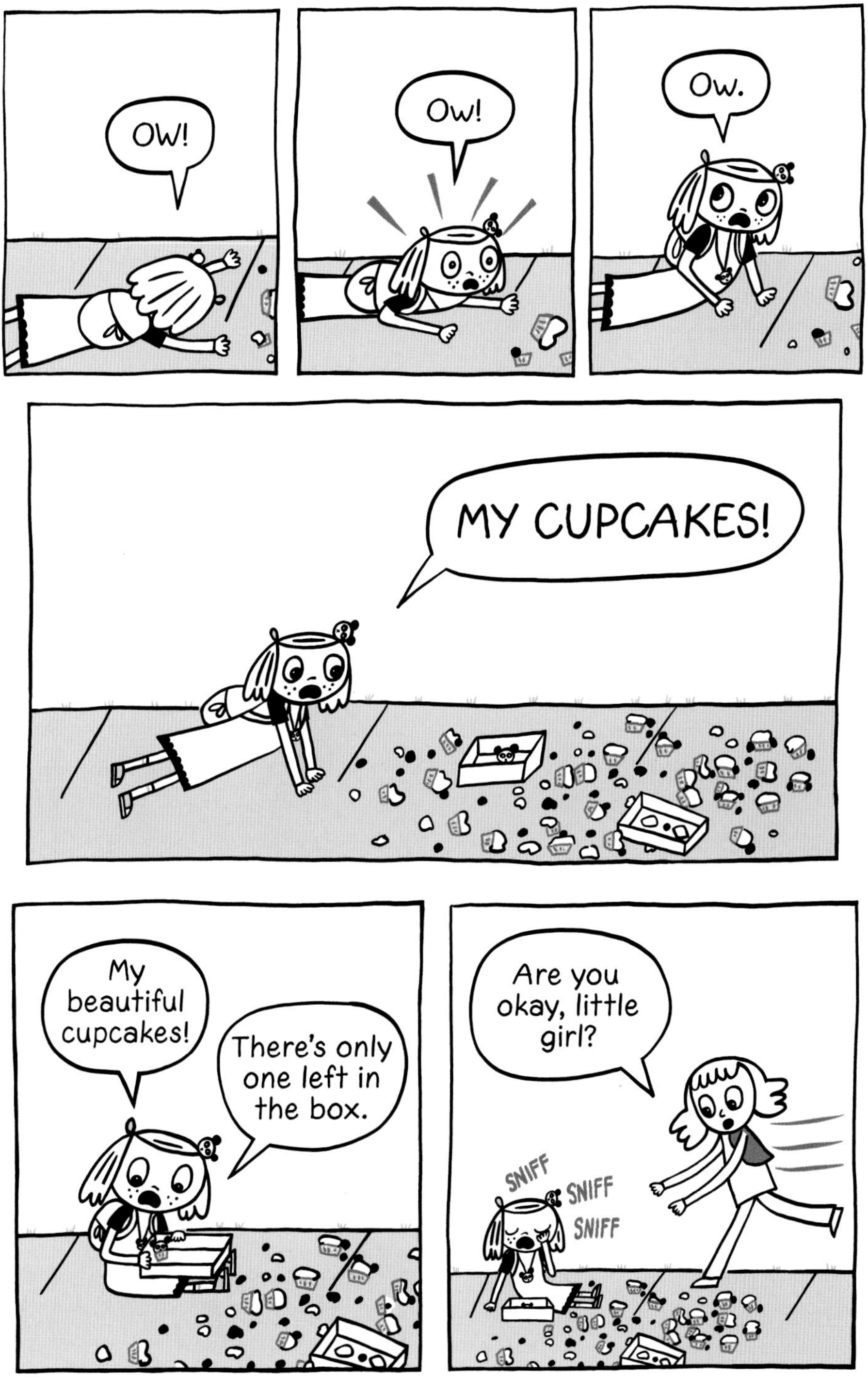
OW!
Ow!
Ow.
MY CUPCAKES!
My beautiful cupcakes!
There's only one left in the box.
Are you okay, little girl?
SNIFF
SNIFF
SNIFF

The lady is a Good Samaritan. That means she cares about helping people.

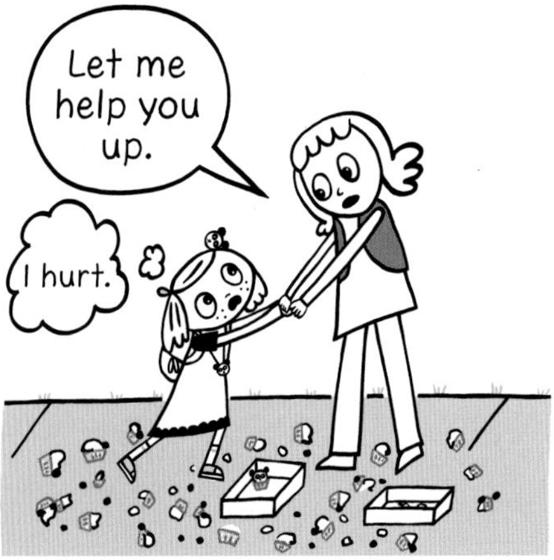
Let me help you up.
I hurt.

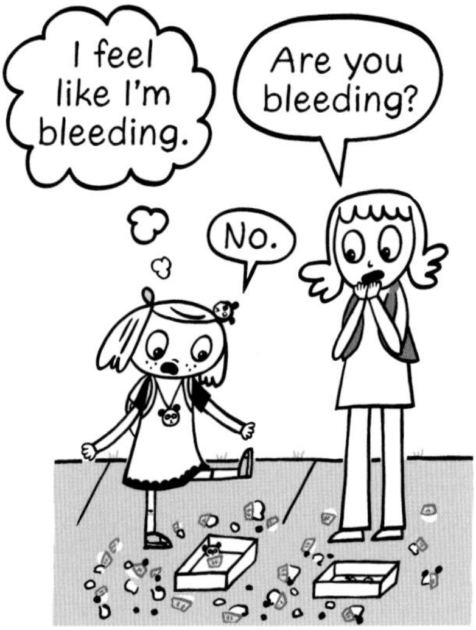
I feel like I'm bleeding.
Are you bleeding?
No.

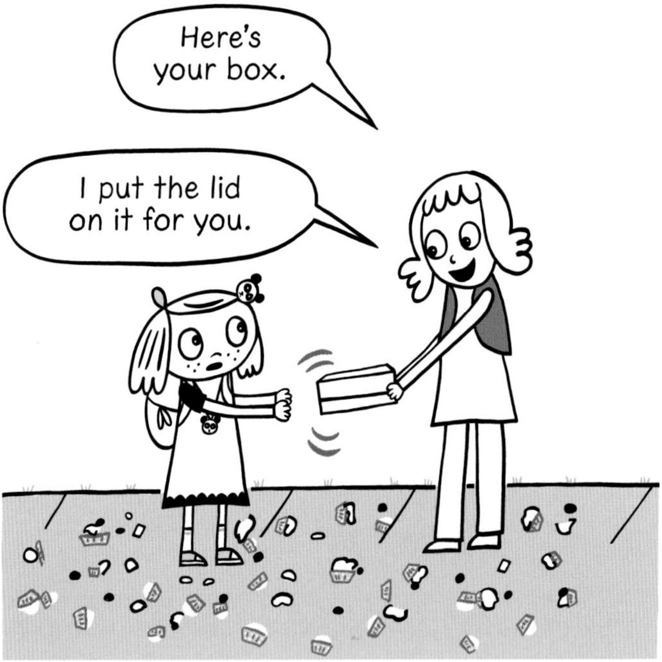
Here's your box.
I put the lid on it for you.

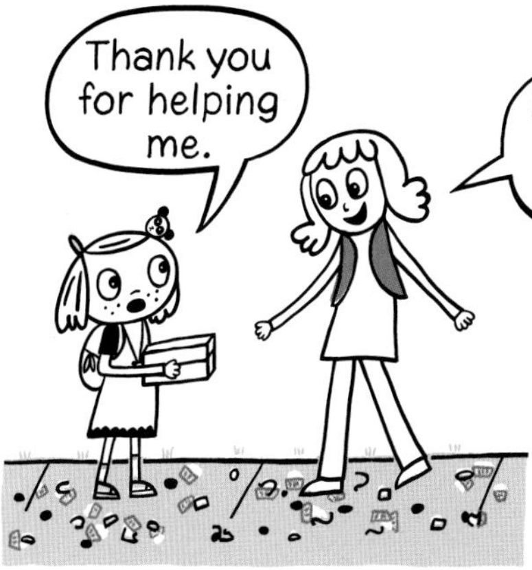
Thank you for helping me.
Happy to help.

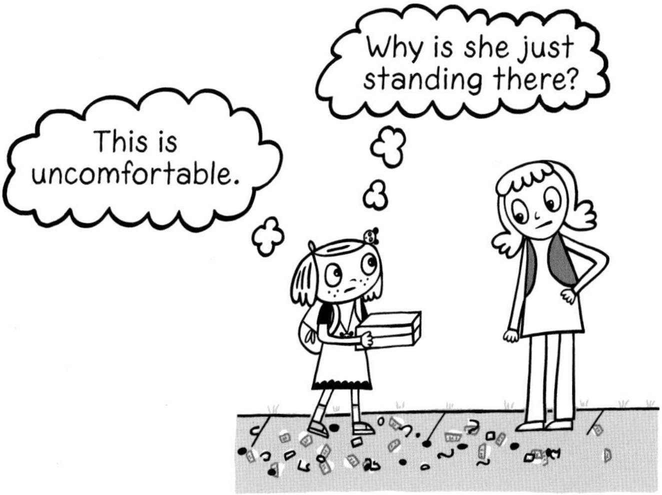
Why is she just standing there?
This is uncomfortable.

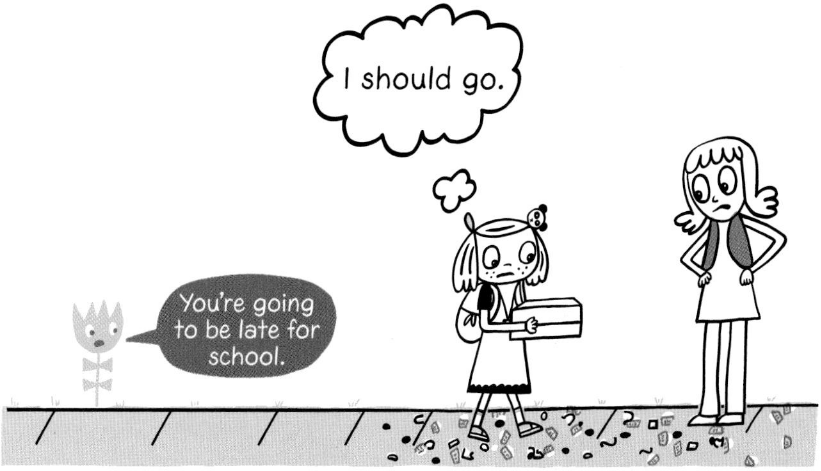
I should go.
You're going to be late for school.

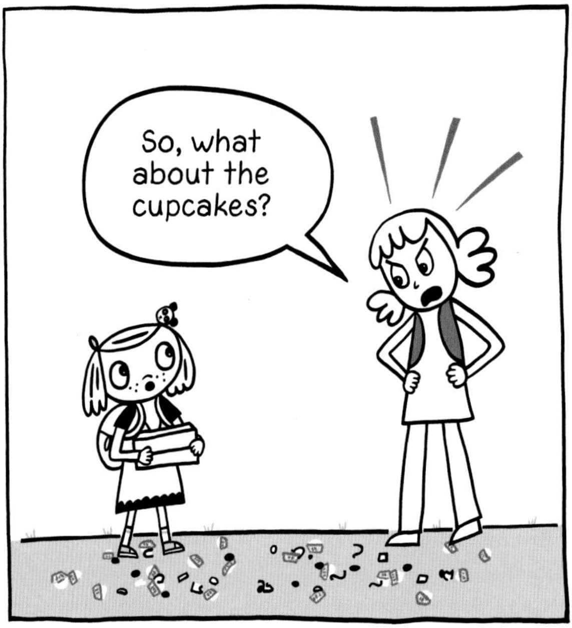
So, what about the cupcakes?

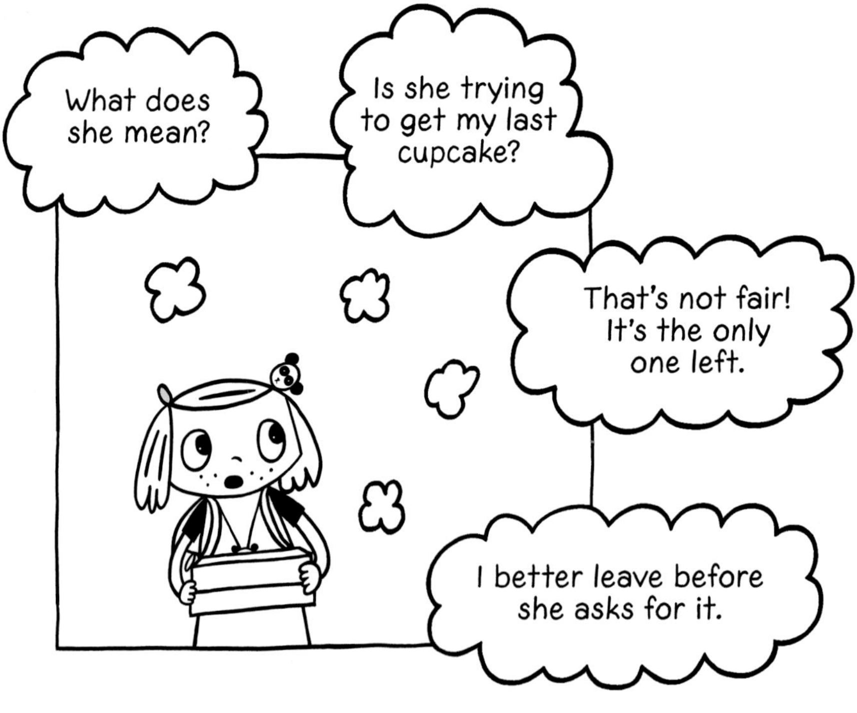
What does she mean?
Is she trying to get my last cupcake?
That's not fair! It's the only one left.
I better leave before she asks for it.

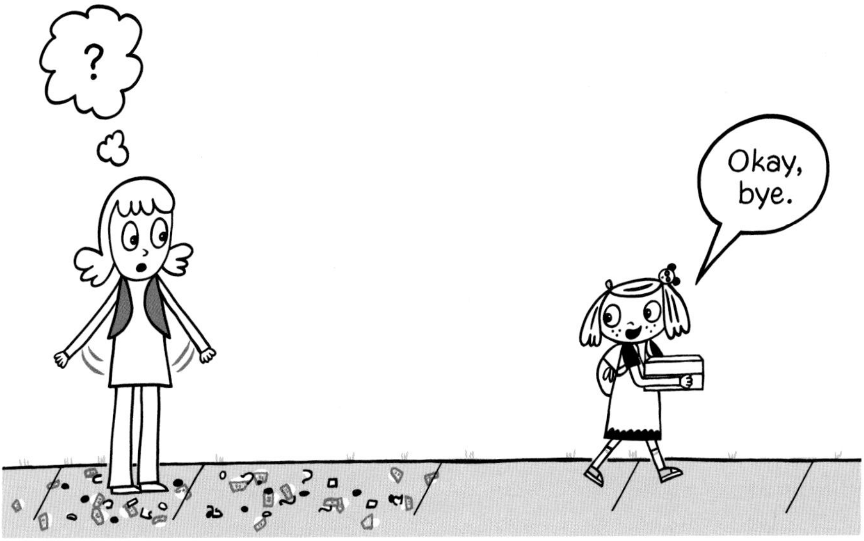
?
Okay, bye.

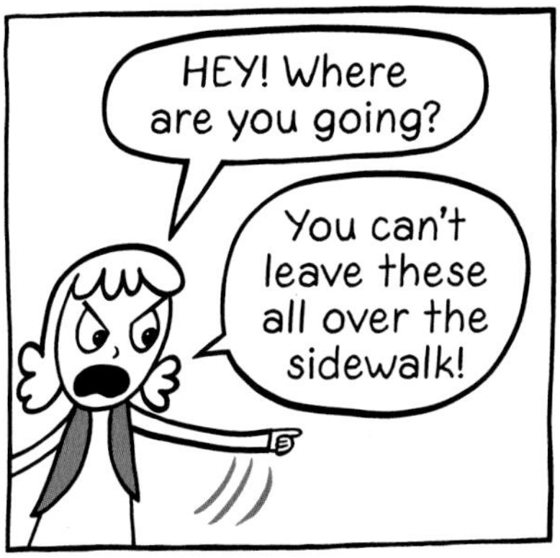
HEY! Where are you going?
You can't leave these all over the sidewalk!

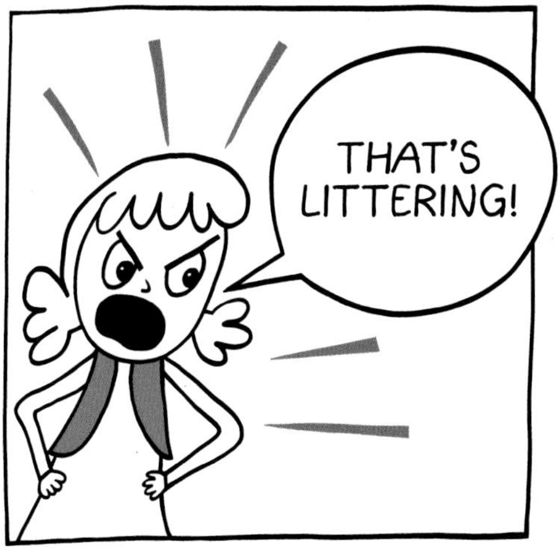
THAT'S LITTERING!

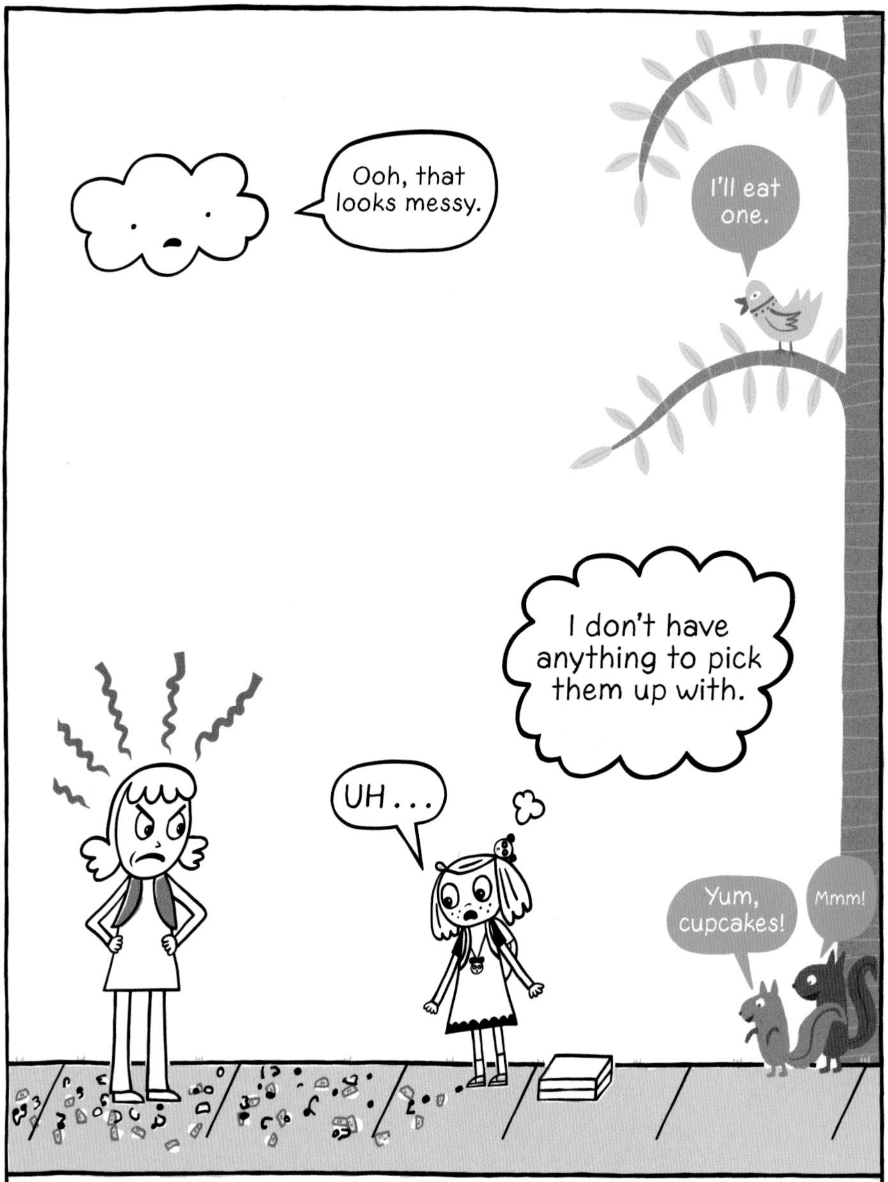
Ooh, that looks messy.
I'll eat one.
I don't have anything to pick them up with.
UH . . .
Yum, cupcakes!
Mmm!

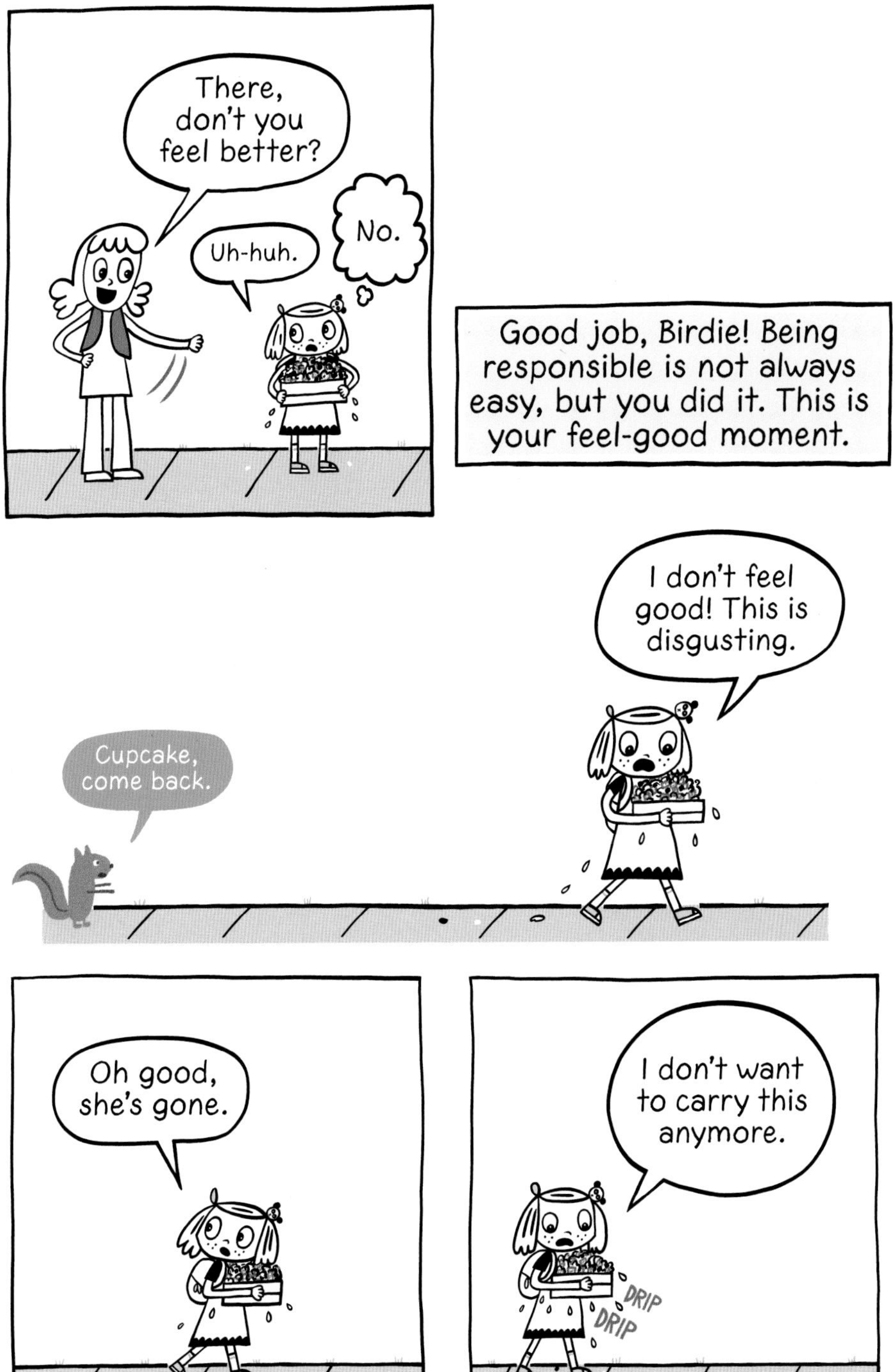
There, don't you feel better?
Uh-huh.
No.
Good job, Birdie! Being responsible is not always easy, but you did it. This is your feel-good moment.
I don't feel good! This is disgusting.
Cupcake, come back.
Oh good, she's gone.
I don't want to carry this anymore.
DRIP
DRIP

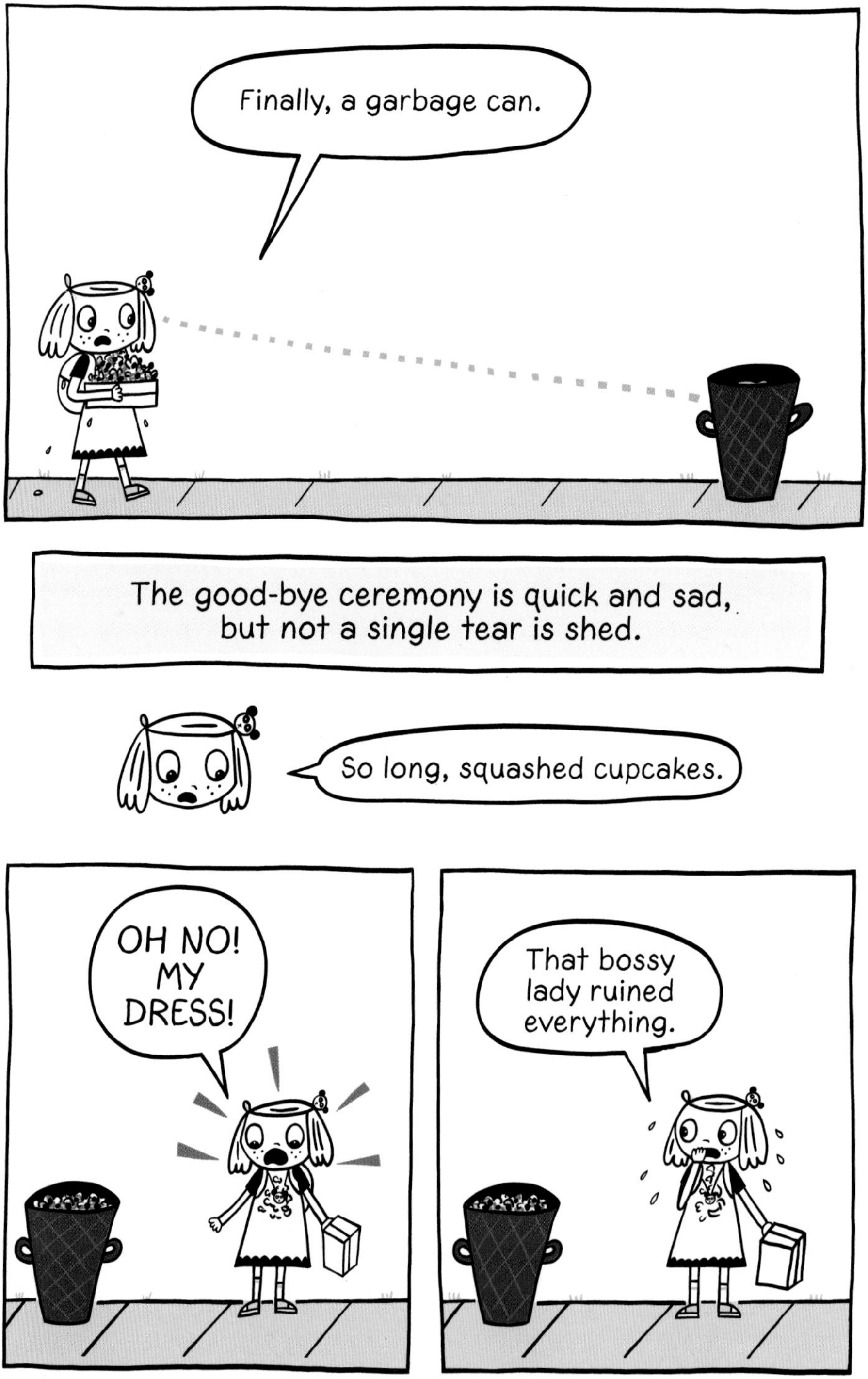
Finally, a garbage can.
The good-bye ceremony is quick and sad, but not a single tear is shed.
So long, squashed cupcakes.
OH NO! MY DRESS!
That bossy lady ruined everything.

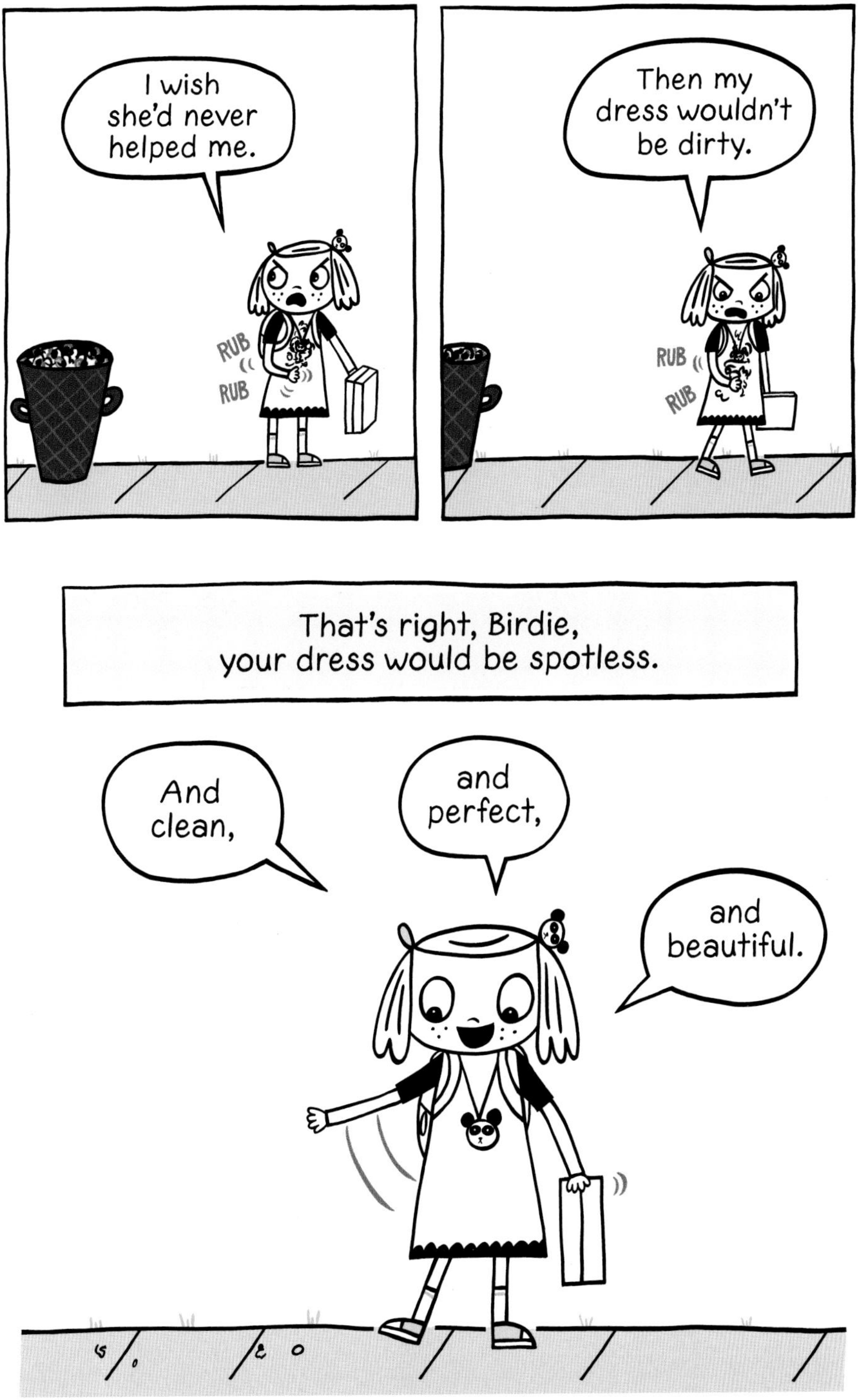
I wish she'd never helped me.
RUB RUB
Then my dress wouldn't be dirty.
RUB RUB
That's right, Birdie, your dress would be spotless.
And clean,
and perfect,
and beautiful.

But what about YOU?
How would YOU look?

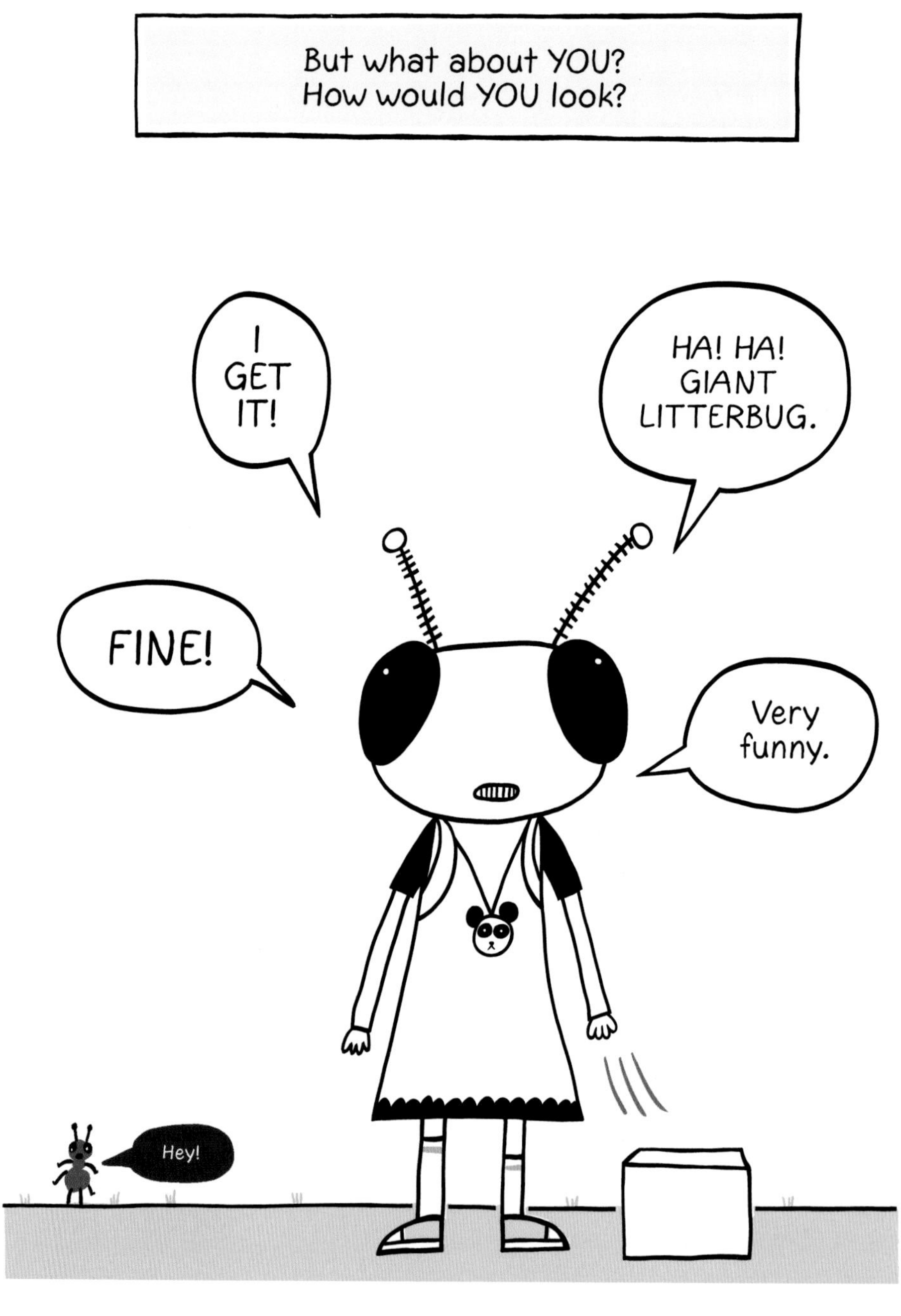
I GET IT!
HA! HA! GIANT LITTERBUG.
FINE!
Very funny.
Hey!

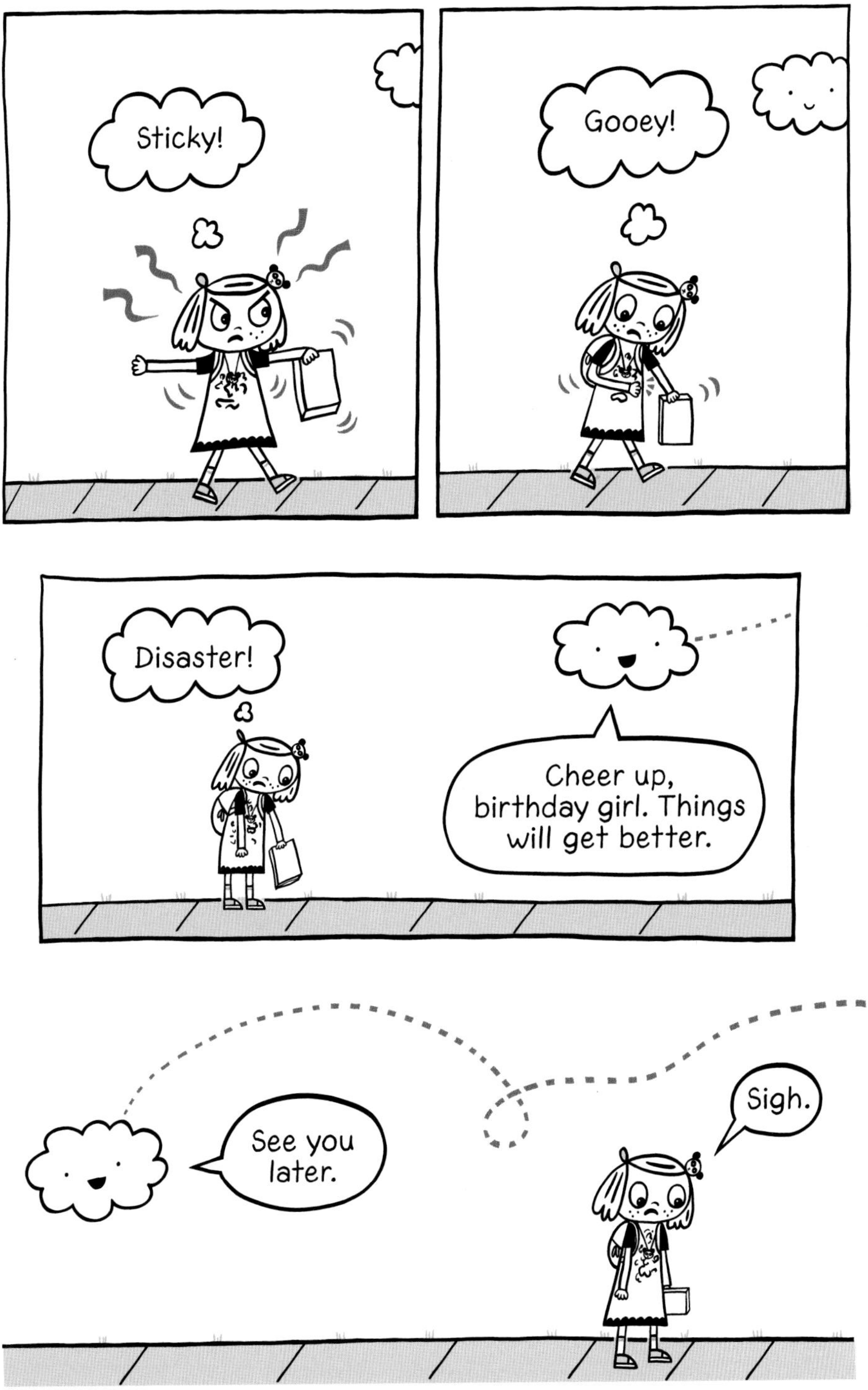
Sticky!
Gooey!
Disaster!
Cheer up, birthday girl. Things will get better.
See you later.
Sigh.

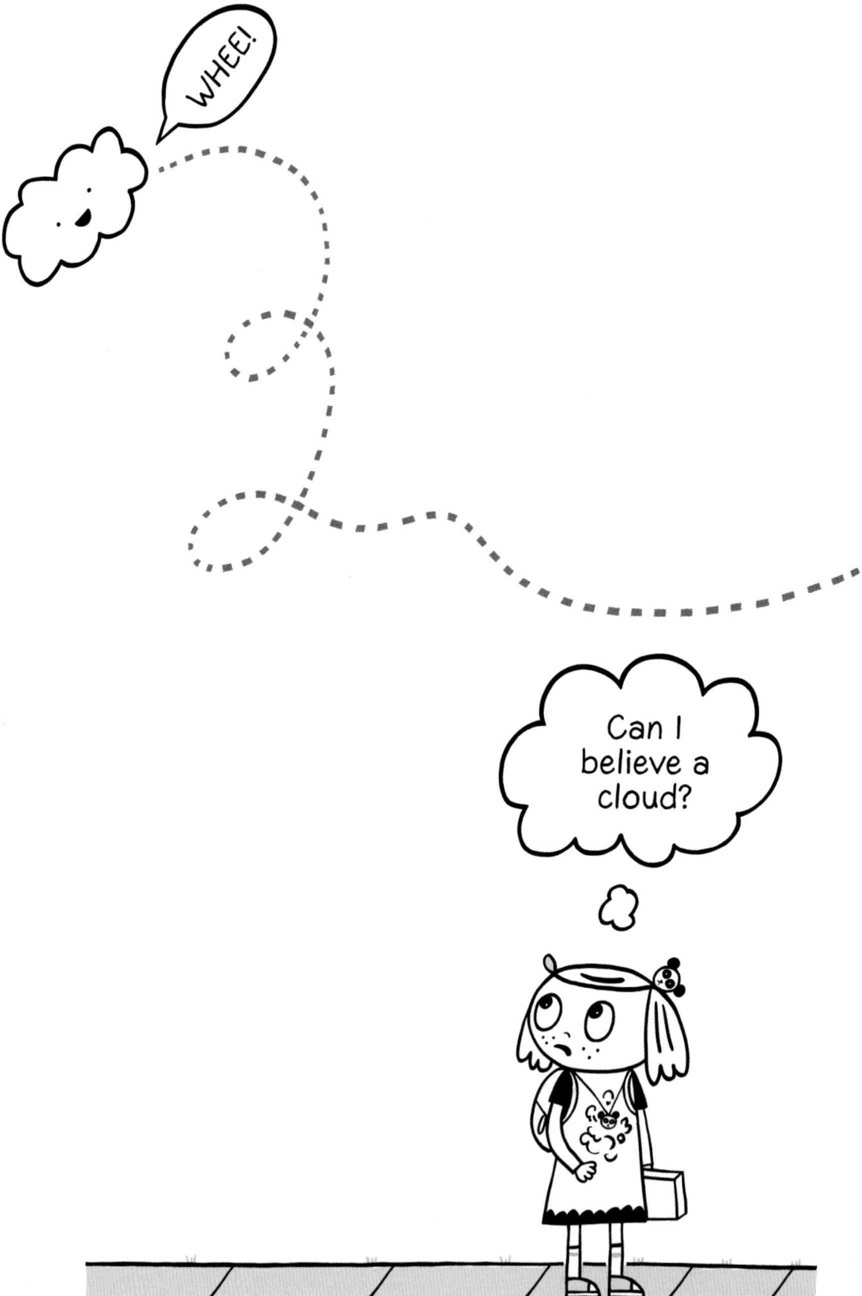
WHEE!
Can I believe a cloud?

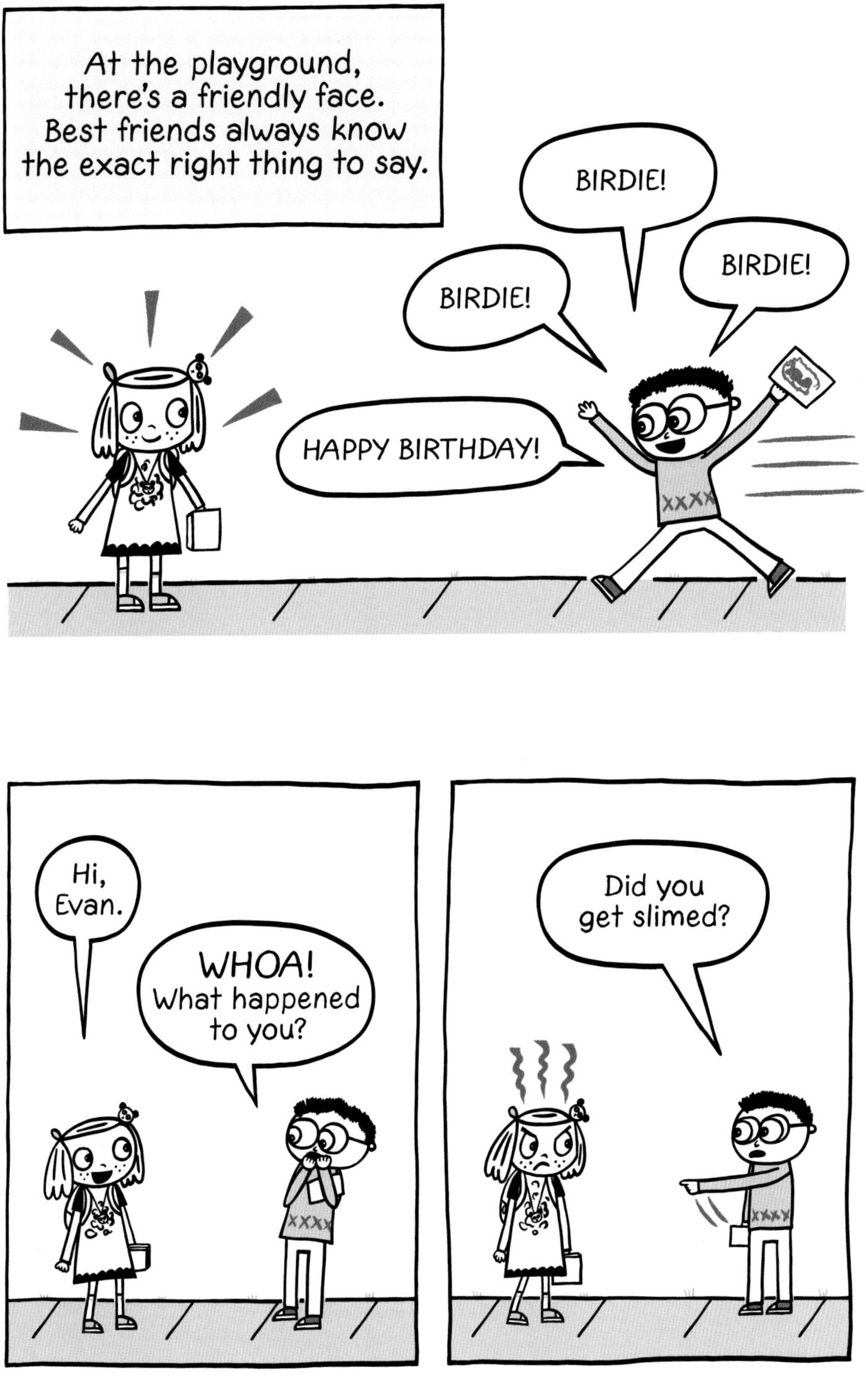
At the playground, there's a friendly face. Best friends always know the exact right thing to say.
BIRDIE!
BIRDIE!
BIRDIE!
HAPPY BIRTHDAY!
Hi, Evan.
WHOA! What happened to you?
Did you get slimed?
XXXX

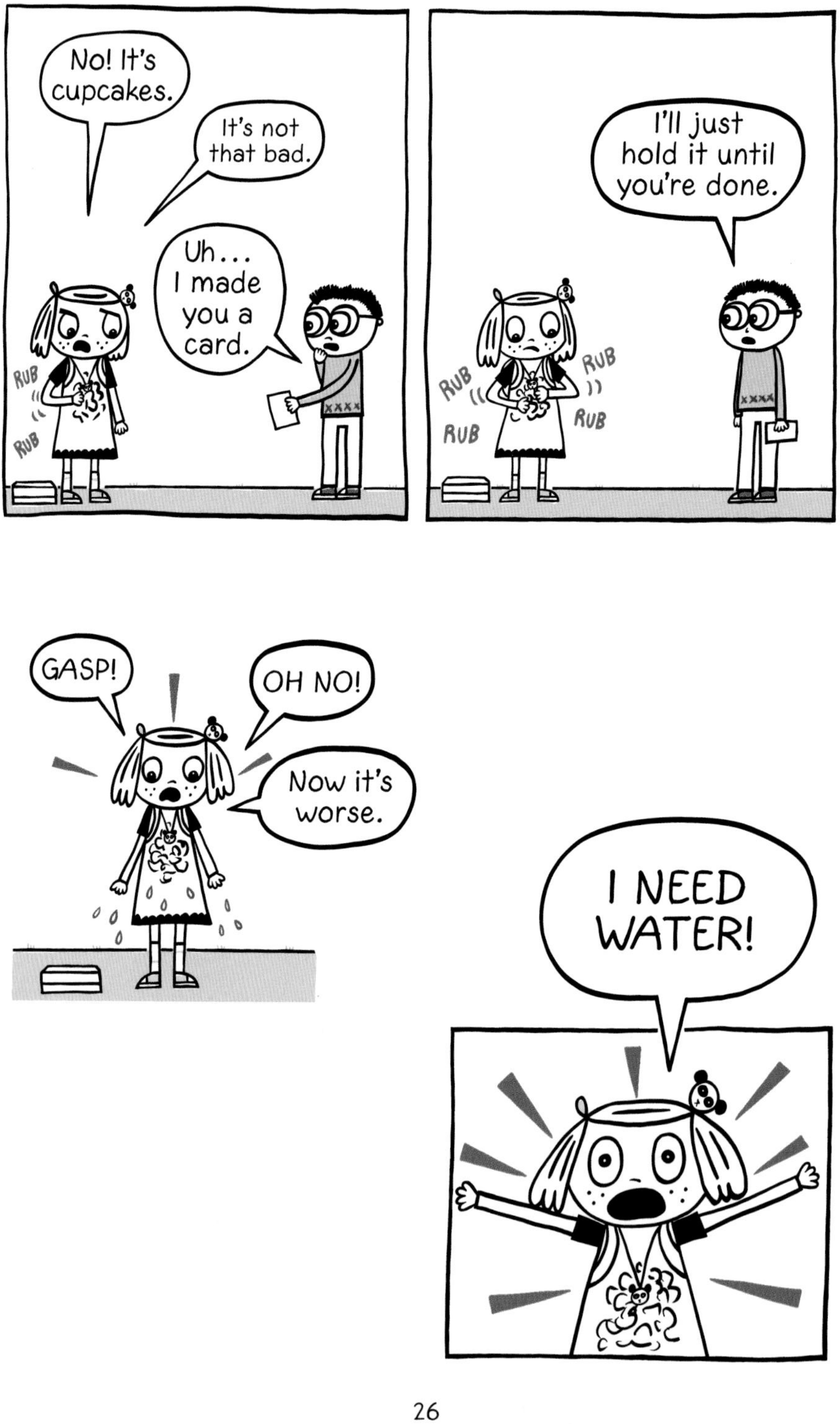
No! It's cupcakes.
It's not that bad.
Uh... I made you a card.
RUB
RUB
I'll just hold it until you're done.
RUB
RUB
RUB
RUB
GASP!
OH NO!
Now it's worse.
I NEED WATER!

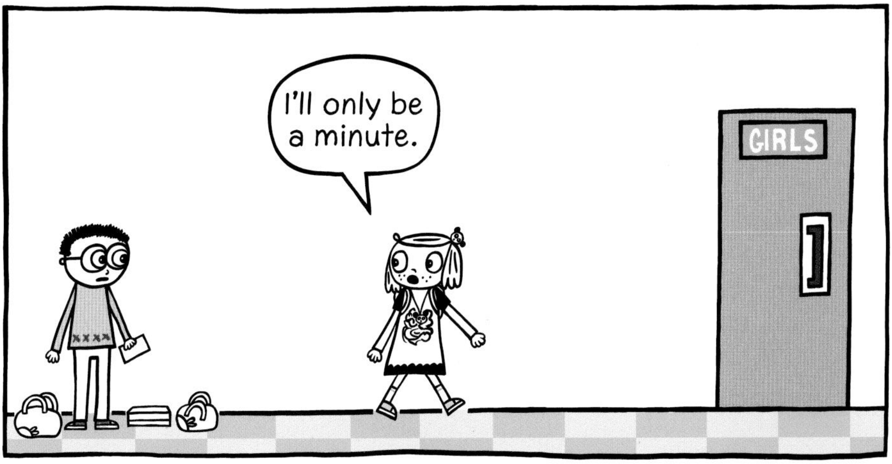
I'll only be a minute.
GIRLS

Inside a closed bathroom stall, a transformation occurs.

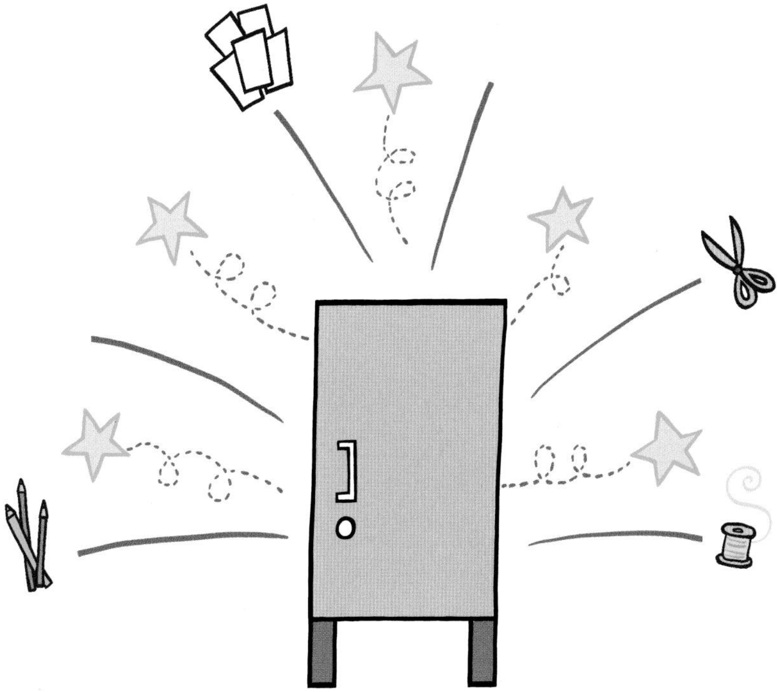

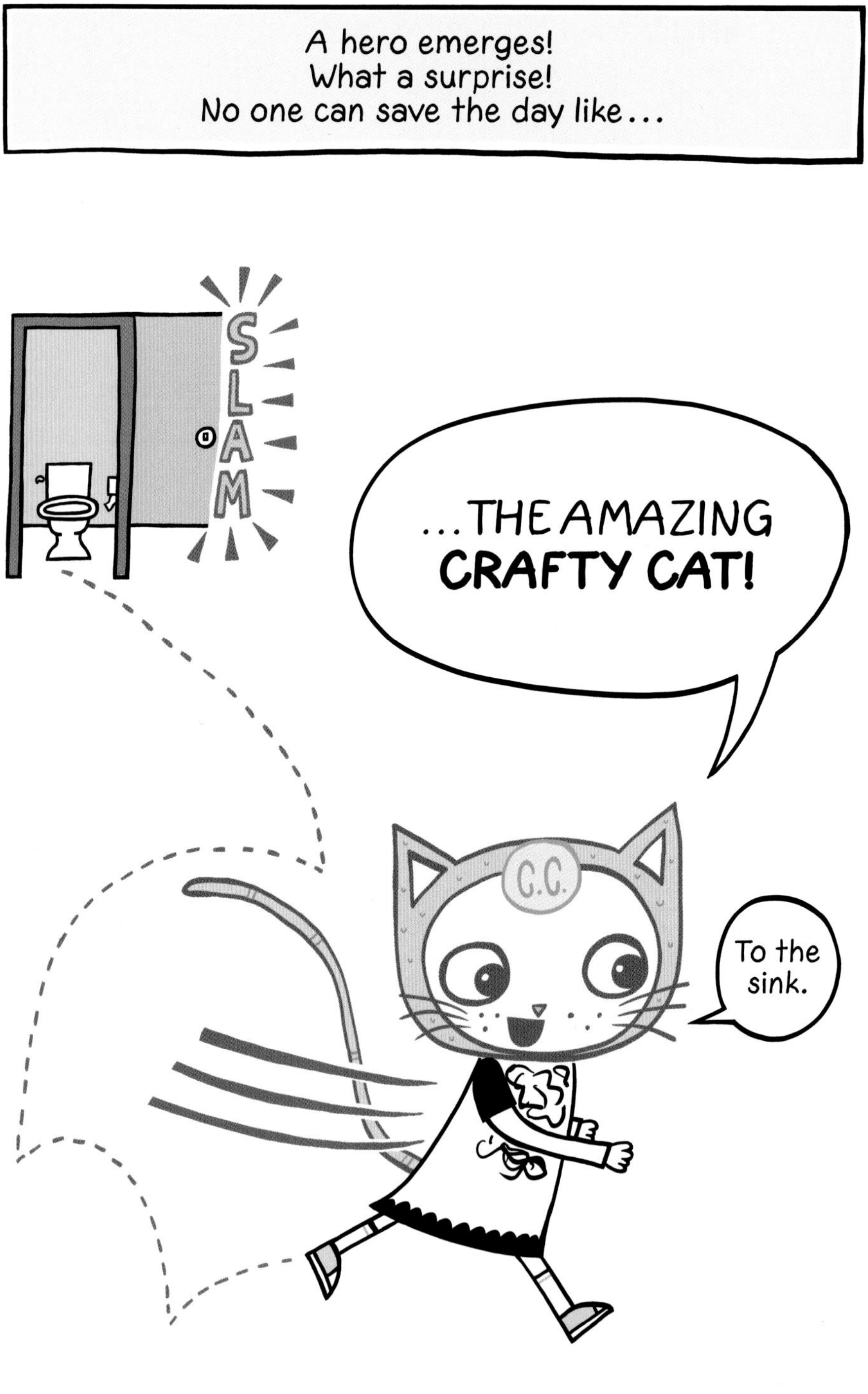
A hero emerges!
What a surprise!
No one can save the day like...
SLAM
...THE AMAZING CRAFTY CAT!
To the sink.

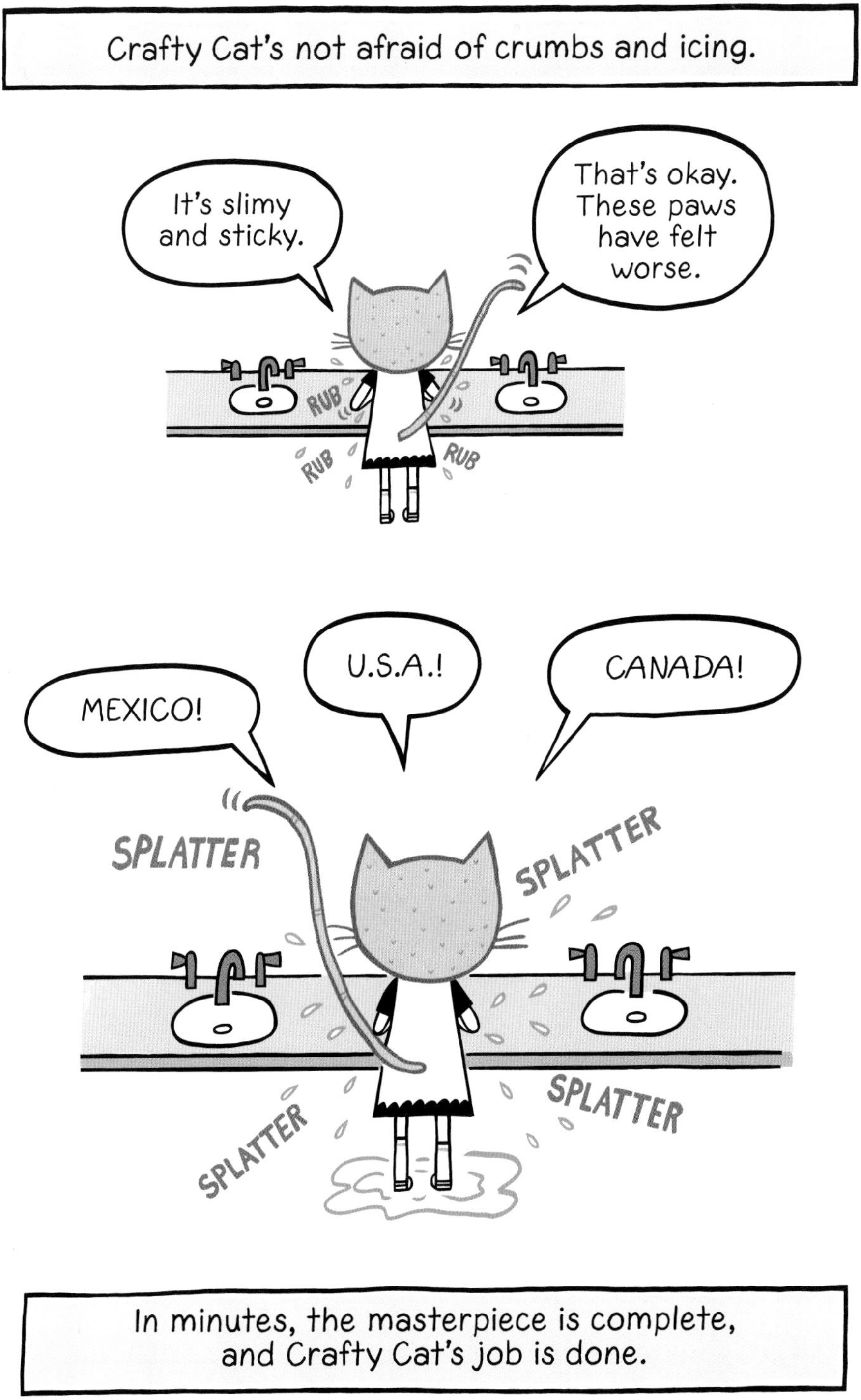
Crafty Cat's not afraid of crumbs and icing.
It's slimy and sticky.
That's okay. These paws have felt worse.
RUB
RUB
RUB
MEXICO!
U.S.A.!
CANADA!
SPLATTER
SPLATTER
SPLATTER
SPLATTER
In minutes, the masterpiece is complete, and Crafty Cat's job is done.

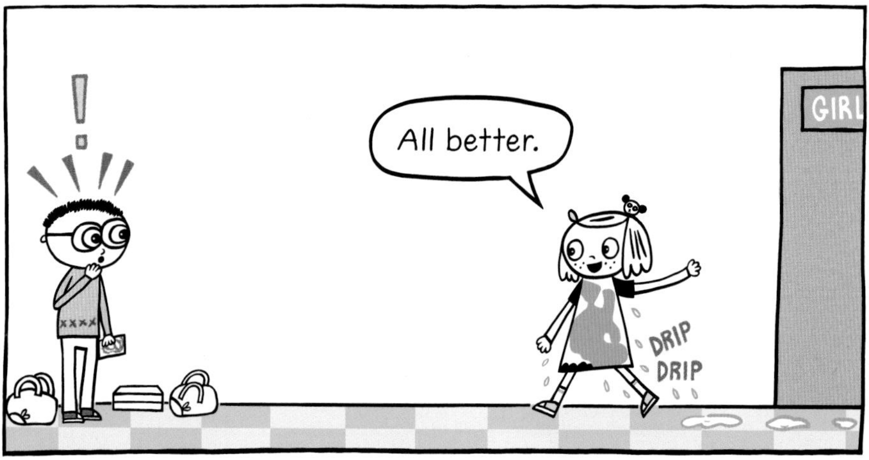
GIRL
All better.
DRIP
DRIP

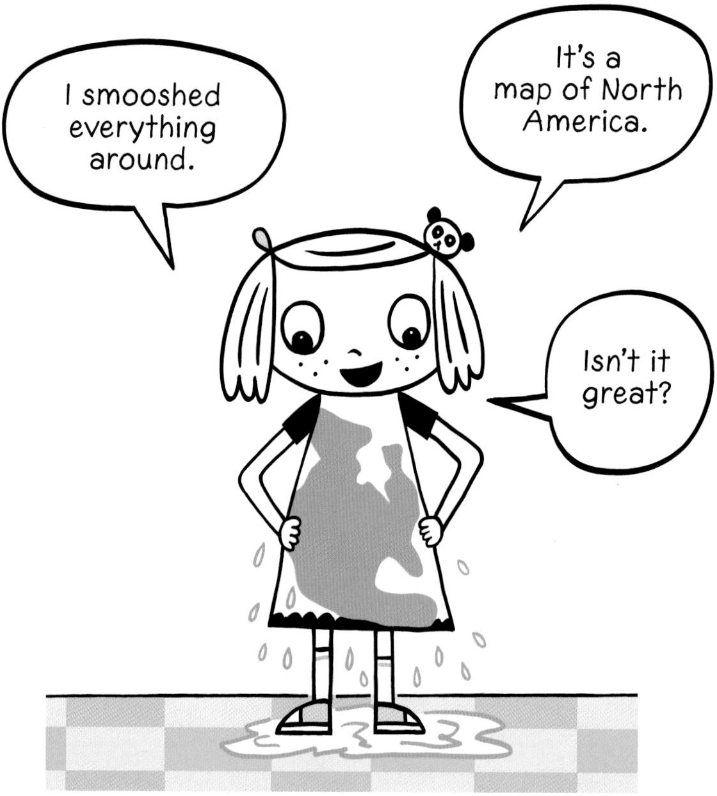
I smooshed everything around.
It's a map of North America.
Isn't it great?

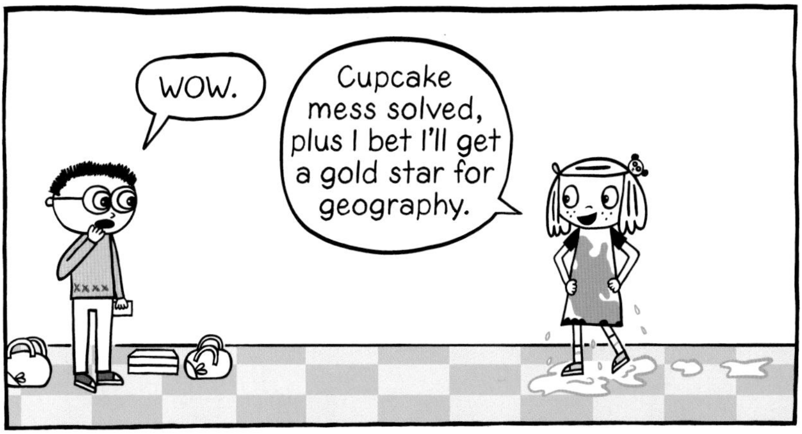
WOW.
Cupcake mess solved, plus I bet I'll get a gold star for geography.

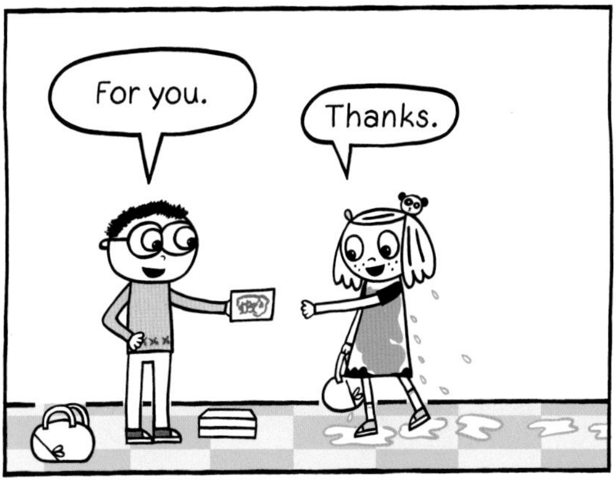
For you.
Thanks.

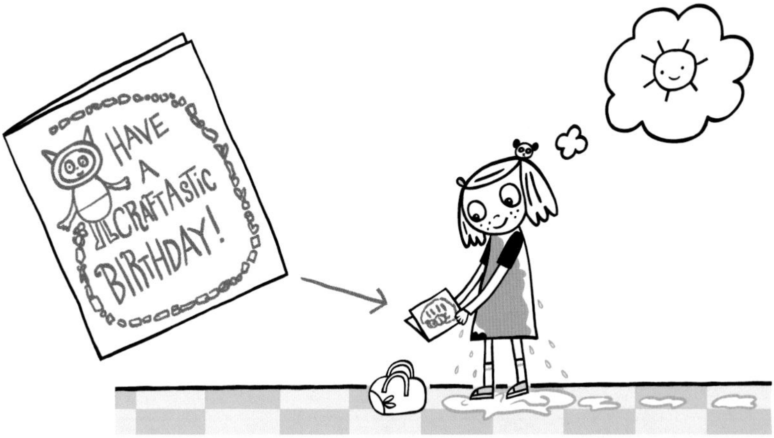
HAVE A CRAFTASTIC BIRTHDAY!

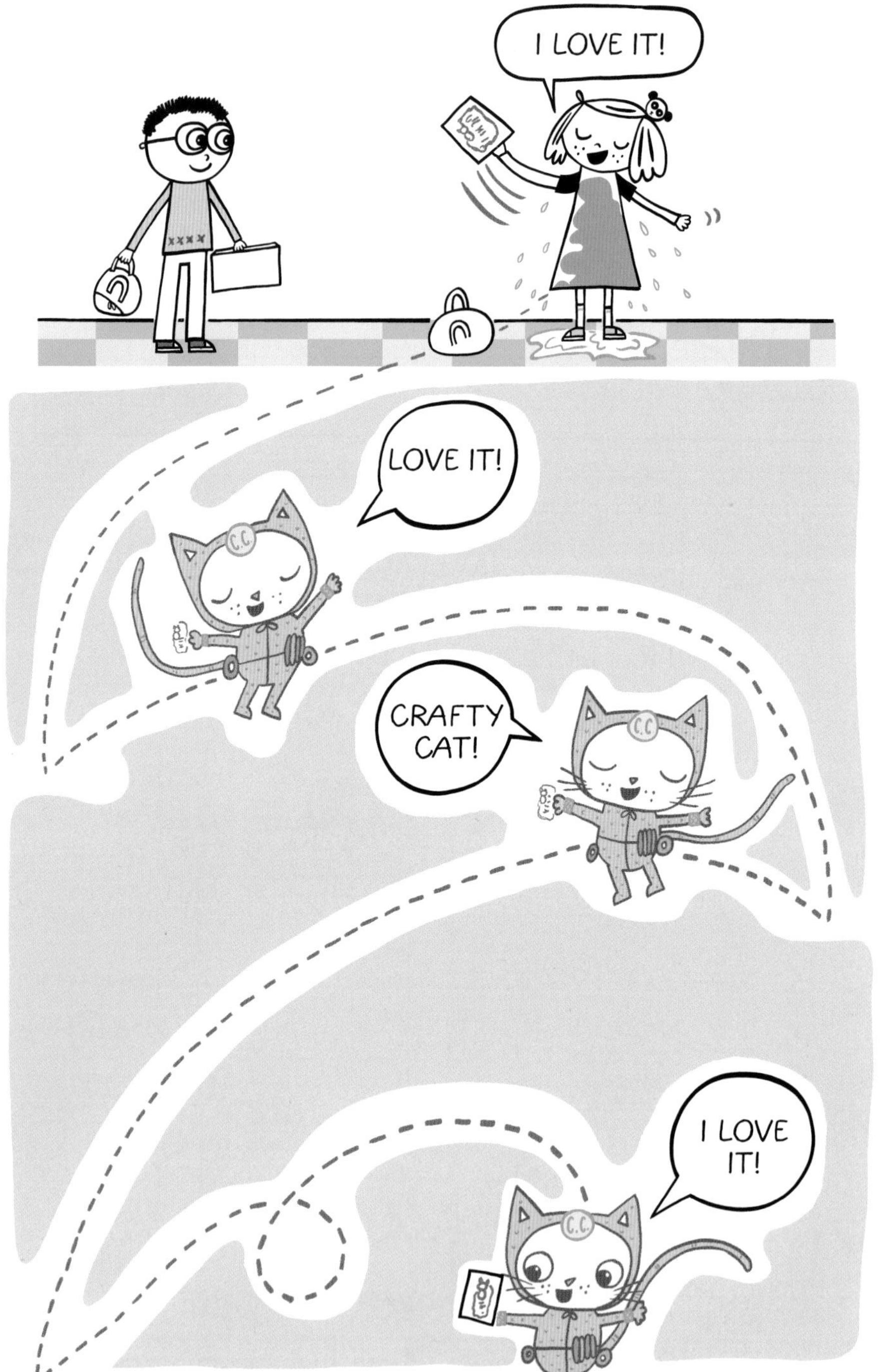
I LOVE IT!
LOVE IT!
CRAFTY CAT!
I LOVE IT!

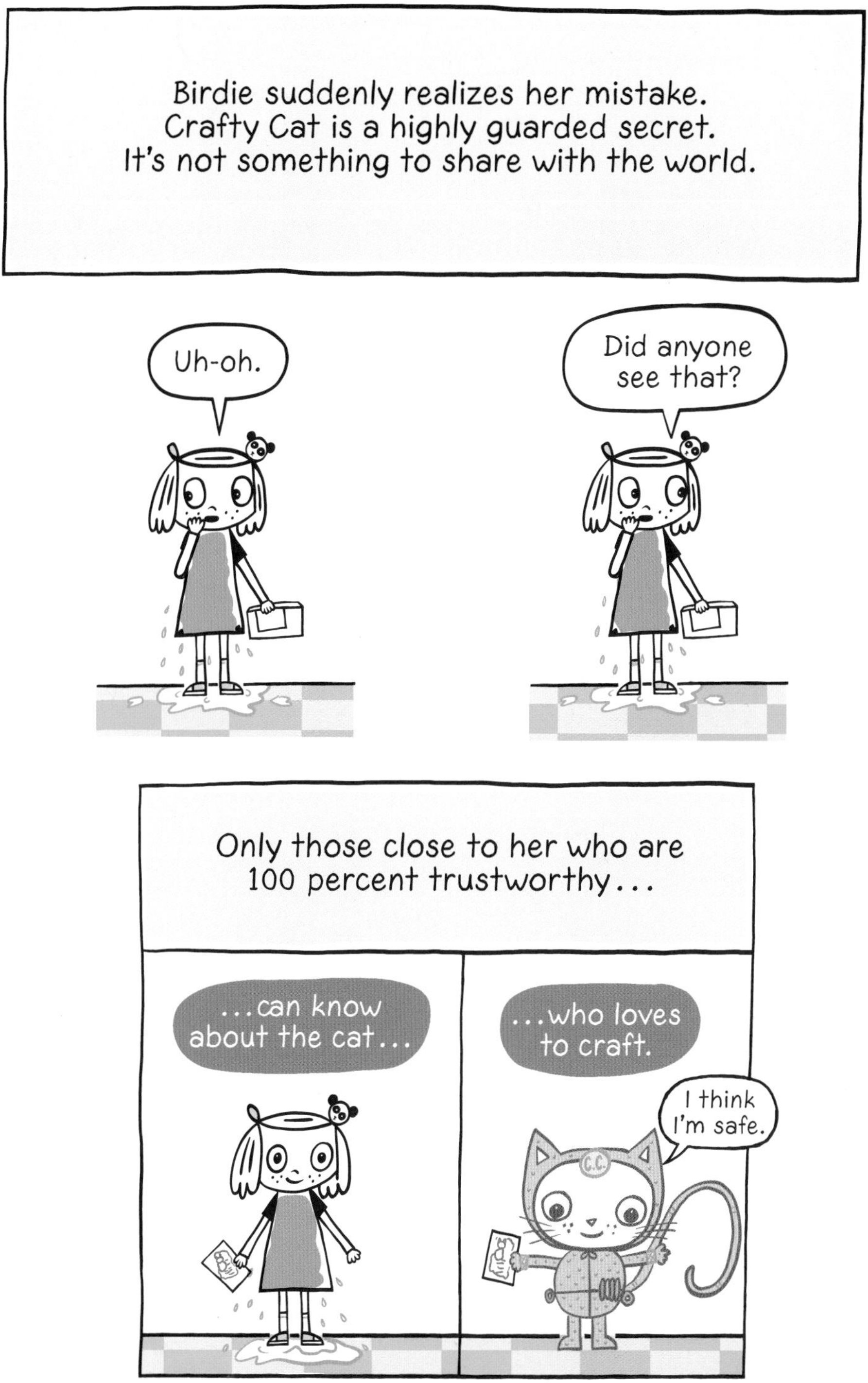
Birdie suddenly realizes her mistake.
Crafty Cat is a highly guarded secret.
It's not something to share with the world.
Uh-oh.
Did anyone see that?
Only those close to her who are 100 percent trustworthy...
...can know about the cat...
...who loves to craft.
I think I'm safe.

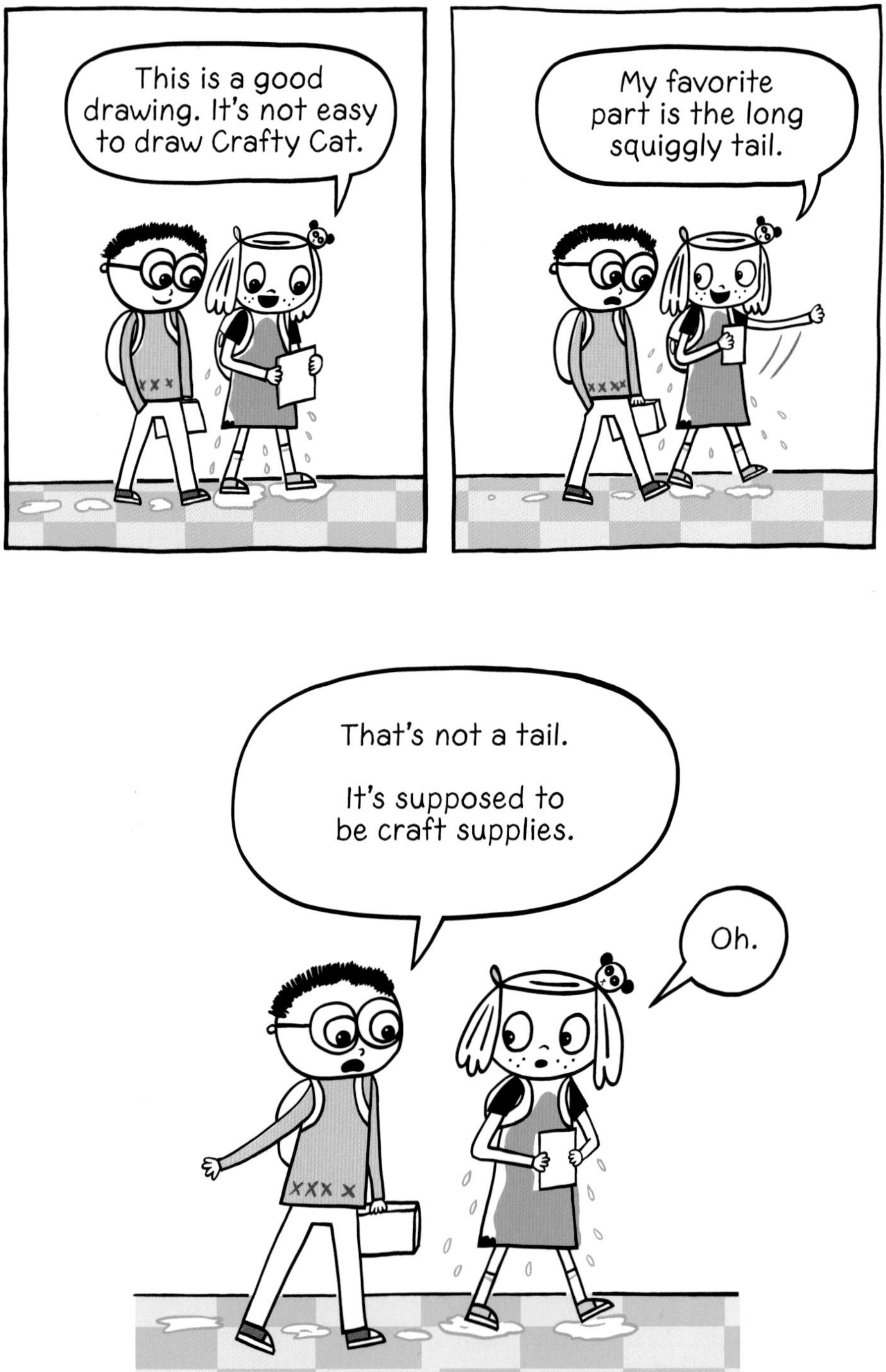
This is a good drawing. It's not easy to draw Crafty Cat.
My favorite part is the long squiggly tail.
That's not a tail.
It's supposed to be craft supplies.
Oh.

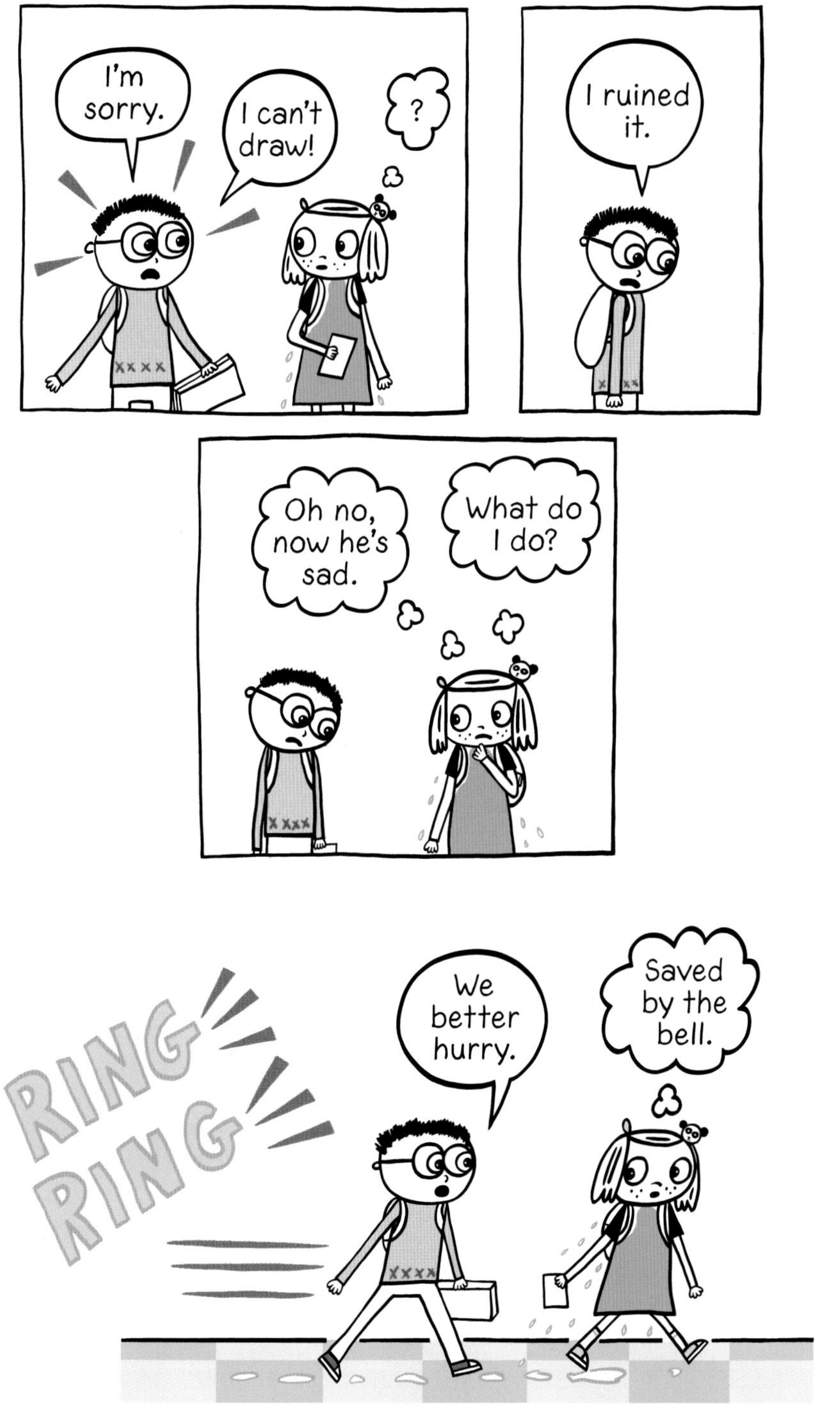
I'm sorry.
I can't draw!
?
I ruined it.
Oh no, now he's sad.
What do I do?
RING RING
We better hurry.
Saved by the bell.

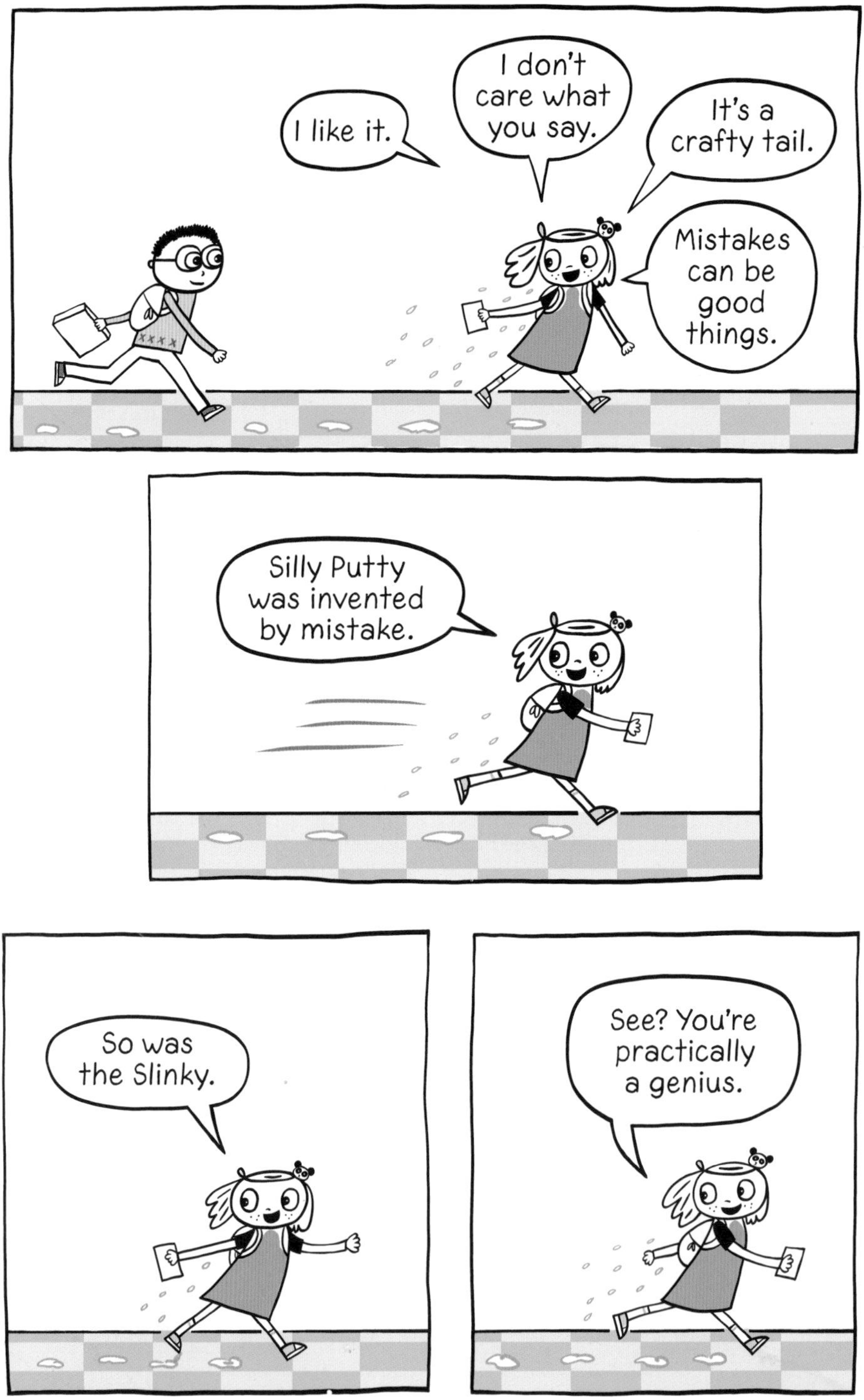
I like it.
I don't care what you say.
It's a crafty tail.
Mistakes can be good things.
Silly Putty was invented by mistake.
So was the Slinky.
See? You're practically a genius.

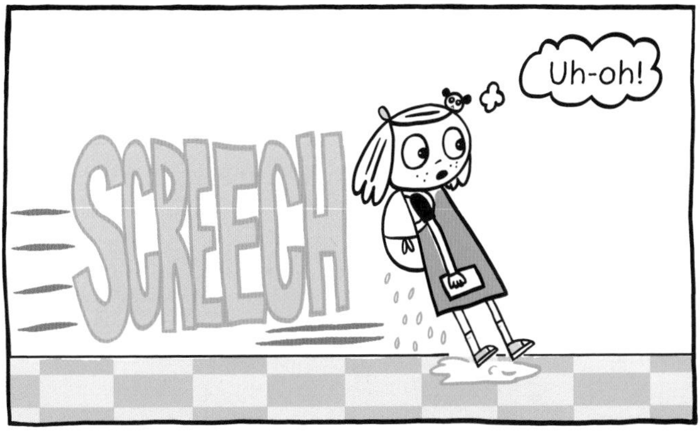
Uh-oh!
SCREECH

"Brave" and "birthday" both start with a "B," but that doesn't mean they always happen at the same time.

Having a birthday is a lot easier than being brave.

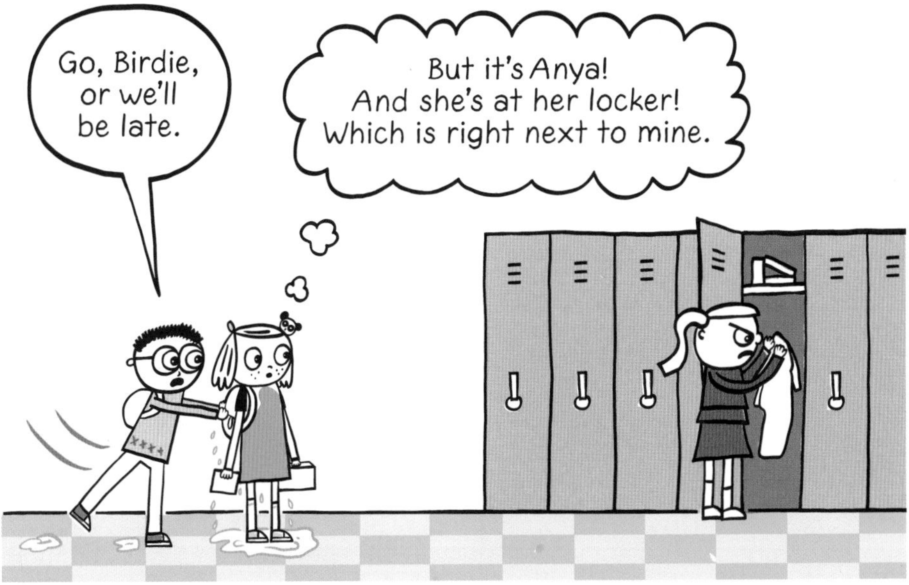
Go, Birdie, or we'll be late.
But it's Anya! And she's at her locker! Which is right next to mine.

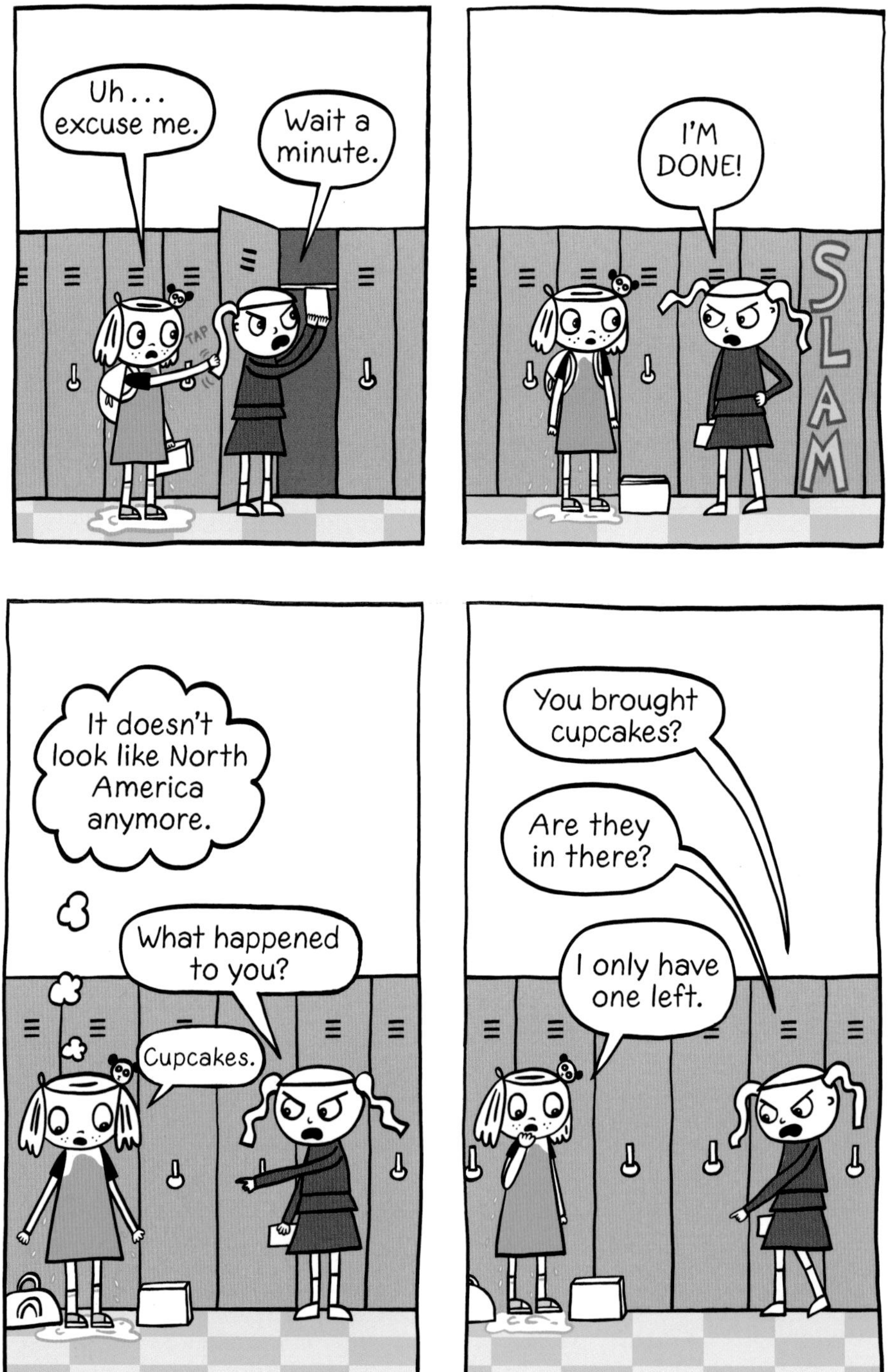

Uh... excuse me.
TAP
Wait a minute.
I'M DONE!
SLAM
It doesn't look like North America anymore.
What happened to you?
Cupcakes.
You brought cupcakes?
Are they in there?
I only have one left.

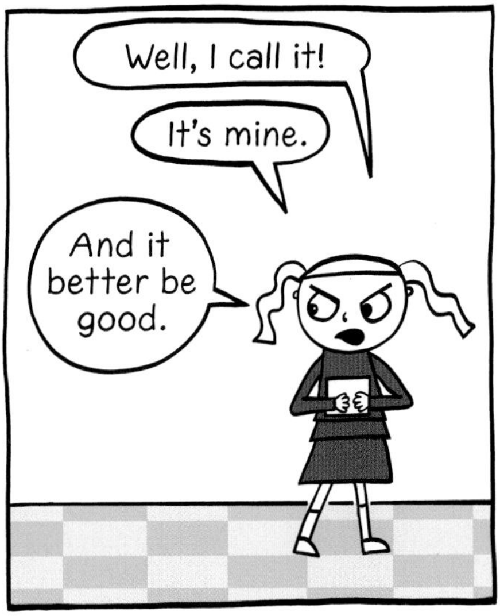
Well, I call it!
It's mine.
And it better be good.

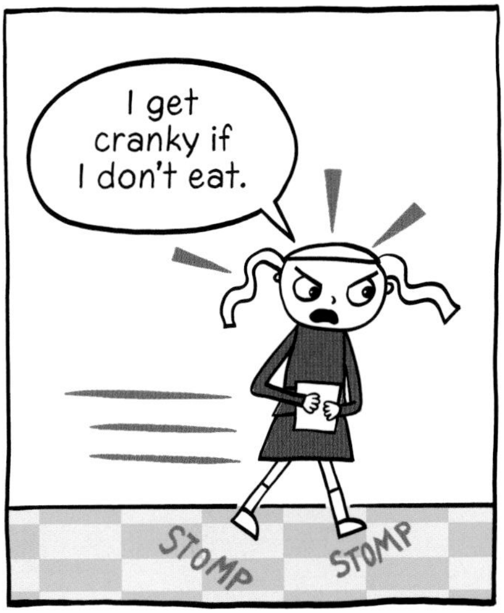
I get cranky if I don't eat.
STOMP
STOMP

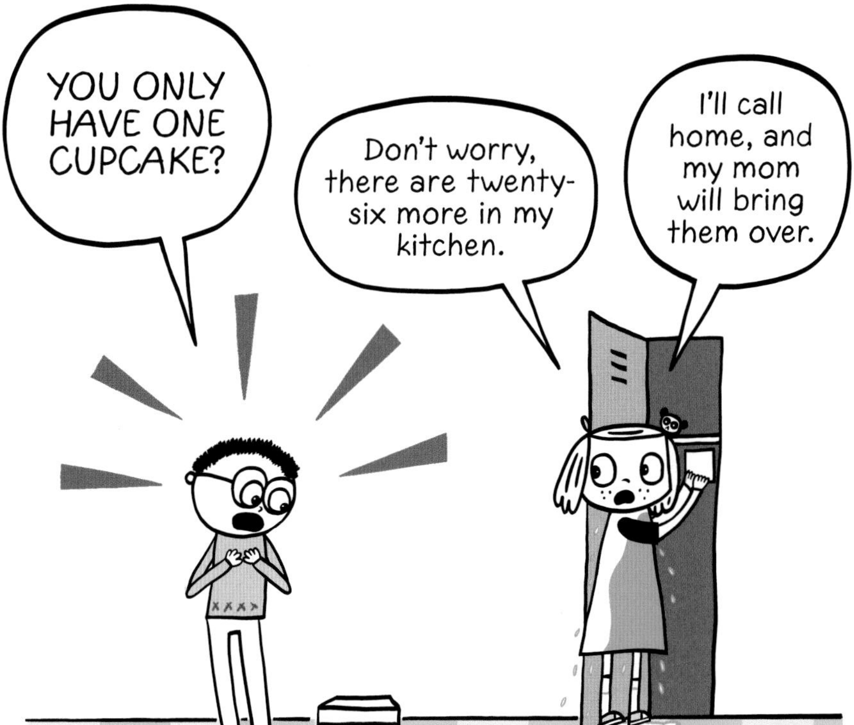
YOU ONLY HAVE ONE CUPCAKE?
Don't worry, there are twenty-six more in my kitchen.
I'll call home, and my mom will bring them over.

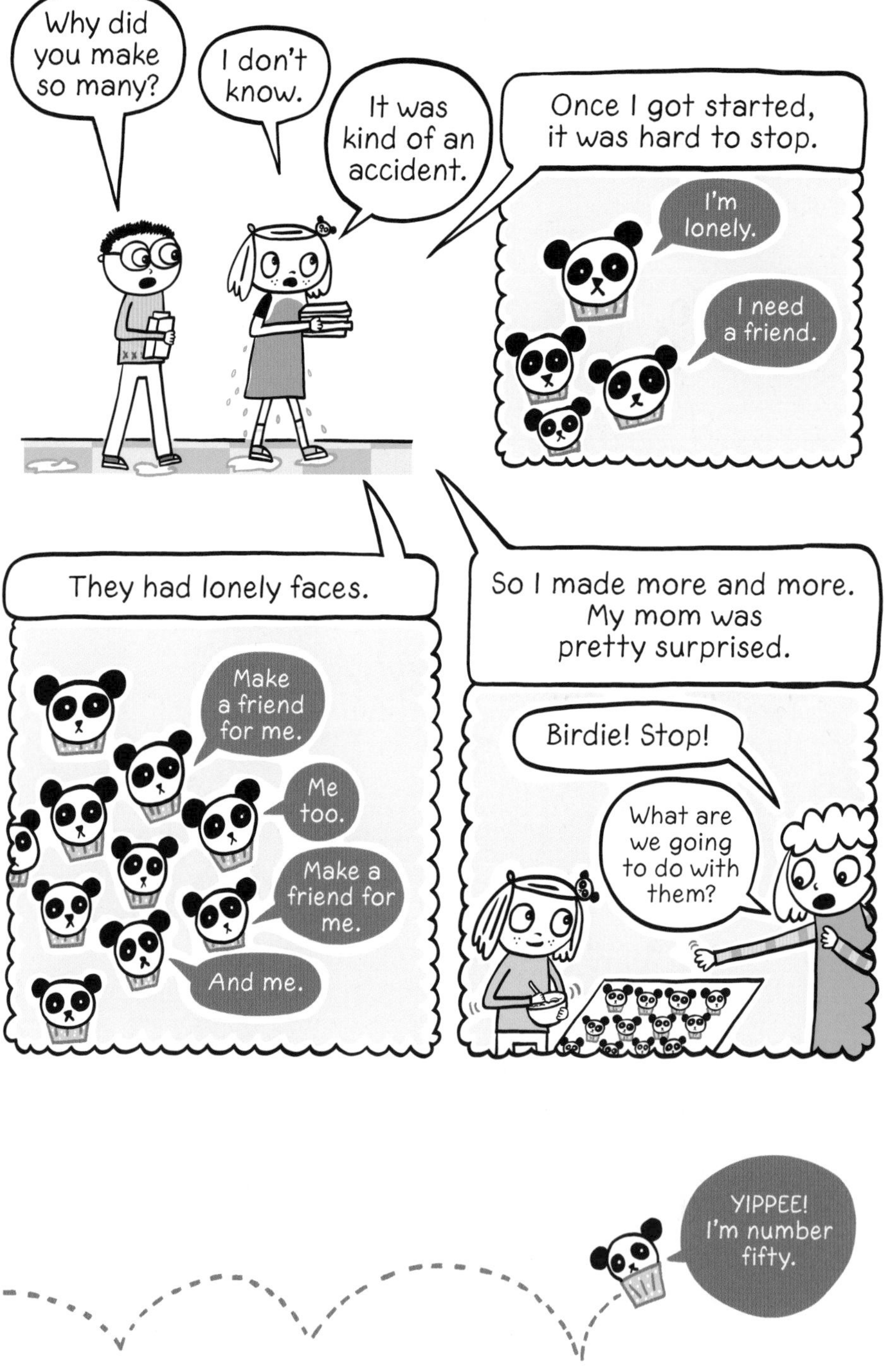
Why did you make so many?
I don't know.
It was kind of an accident.
Once I got started, it was hard to stop.
I'm lonely.
I need a friend.
They had lonely faces.
Make a friend for me.
Me too.
Make a friend for me.
And me.
So I made more and more. My mom was pretty surprised.
Birdie! Stop!
What are we going to do with them?
YIPPEE! I'm number fifty.

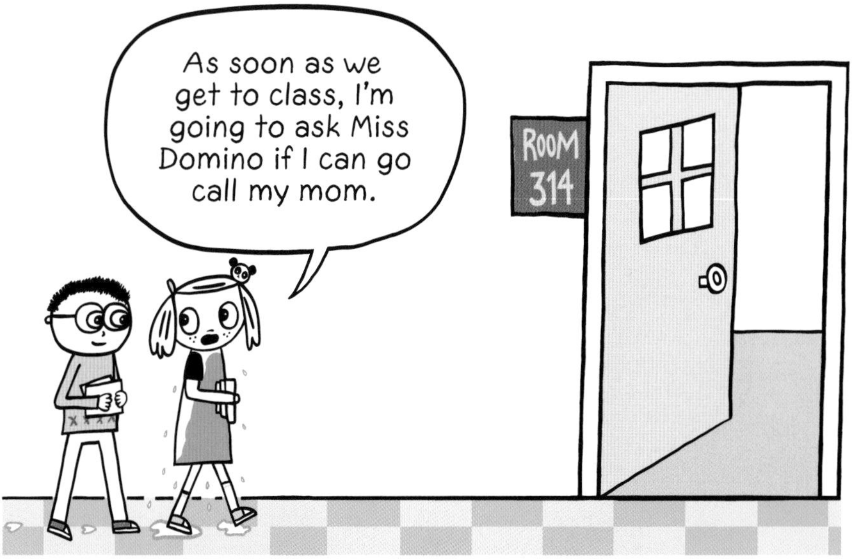
As soon as we get to class, I'm going to ask Miss Domino if I can go call my mom.
ROOM 314

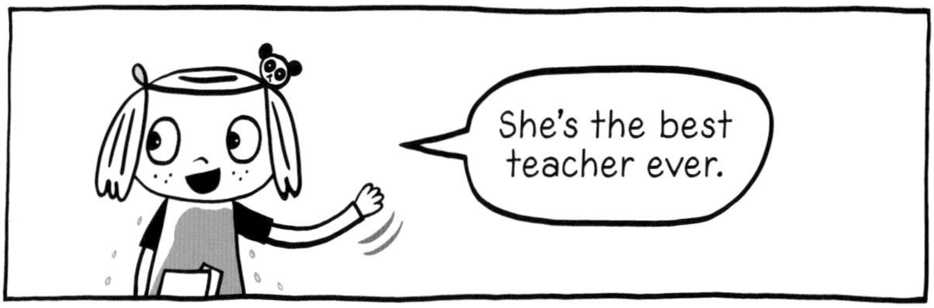
She's the best teacher ever.

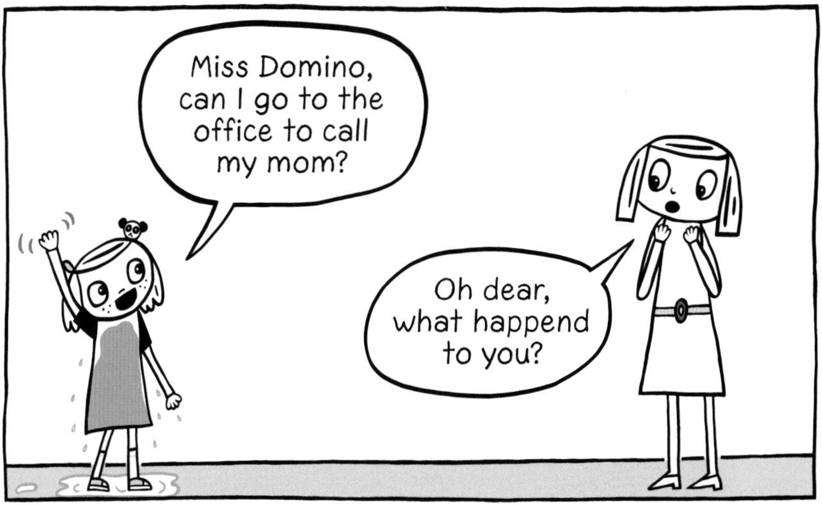
Miss Domino, can I go to the office to call my mom?
Oh dear, what happend to you?

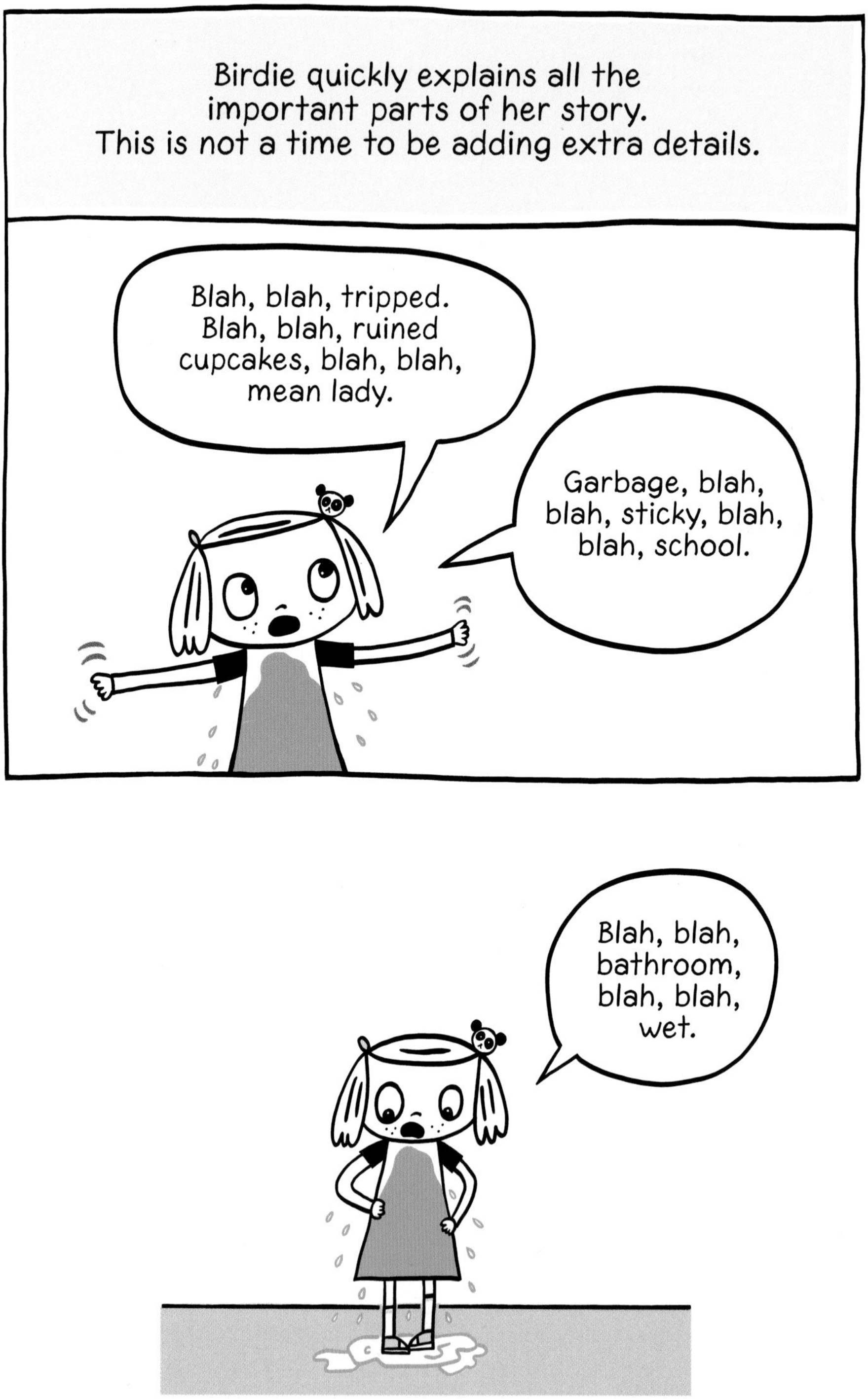
Birdie quickly explains all the important parts of her story. This is not a time to be adding extra details.
Blah, blah, tripped. Blah, blah, ruined cupcakes, blah, blah, mean lady.
Garbage, blah, blah, sticky, blah, blah, school.
Blah, blah, bathroom, blah, blah, wet.

Miss Domino is an expert at solving problems.

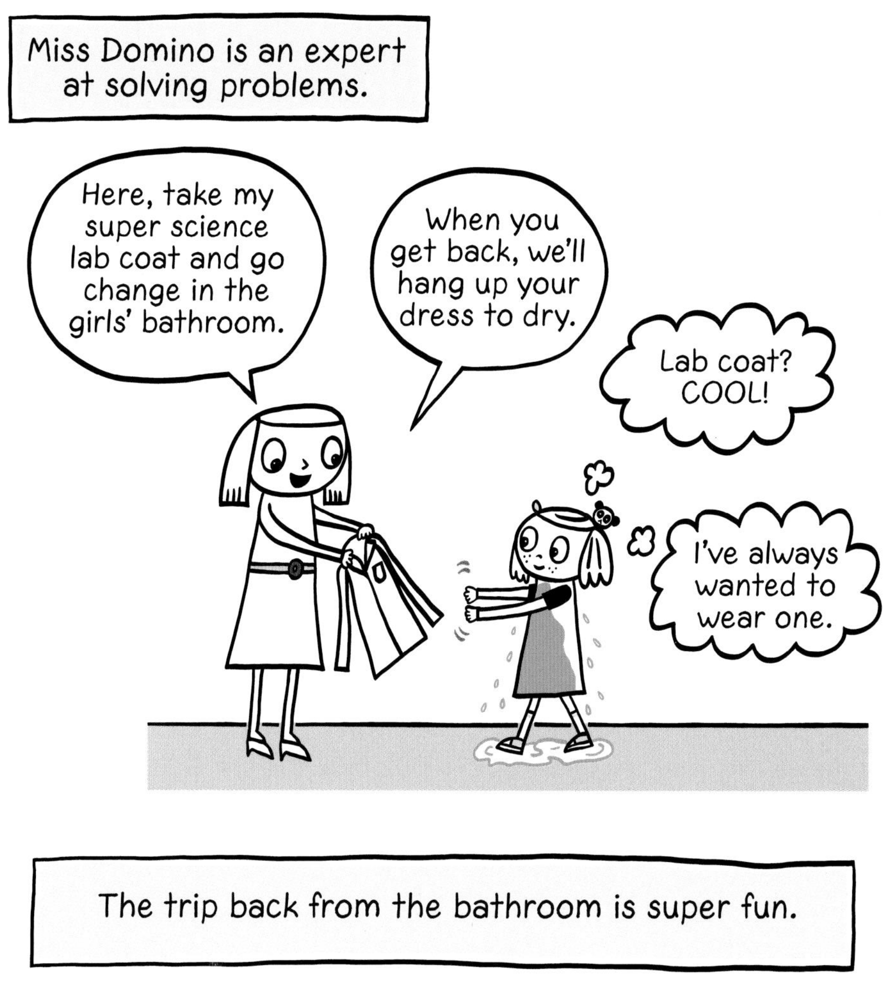
Here, take my super science lab coat and go change in the girls' bathroom.
When you get back, we'll hang up your dress to dry.
Lab coat? COOL!
I've always wanted to wear one.

The trip back from the bathroom is super fun.

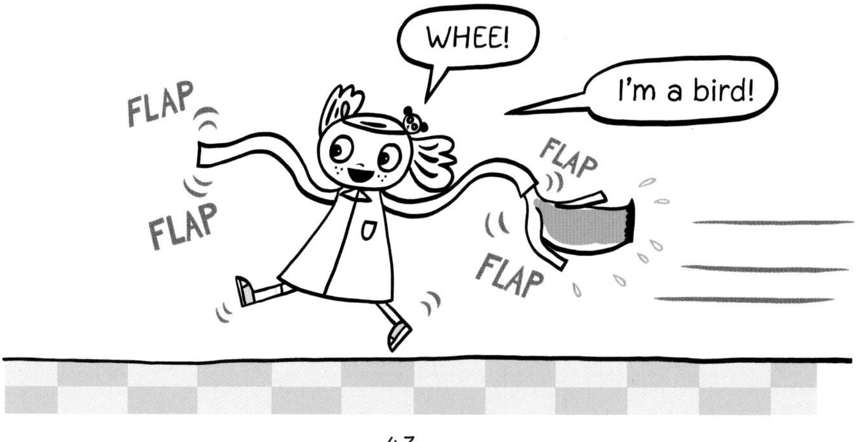
WHEE!
I'm a bird!
FLAP
FLAP
FLAP
FLAP

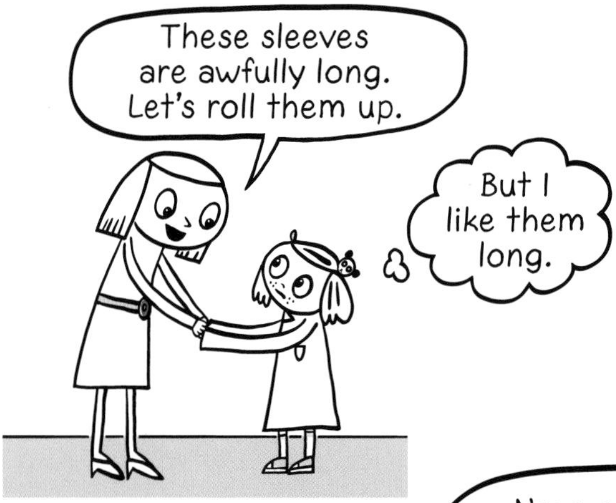
These sleeves are awfully long. Let's roll them up.
But I like them long.

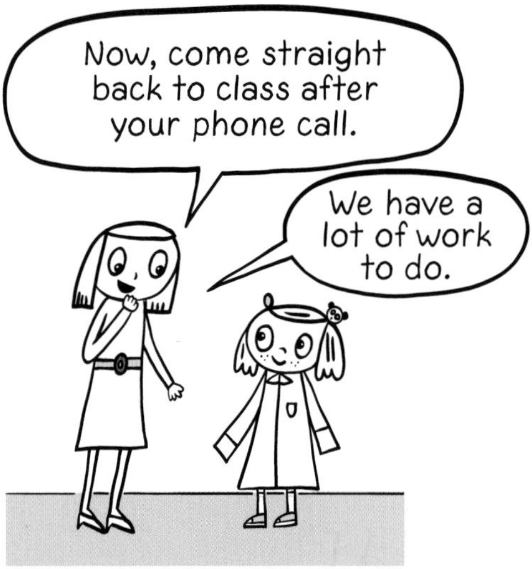
Now, come straight back to class after your phone call.
We have a lot of work to do.

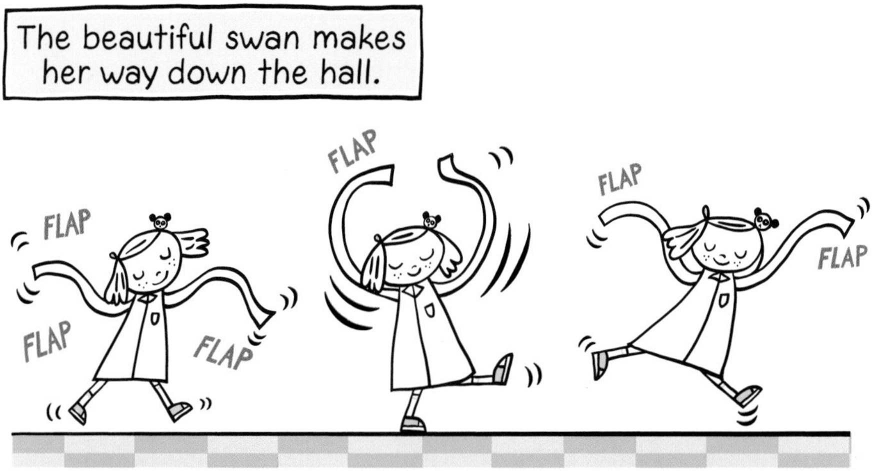
The beautiful swan makes her way down the hall.
FLAP
FLAP
FLAP
FLAP
FLAP
FLAP

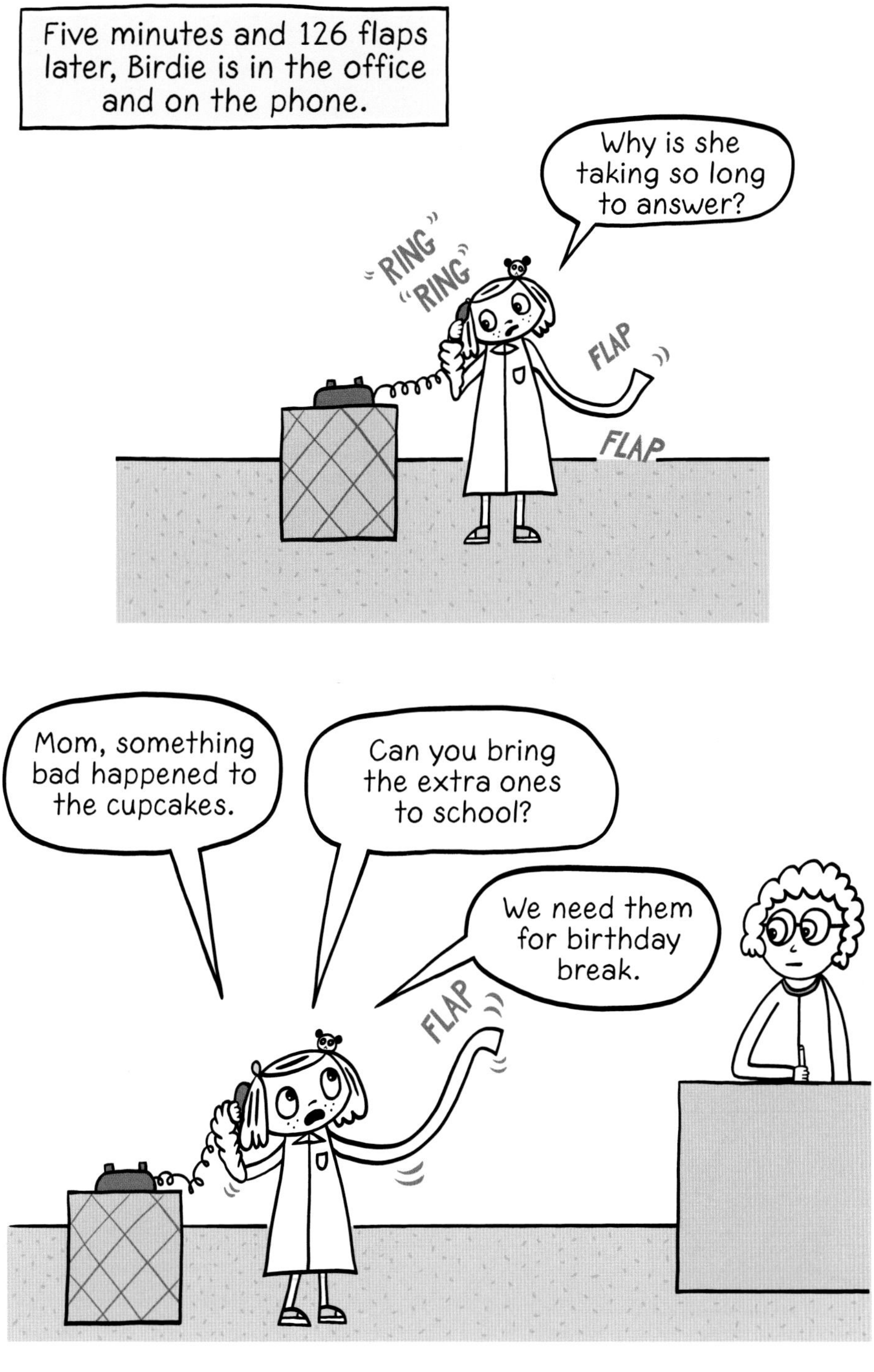
Five minutes and 126 flaps later, Birdie is in the office and on the phone.
Why is she taking so long to answer?
RING
RING
FLAP
FLAP
Mom, something bad happened to the cupcakes.
Can you bring the extra ones to school?
We need them for birthday break.
FLAP

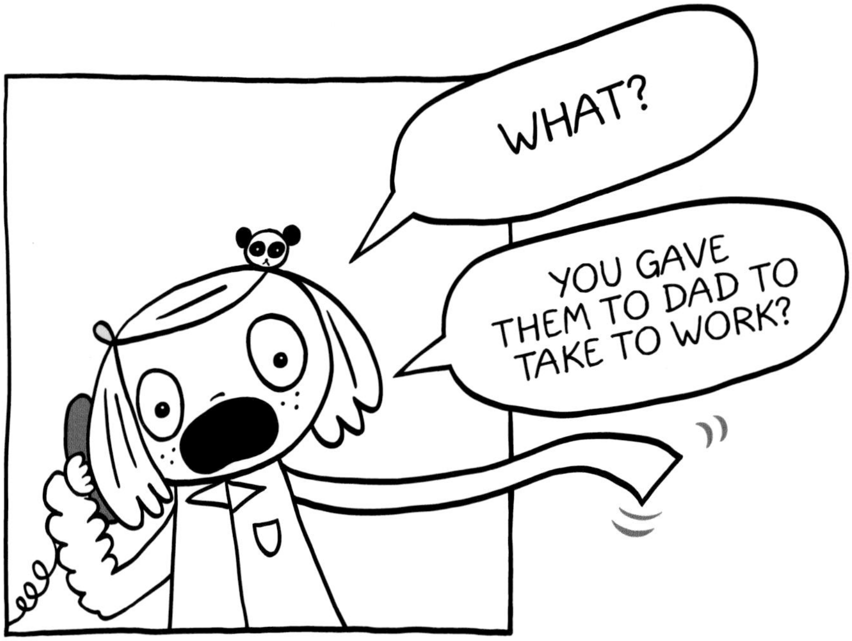
WHAT?
YOU GAVE THEM TO DAD TO TAKE TO WORK?

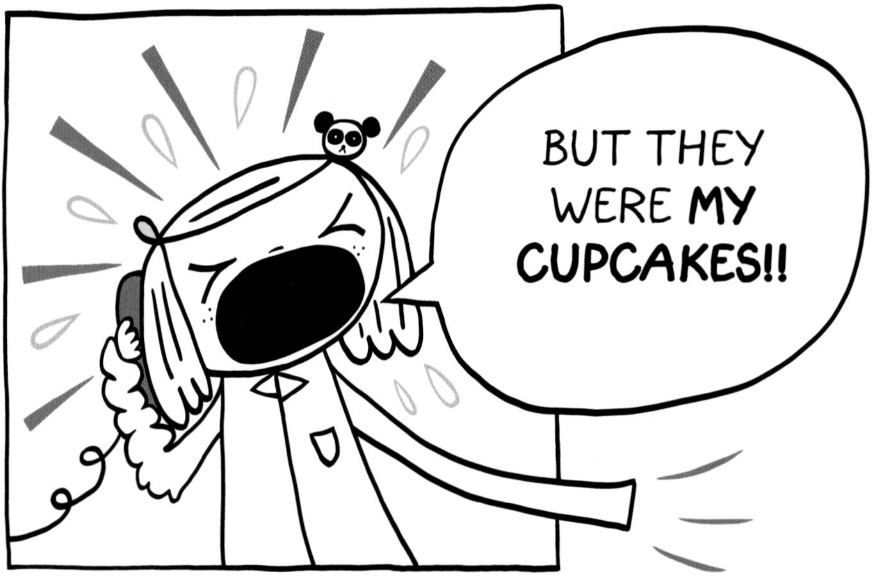
BUT THEY WERE **MY CUPCAKES!!**

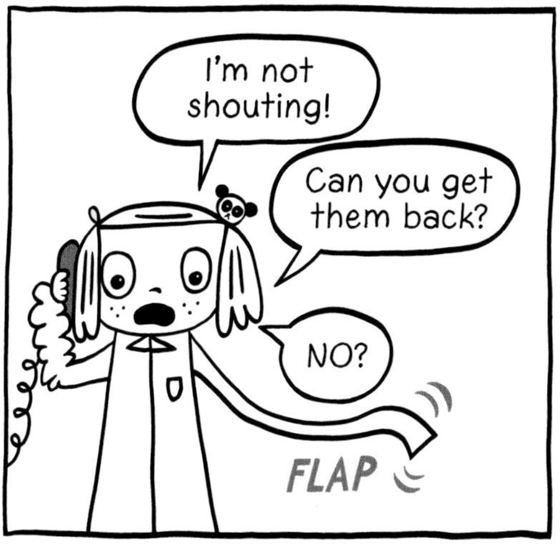
I'm not shouting!
Can you get them back?
NO?
FLAP

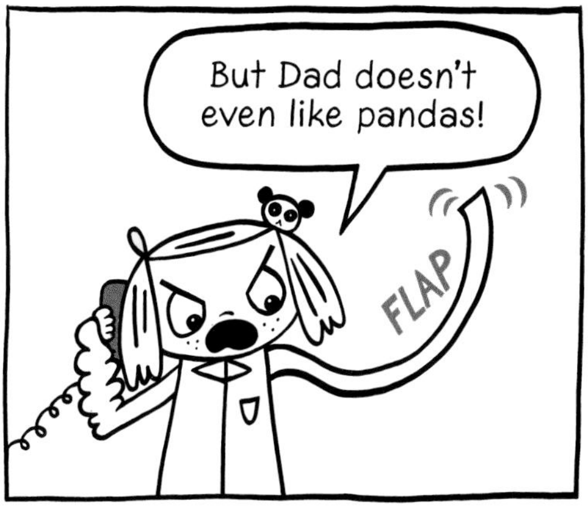
But Dad doesn't even like pandas!
FLAP

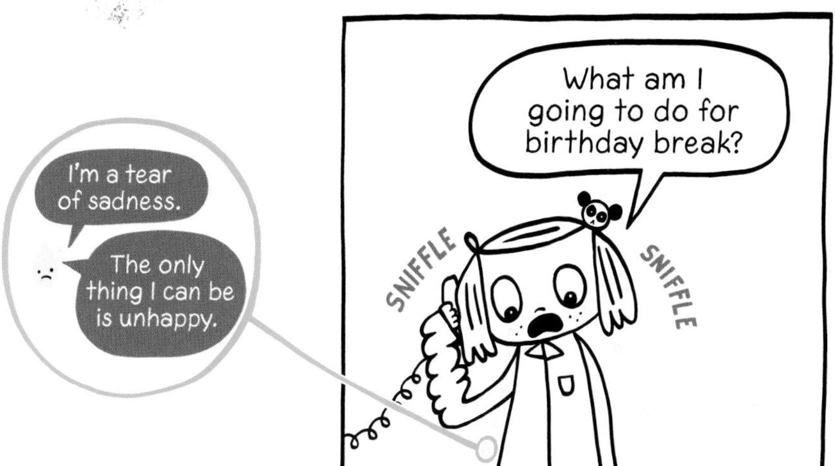
What am I going to do for birthday break?
SNIFFLE
SNIFFLE
I'm a tear of sadness.
The only thing I can be is unhappy.

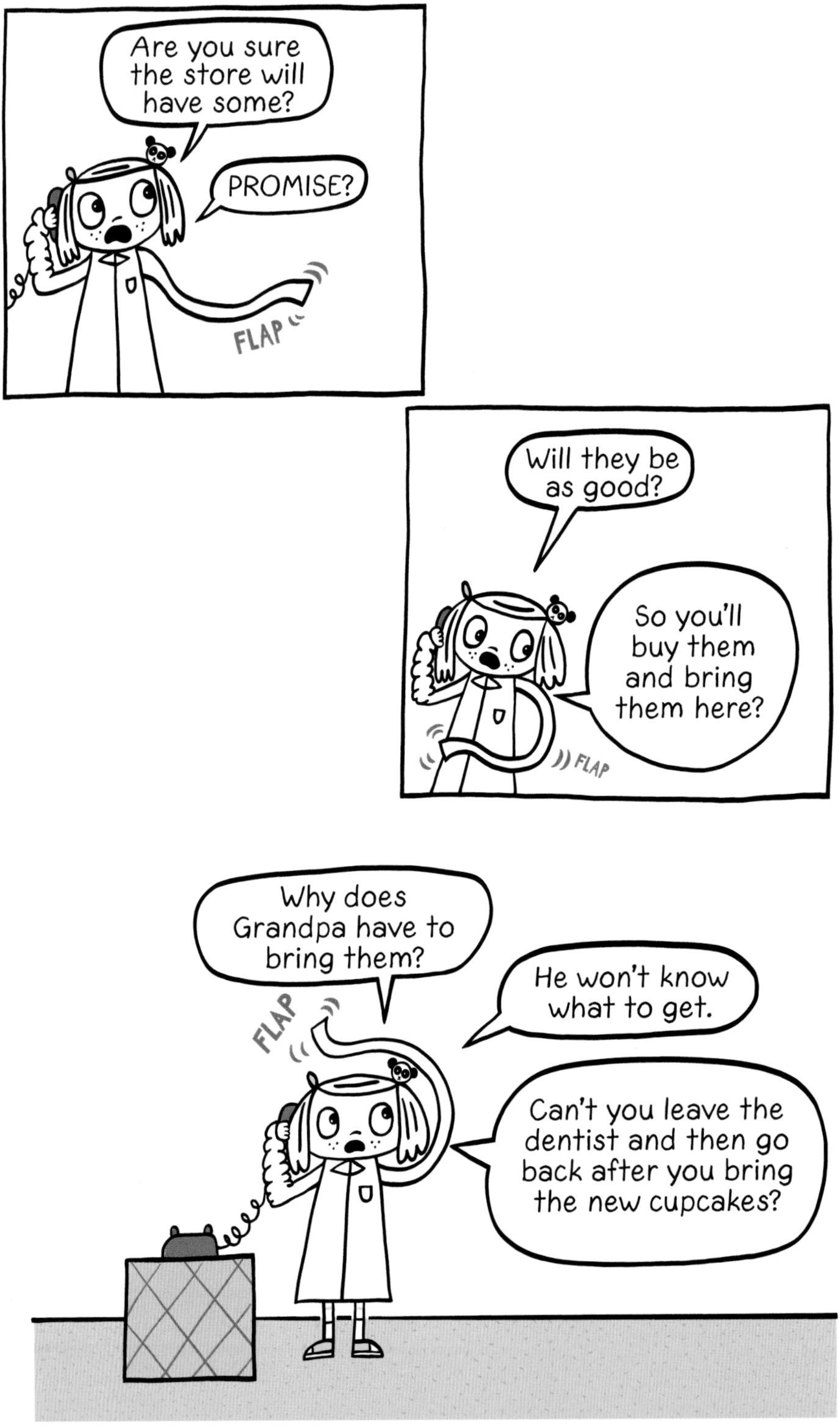
Are you sure the store will have some?
PROMISE?
FLAP
Will they be as good?
So you'll buy them and bring them here?
FLAP
Why does Grandpa have to bring them?
He won't know what to get.
FLAP
Can't you leave the dentist and then go back after you bring the new cupcakes?

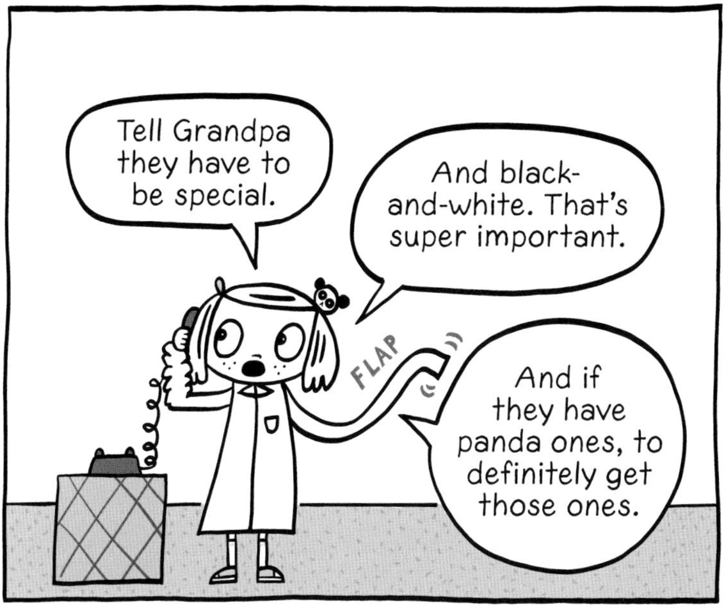
Tell Grandpa they have to be special.
And black-and-white. That's super important.
FLAP
And if they have panda ones, to definitely get those ones.

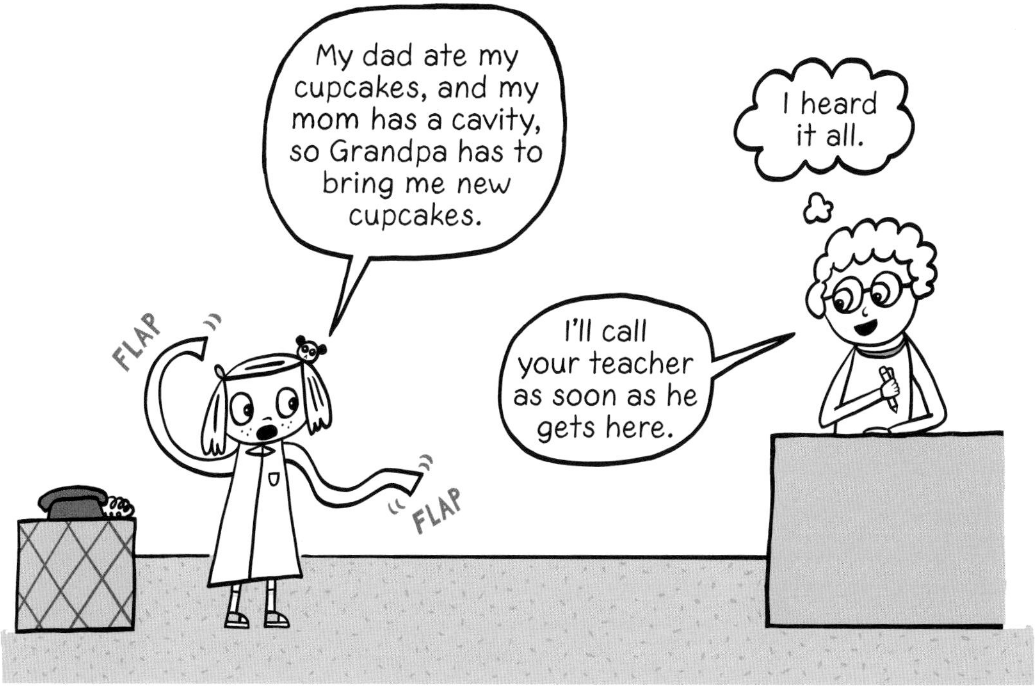
My dad ate my cupcakes, and my mom has a cavity, so Grandpa has to bring me new cupcakes.
FLAP
FLAP
I heard it all.
I'll call your teacher as soon as he gets here.

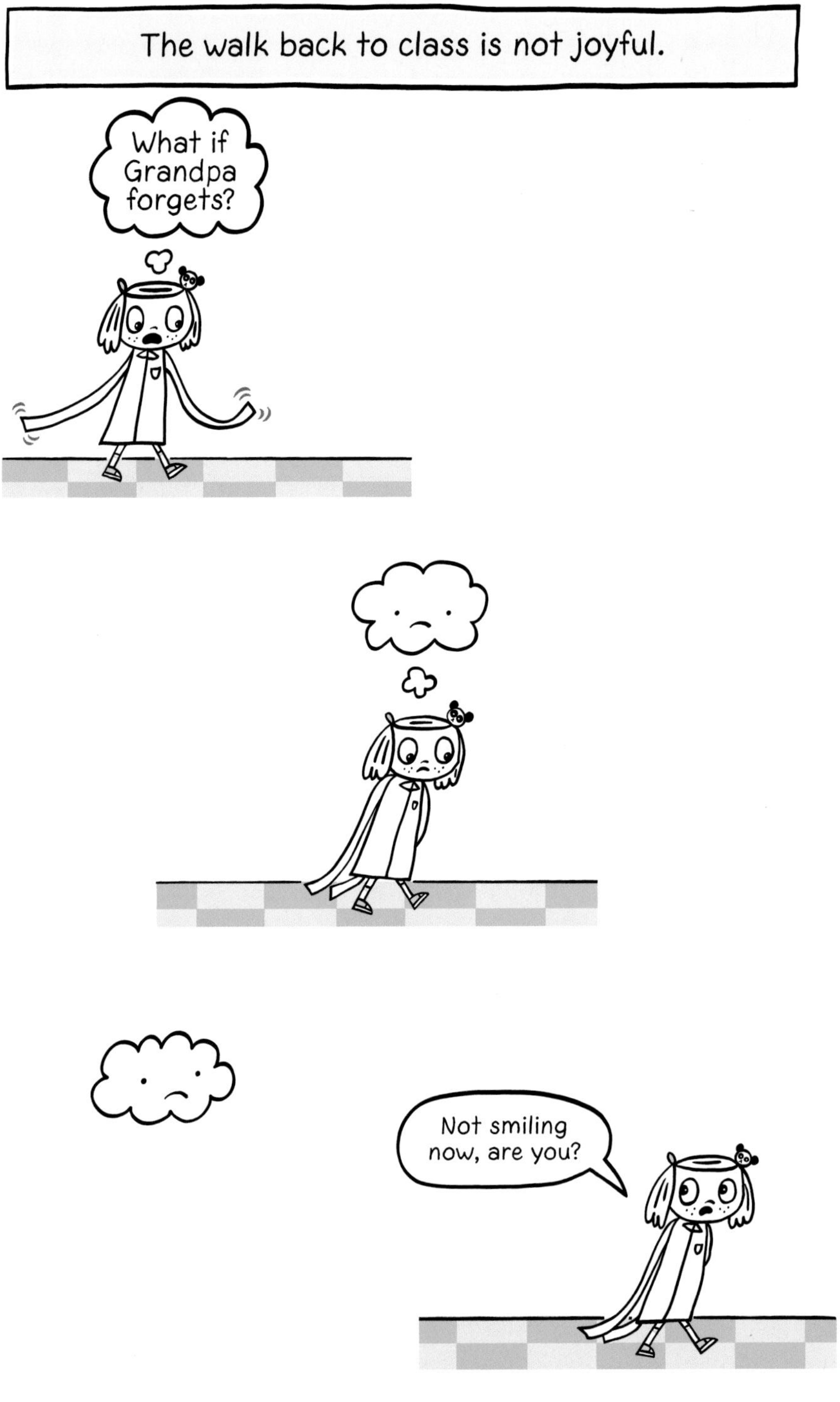
The walk back to class is not joyful.
What if Grandpa forgets?
Not smiling now, are you?

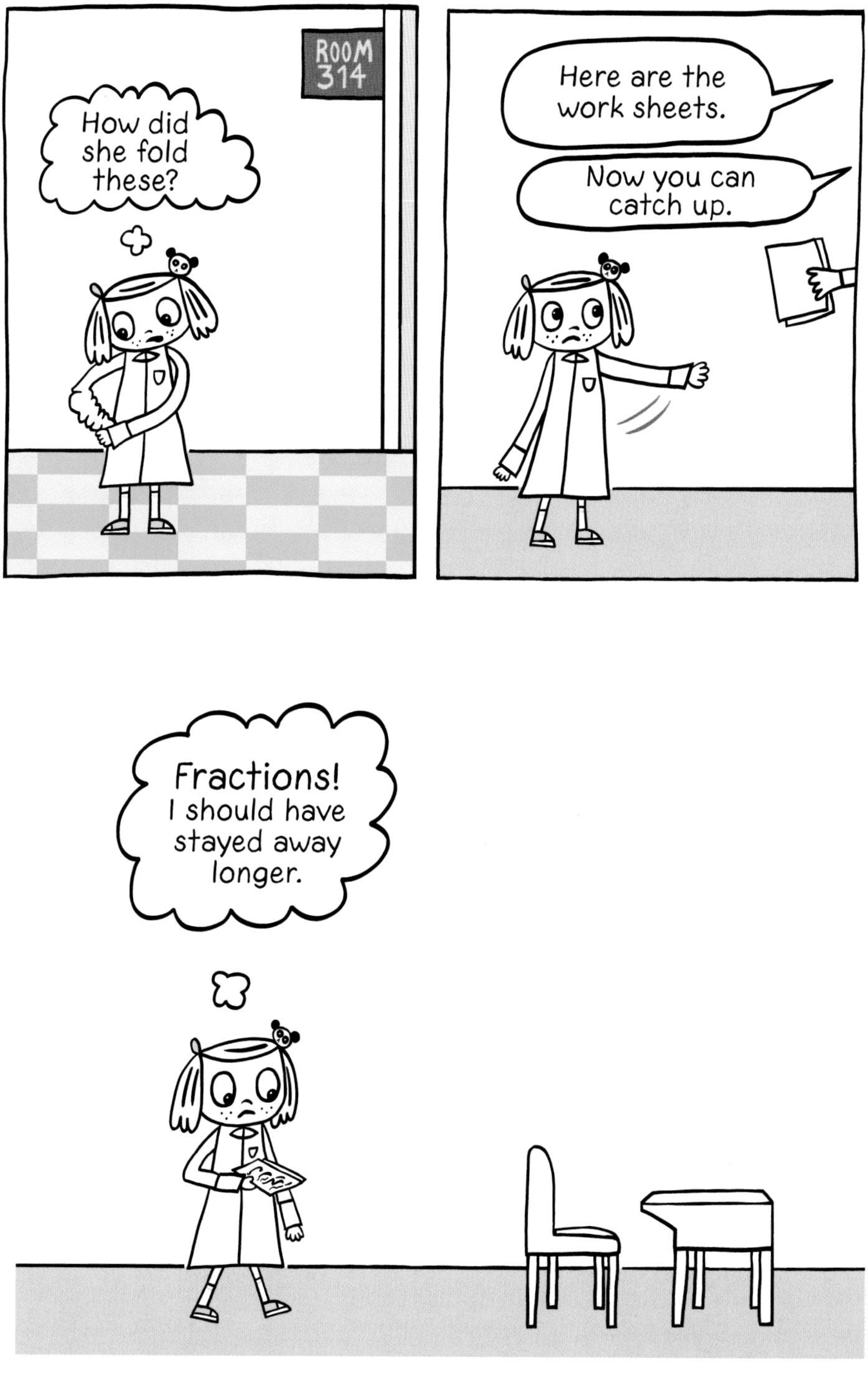
ROOM 314
How did she fold these?
Here are the work sheets.
Now you can catch up.
Fractions! I should have stayed away longer.

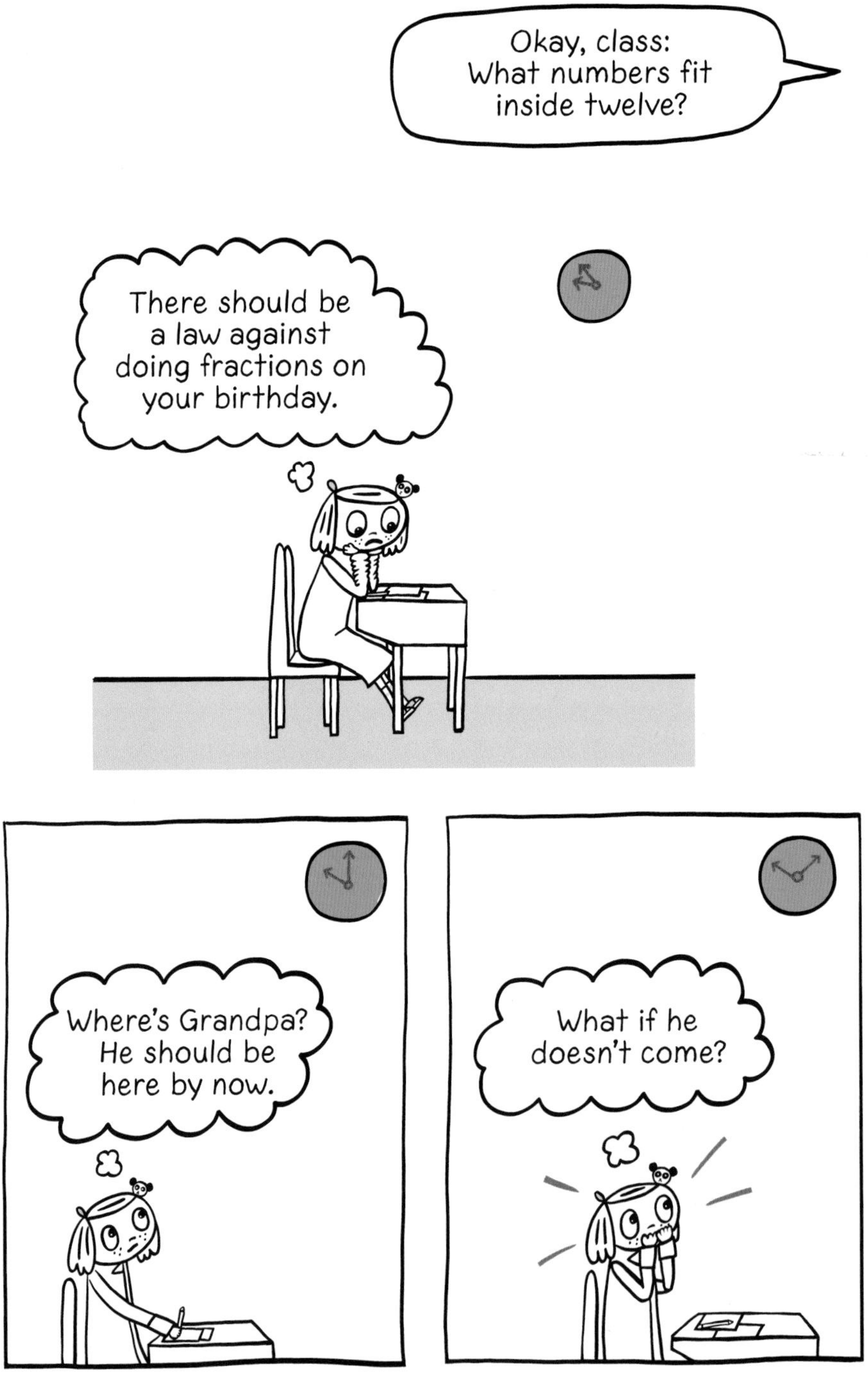
Okay, class:
What numbers fit
inside twelve?
There should be
a law against
doing fractions on
your birthday.
Where's Grandpa?
He should be
here by now.
What if he
doesn't come?

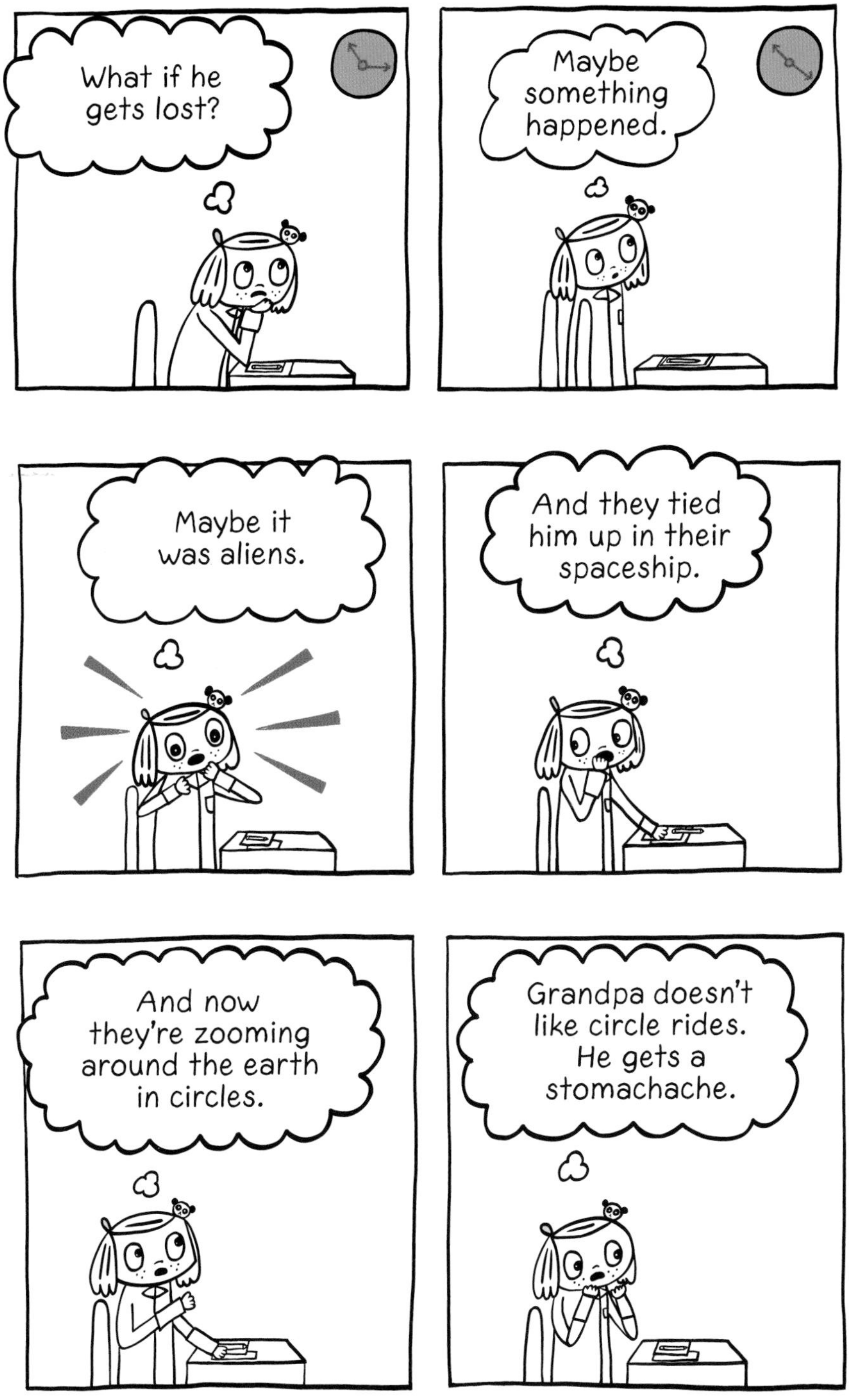
What if he gets lost?
Maybe something happened.
Maybe it was aliens.
And they tied him up in their spaceship.
And now they're zooming around the earth in circles.
Grandpa doesn't like circle rides. He gets a stomachache.

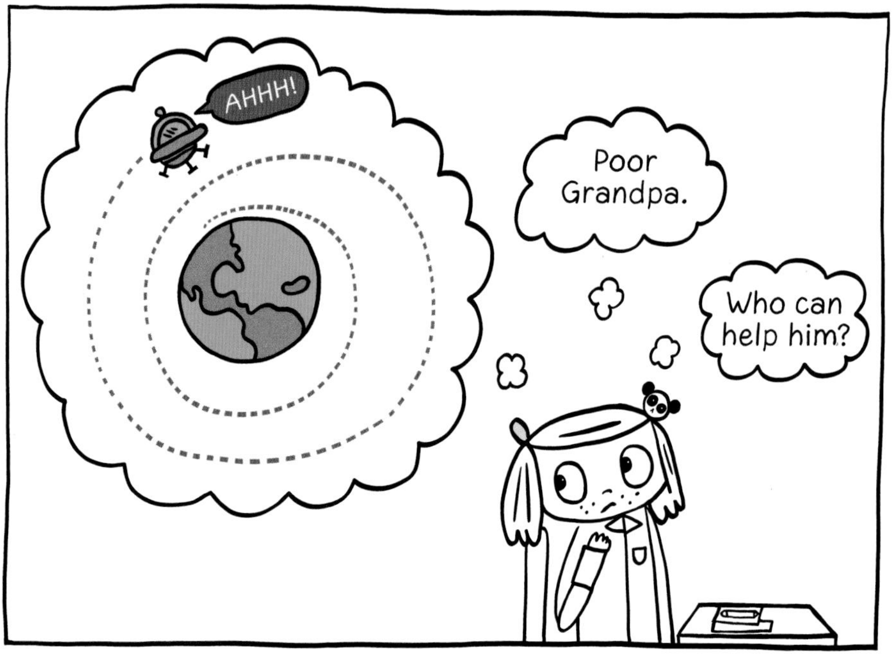
AHHH!
Poor Grandpa.
Who can help him?

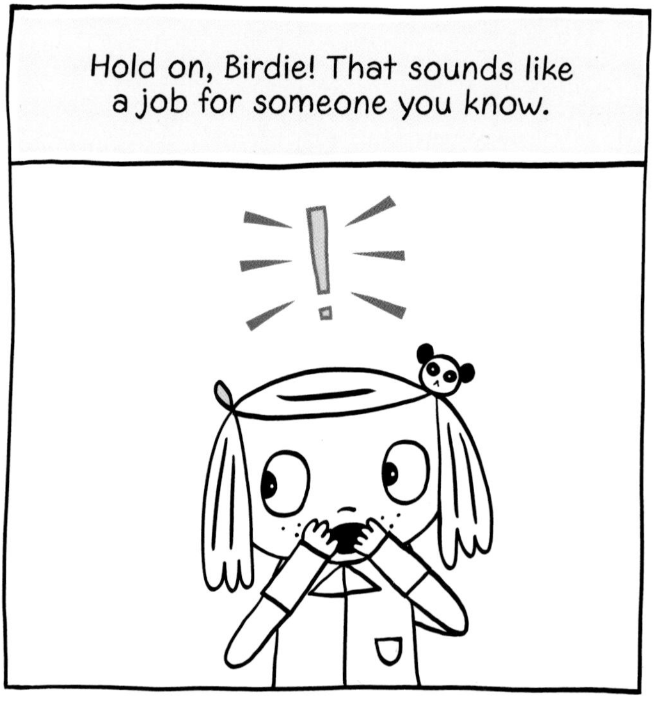
Hold on, Birdie! That sounds like a job for someone you know.
!

Someone who's not afraid of paper cuts.

Someone who can handle a stapler in one hand and glue in the other.

Someone who can fold a perfectly straight line without a ruler.

Someone who can cut tape without getting stuck.
Someone who can sew, knot, and tie without tangles.
Someone who is not afraid of the word "homemade."

Who is that someone?

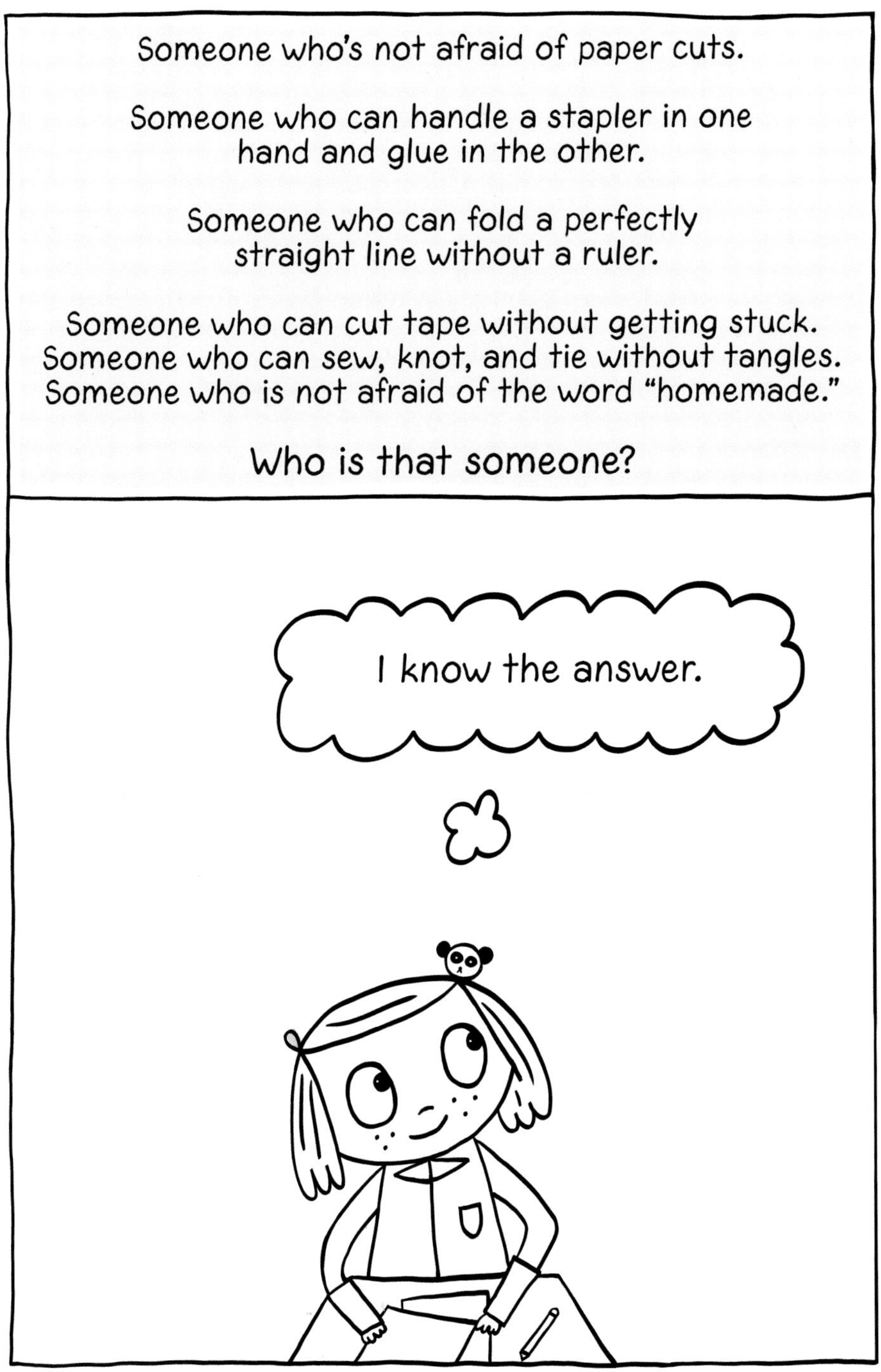
I know the answer.

PATTERNED PAPERS

SWIRLING STRING

GLOPPY GLUE

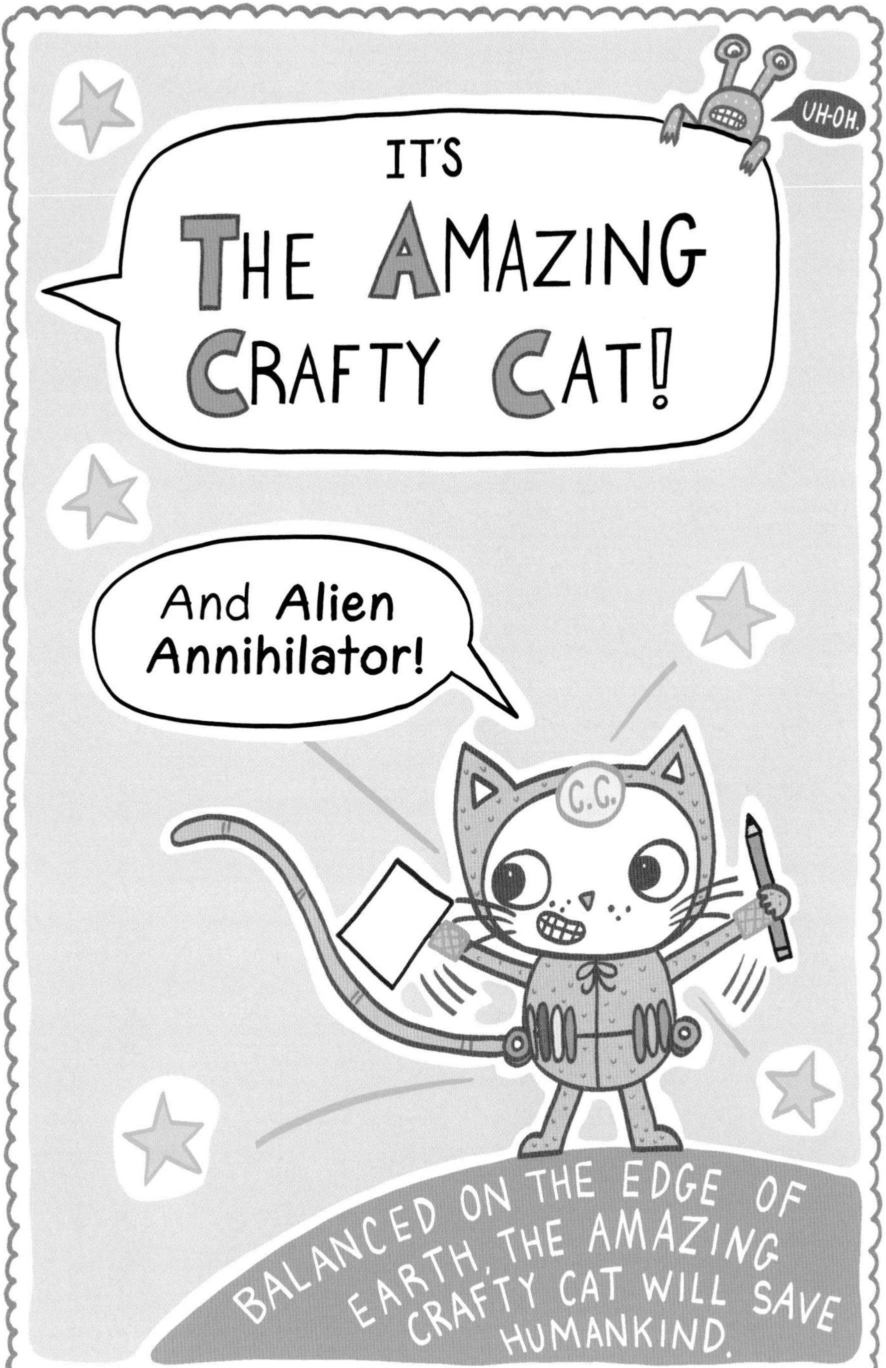
UH-OH.
IT'S THE AMAZING CRAFTY CAT!
And Alien Annihilator!
C.C.
BALANCED ON THE EDGE OF EARTH, THE AMAZING CRAFTY CAT WILL SAVE HUMANKIND.

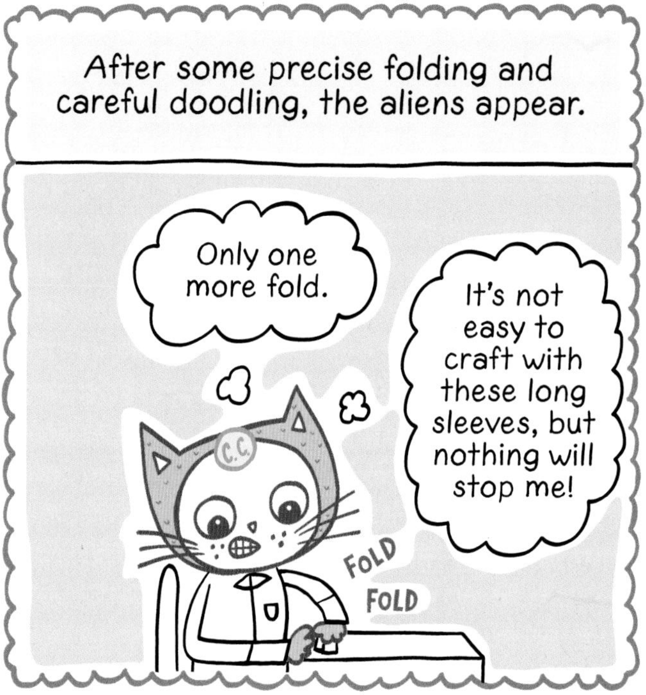
After some precise folding and careful doodling, the aliens appear.
Only one more fold.
It's not easy to craft with these long sleeves, but nothing will stop me!
FOLD
FOLD
C.C.

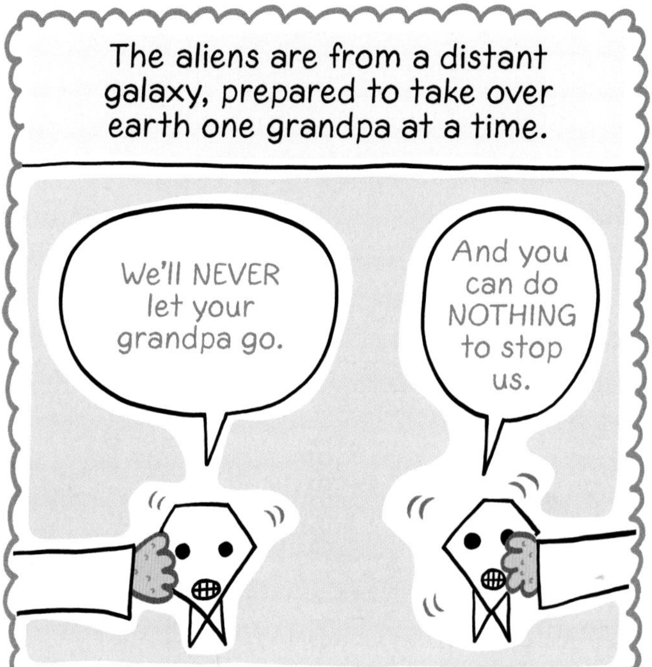
The aliens are from a distant galaxy, prepared to take over earth one grandpa at a time.
We'll NEVER let your grandpa go.
And you can do NOTHING to stop us.

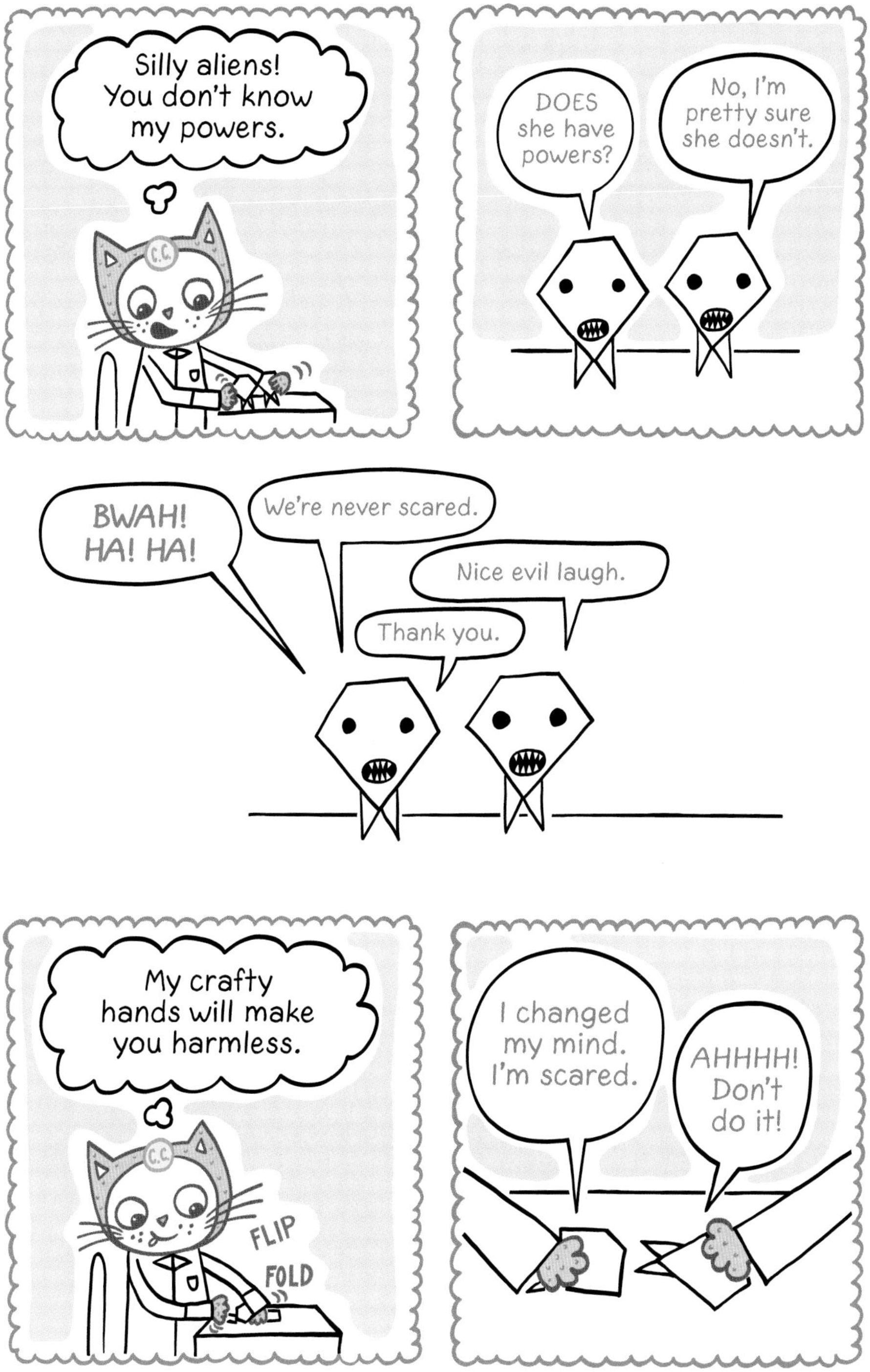
Silly aliens! You don't know my powers.
DOES she have powers?
No, I'm pretty sure she doesn't.
BWAH! HA! HA!
We're never scared.
Nice evil laugh.
Thank you.
My crafty hands will make you harmless.
FLIP
FOLD
I changed my mind. I'm scared.
AHHHH! Don't do it!

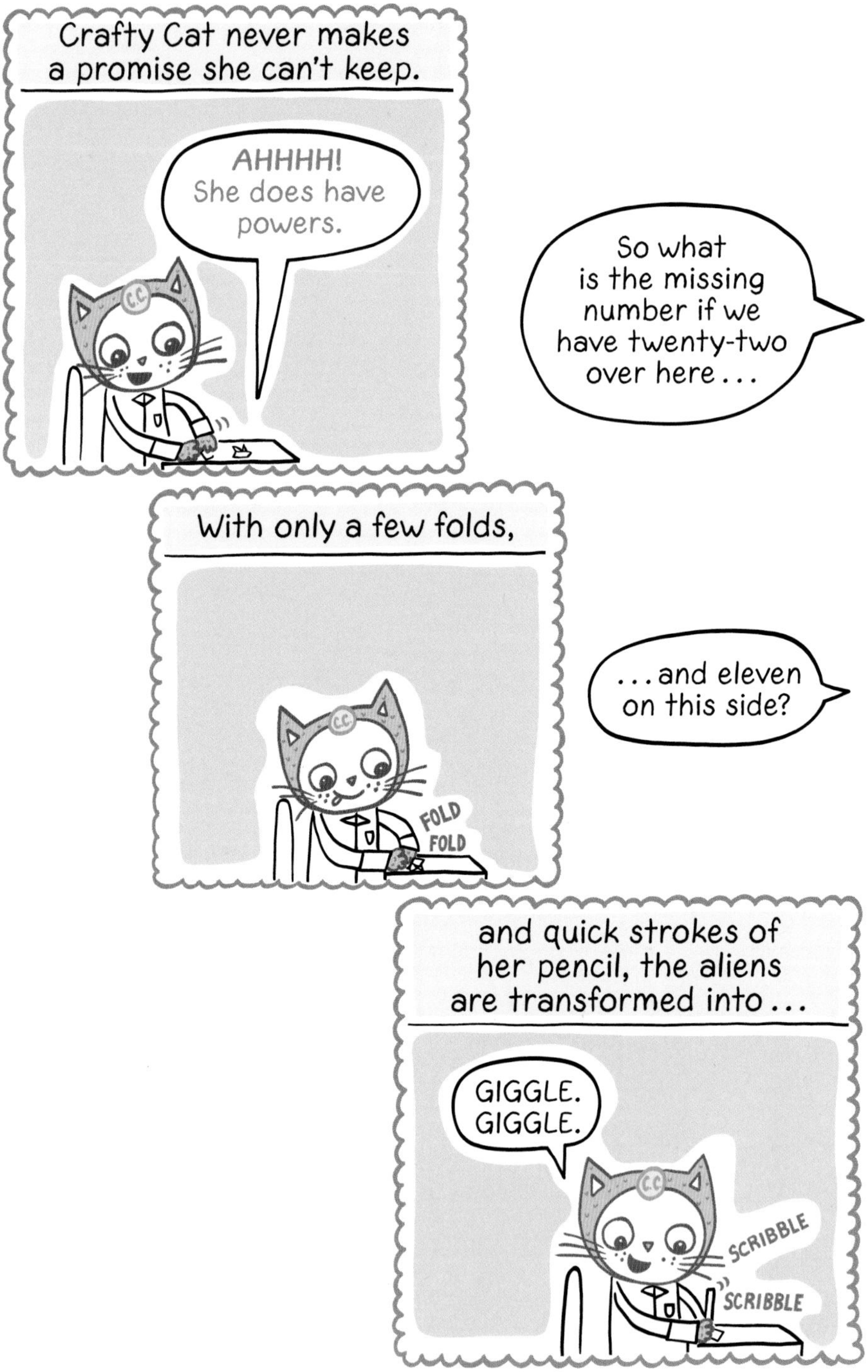
Crafty Cat never makes a promise she can't keep.
AHHHH! She does have powers.
So what is the missing number if we have twenty-two over here . . .
With only a few folds,
FOLD
FOLD
. . . and eleven on this side?
and quick strokes of her pencil, the aliens are transformed into . . .
GIGGLE. GIGGLE.
SCRIBBLE
SCRIBBLE

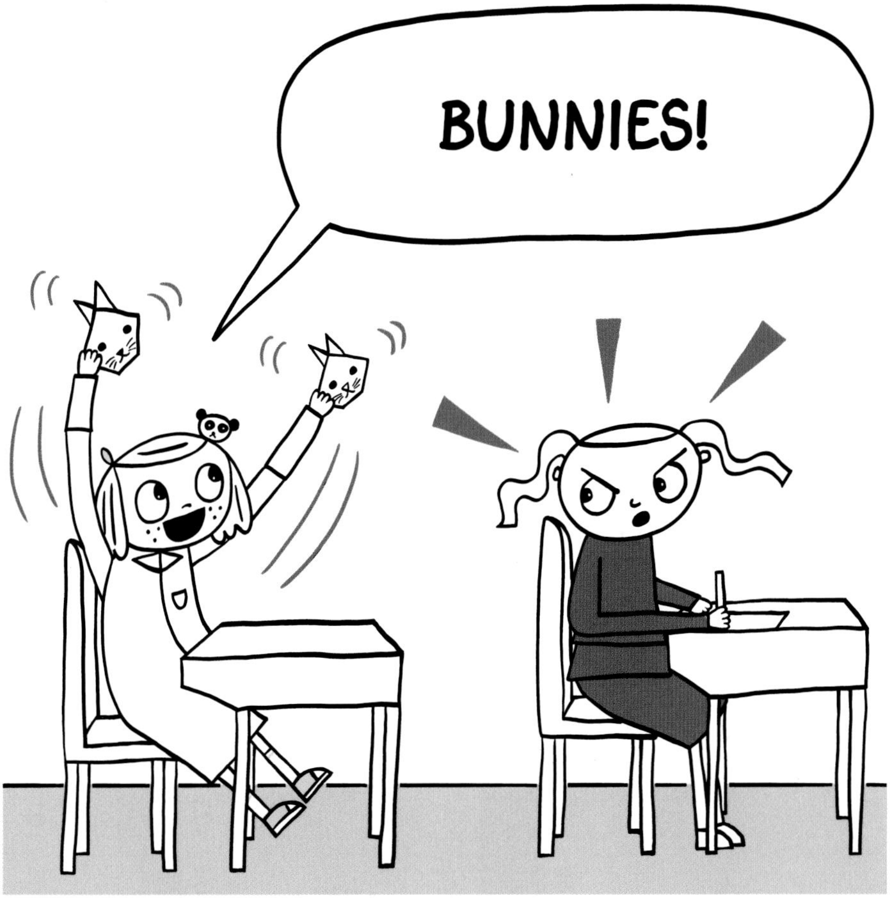
BUNNIES!

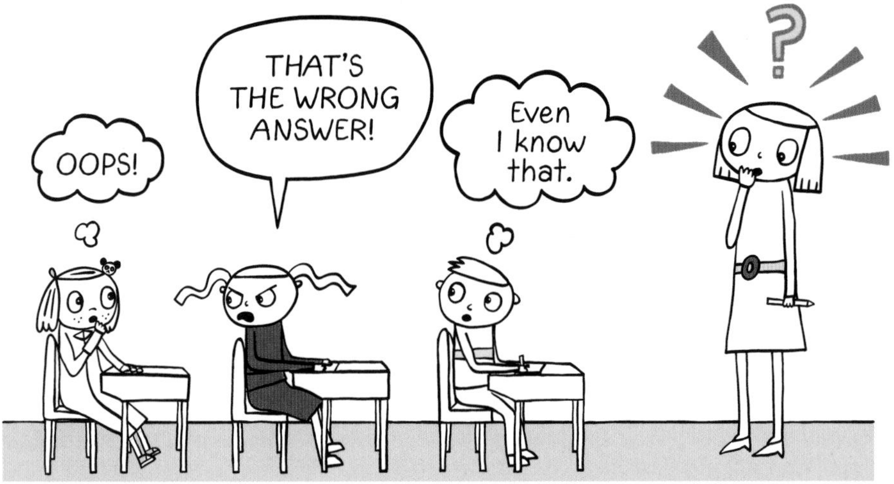
OOPS!
THAT'S THE WRONG ANSWER!
Even I know that.
?

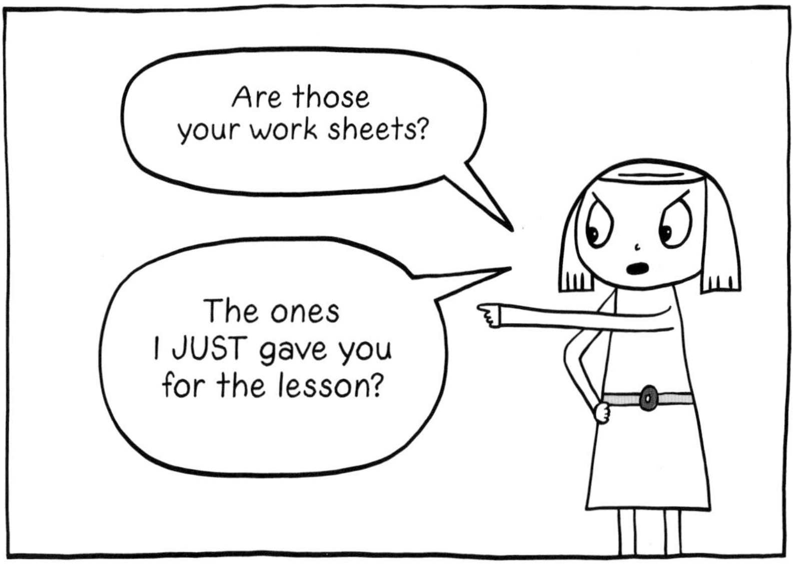
Are those your work sheets?
The ones I JUST gave you for the lesson?

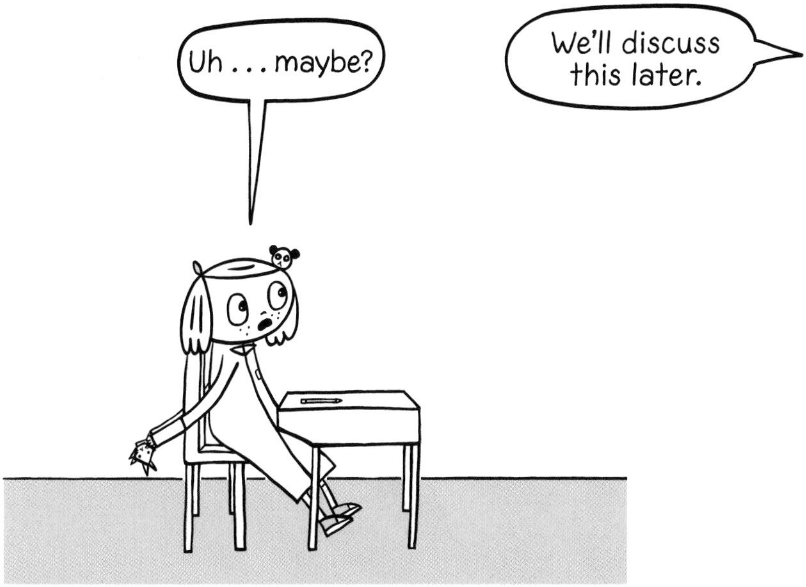
Uh . . . maybe?
We'll discuss this later.

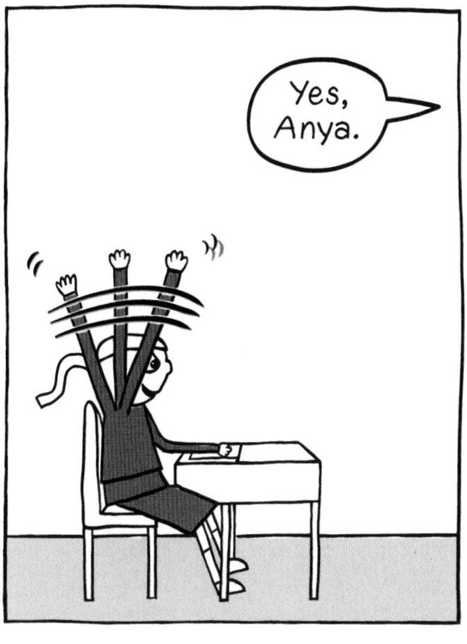
Yes, Anya.

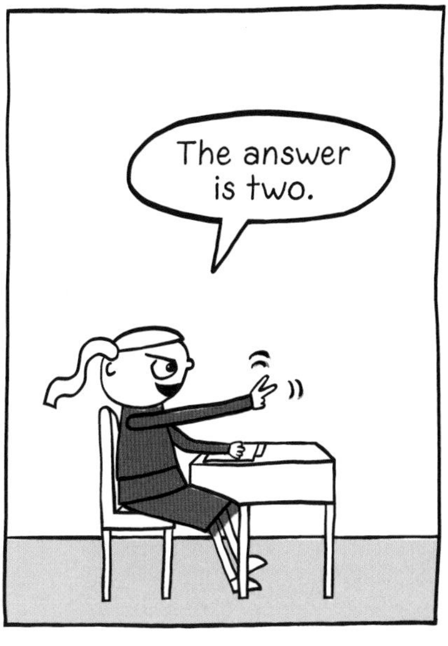
The answer is two.

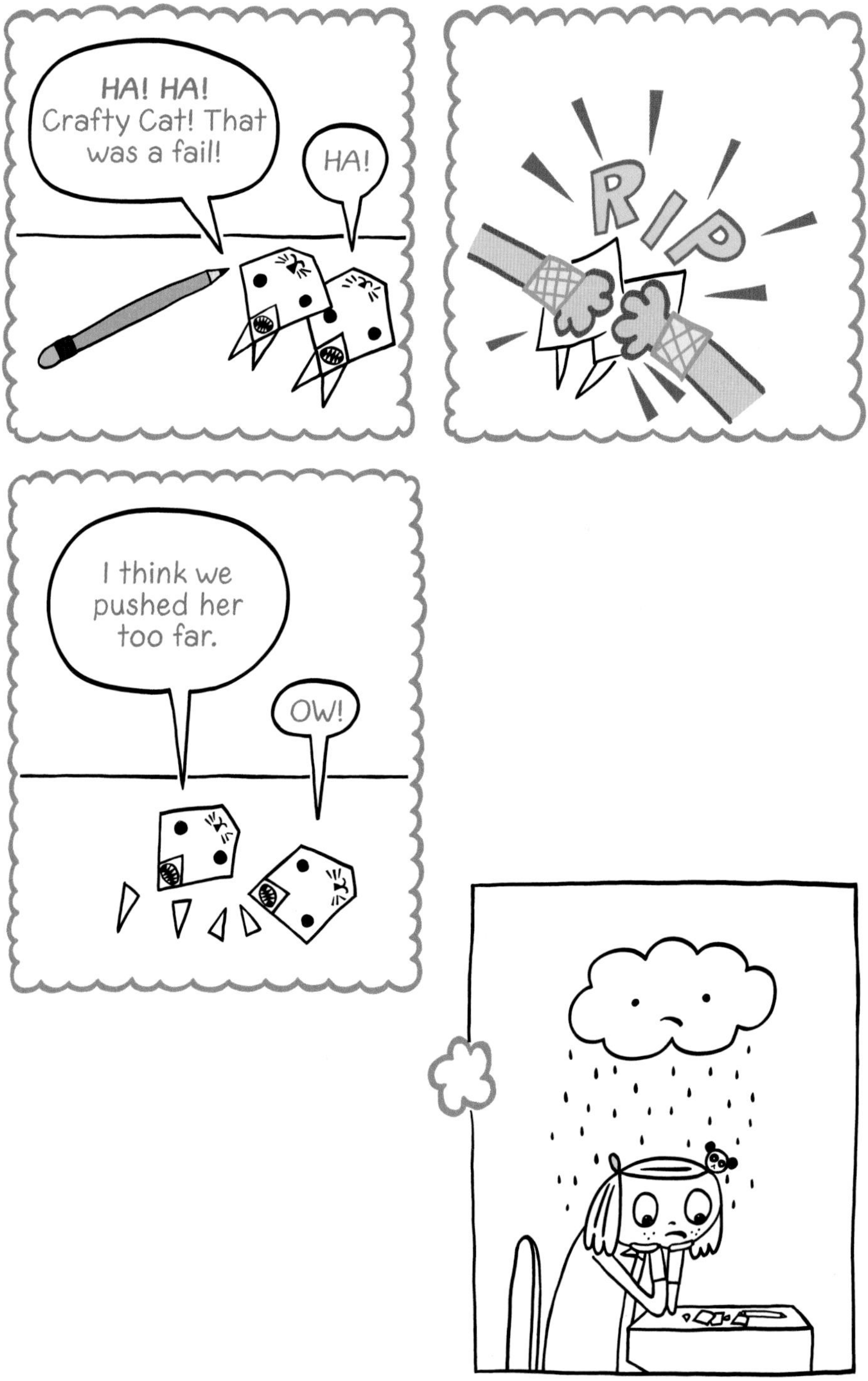

HA! HA!
Crafty Cat! That was a fail!
HA!
RIP
I think we pushed her too far.
OW!

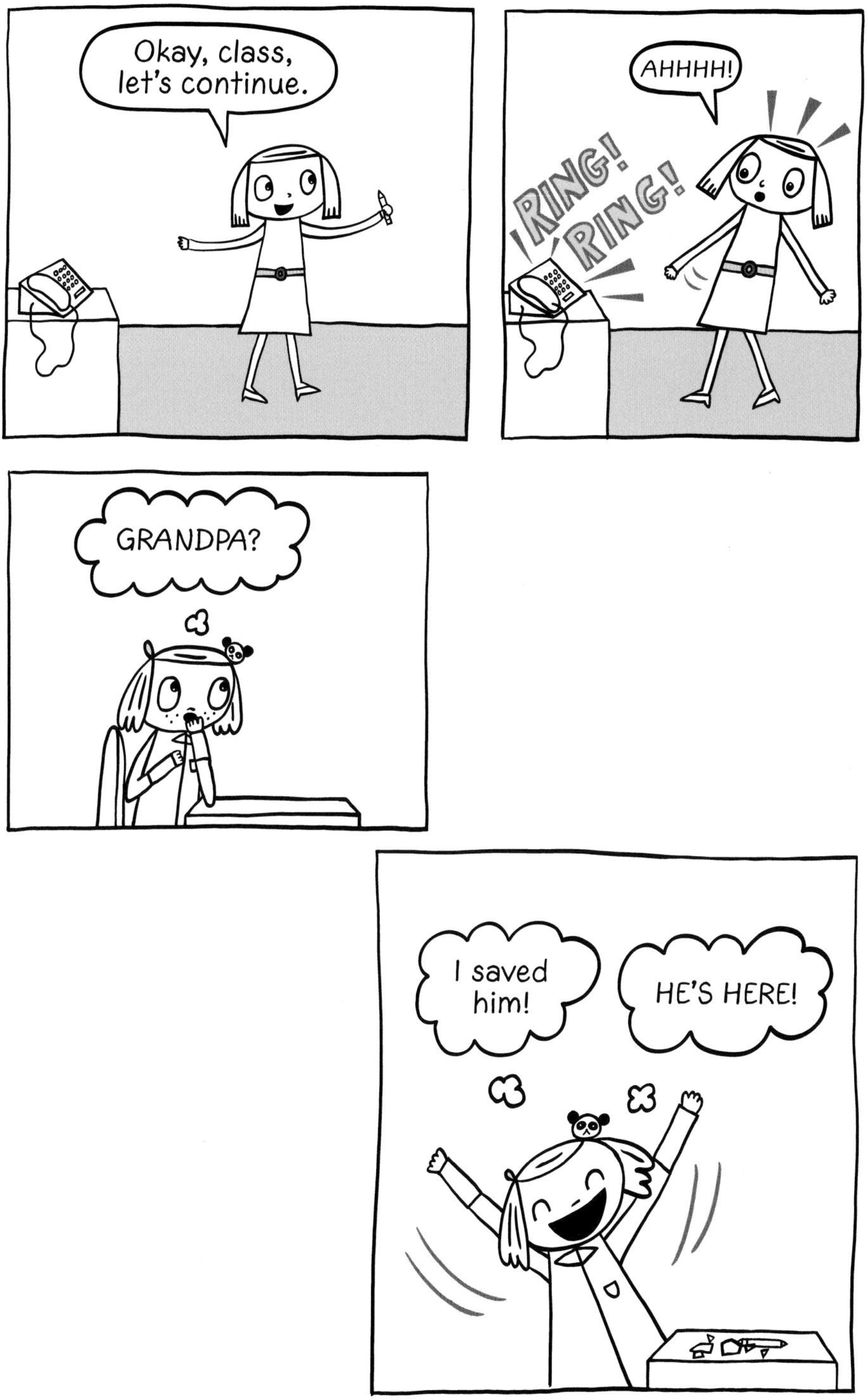
Okay, class, let's continue.
AHHHH!
RING! RING!
GRANDPA?
I saved him!
HE'S HERE!

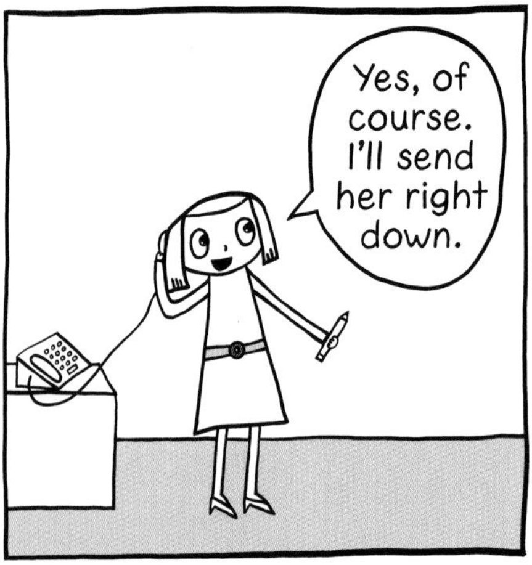
Yes, of course. I'll send her right down.

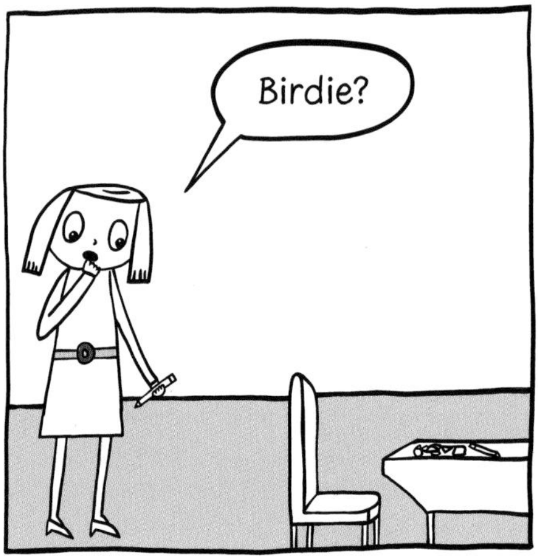
Birdie?

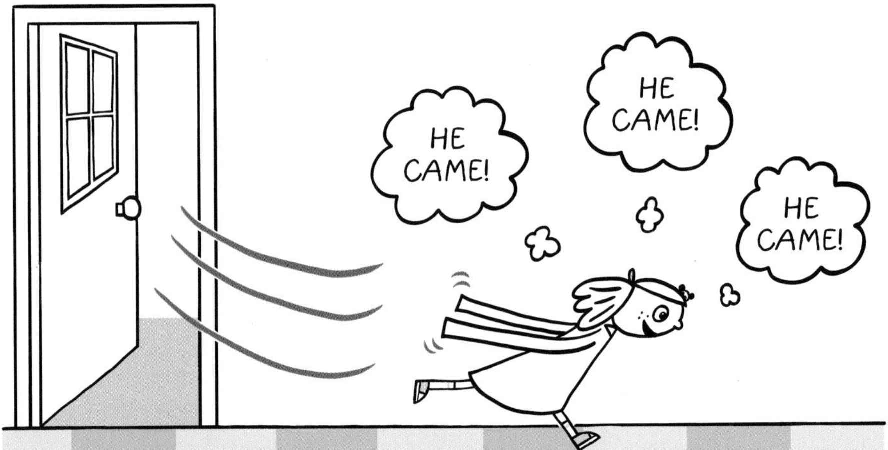
HE CAME!
HE CAME!
HE CAME!

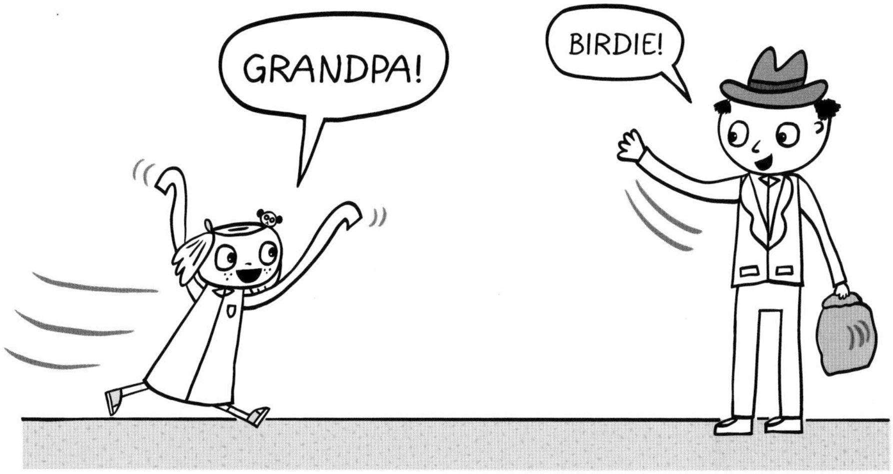
GRANDPA!
BIRDIE!

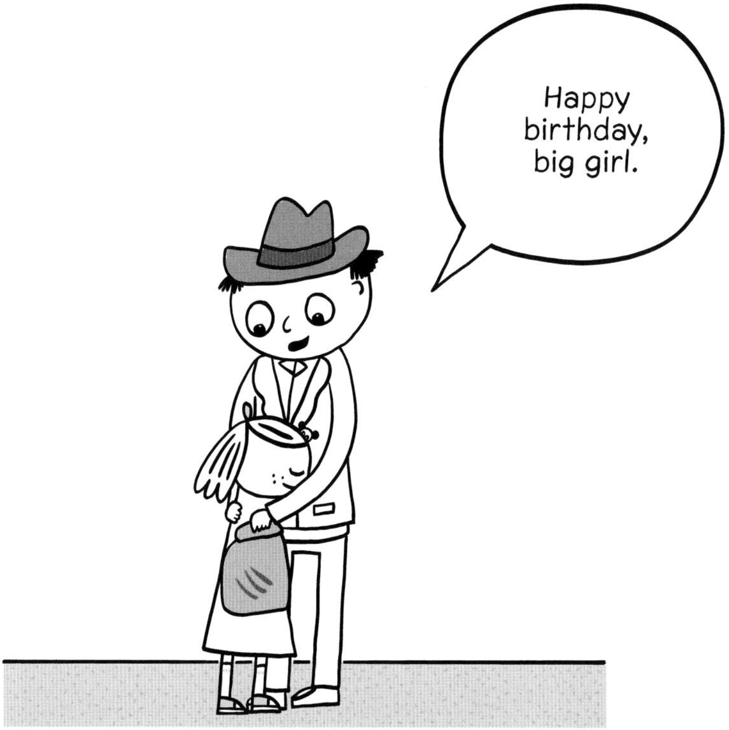
Happy birthday, big girl.

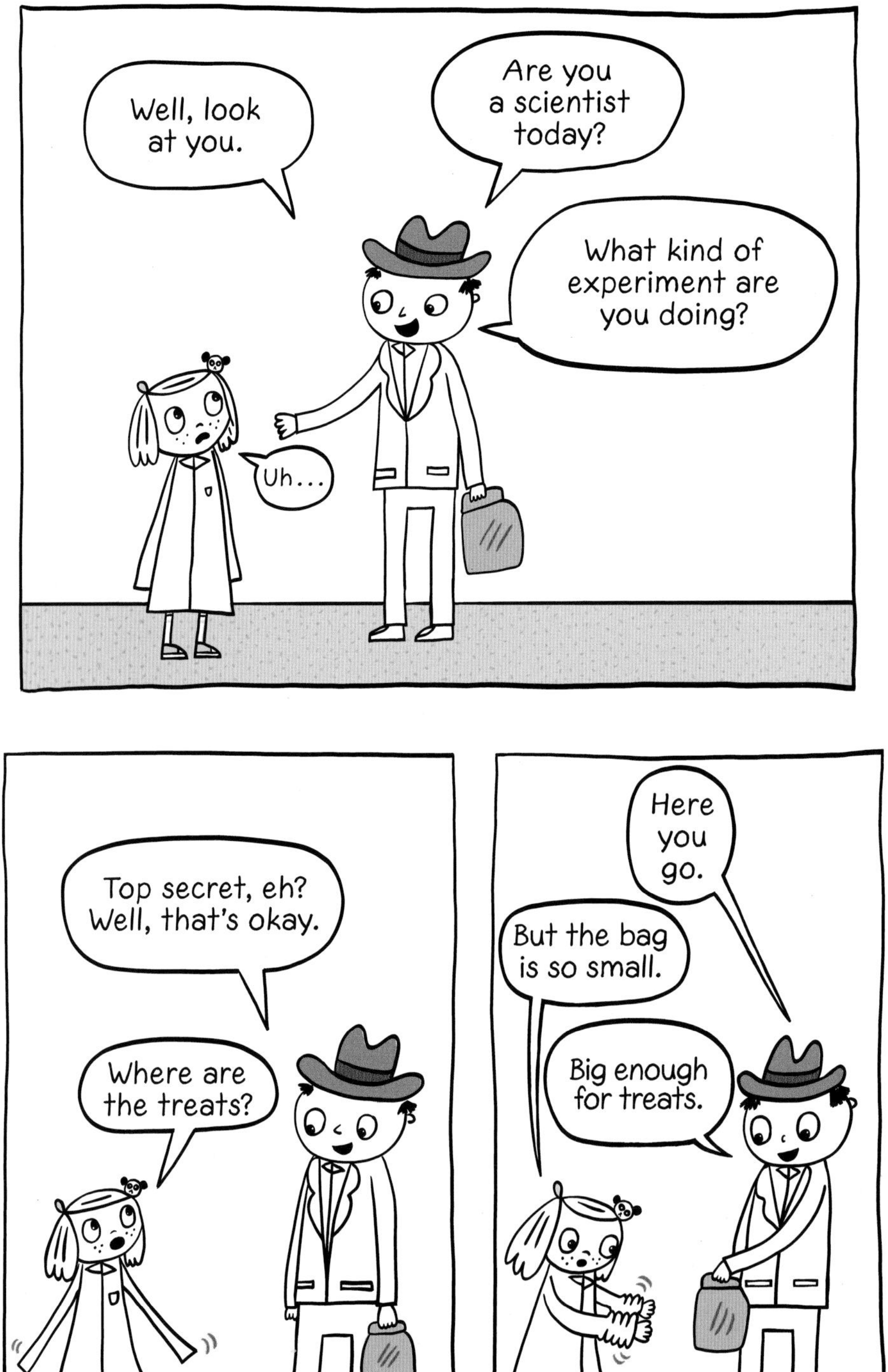
Well, look at you.
Are you a scientist today?
What kind of experiment are you doing?
Uh...
Top secret, eh? Well, that's okay.
Where are the treats?
Here you go.
But the bag is so small.
Big enough for treats.

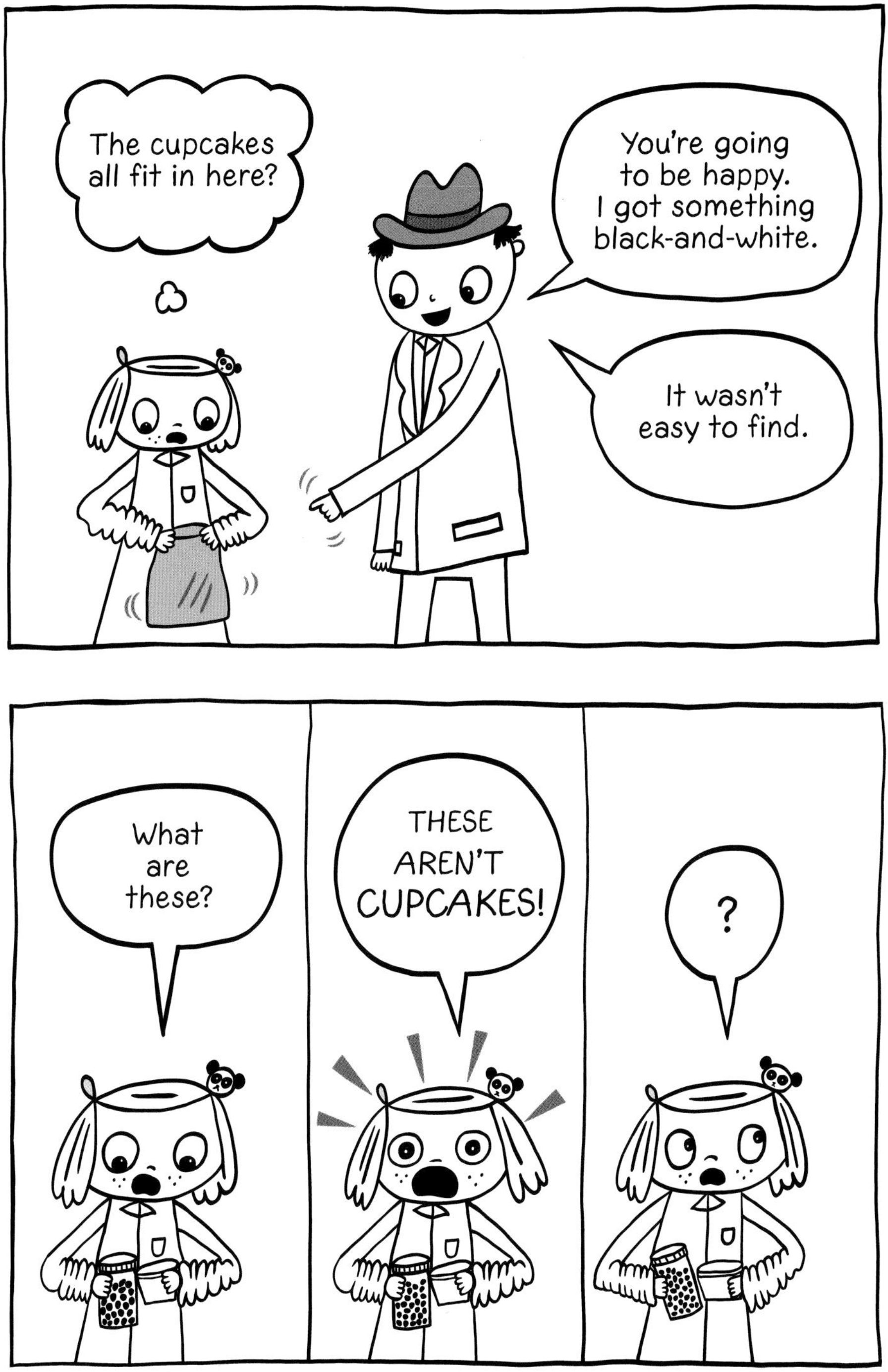
The cupcakes all fit in here?
You're going to be happy. I got something black-and-white.
It wasn't easy to find.
What are these?
THESE AREN'T CUPCAKES!
?

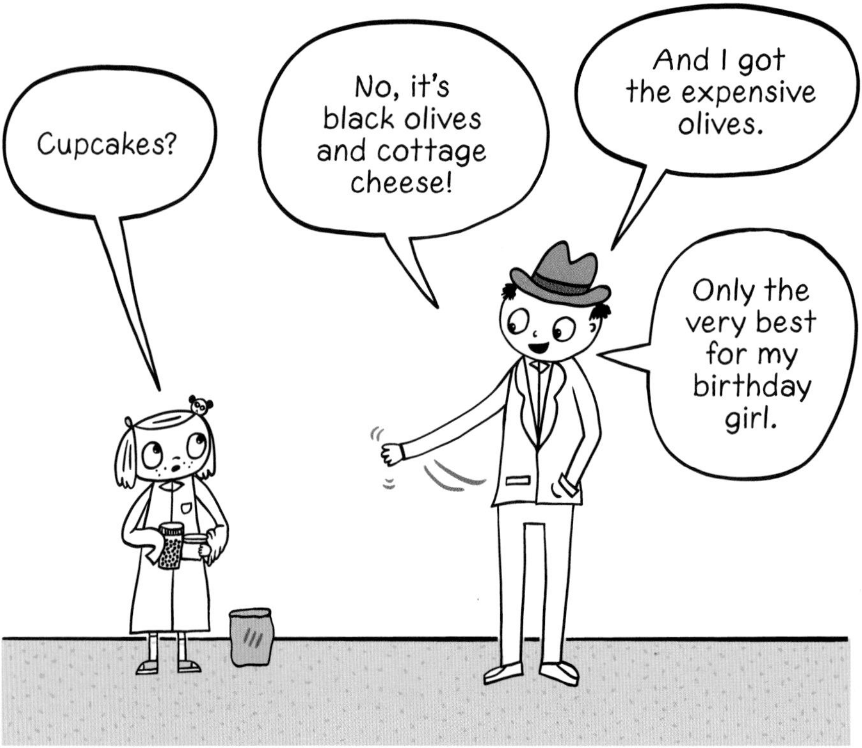
Cupcakes?
No, it's black olives and cottage cheese!
And I got the expensive olives.
Only the very best for my birthday girl.

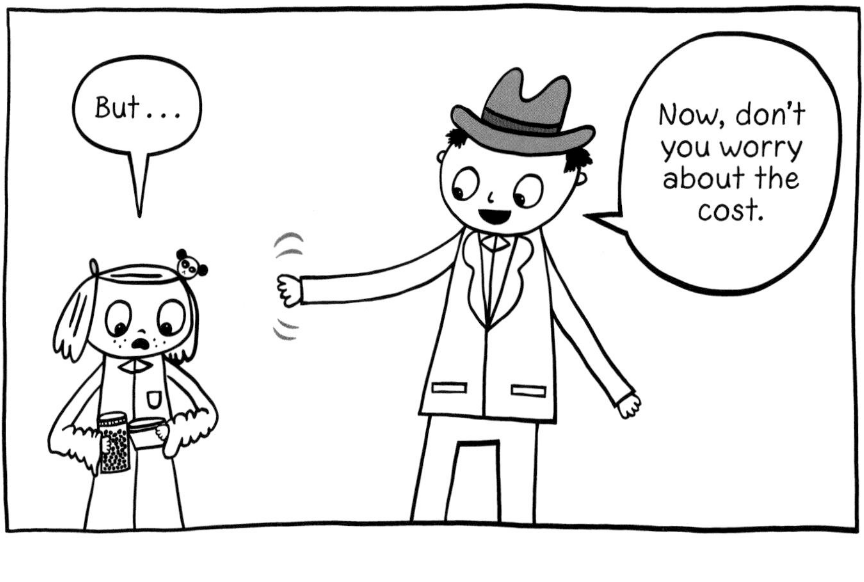
But . . .
Now, don't you worry about the cost.

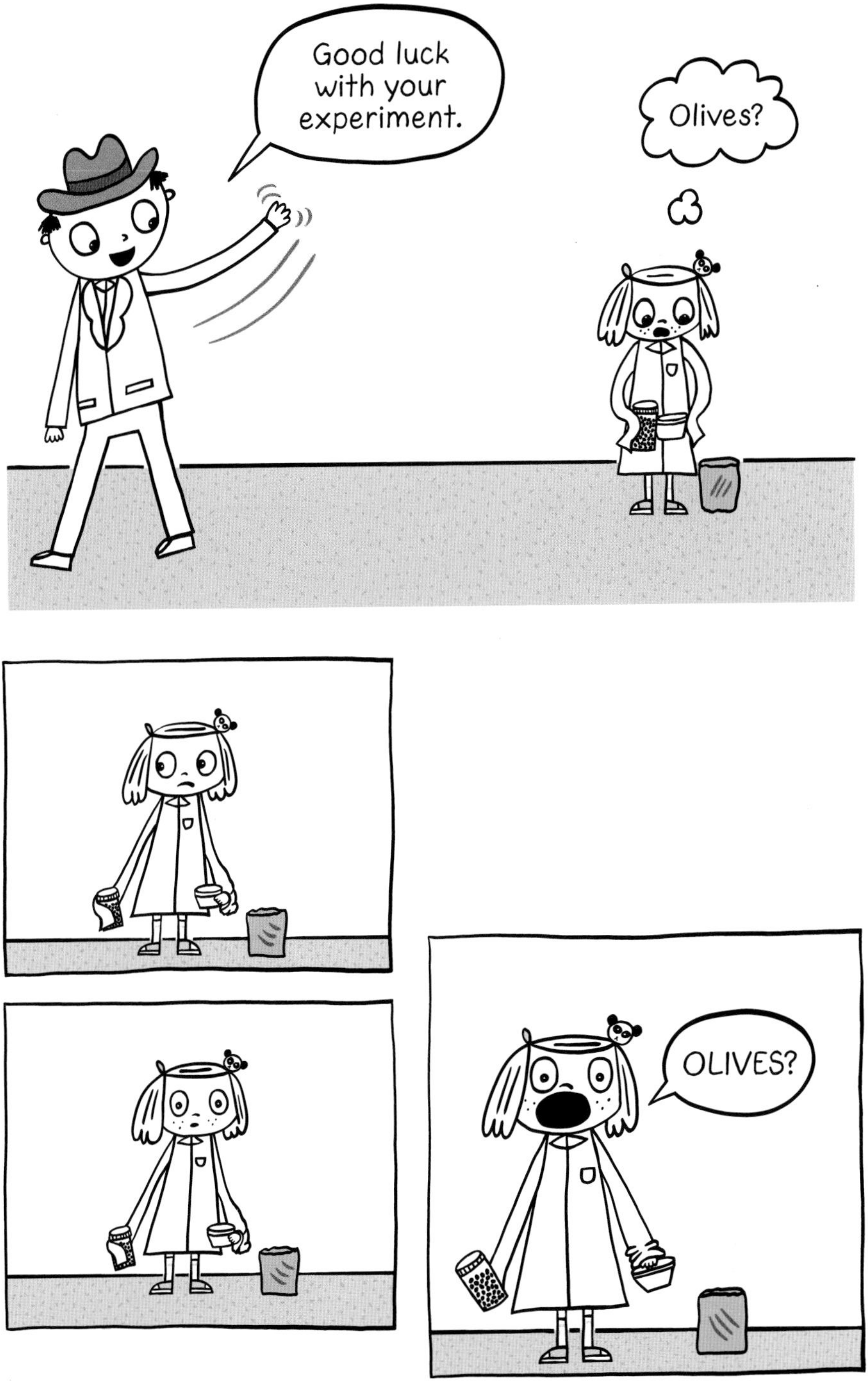
Good luck with your experiment.
Olives?
OLIVES?

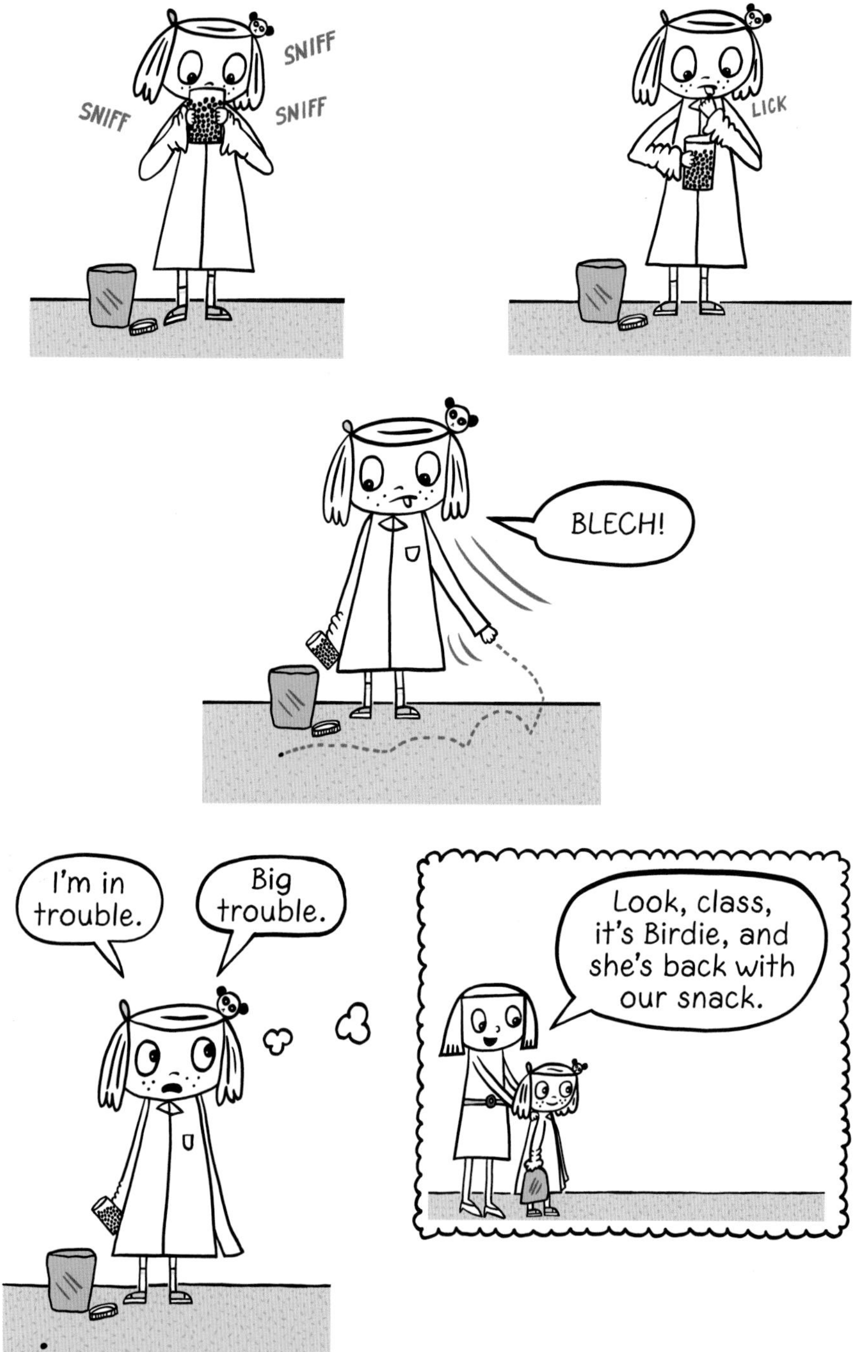
SNIFF
SNIFF
SNIFF
LICK
BLECH!
I'm in trouble.
Big trouble.
Look, class, it's Birdie, and she's back with our snack.

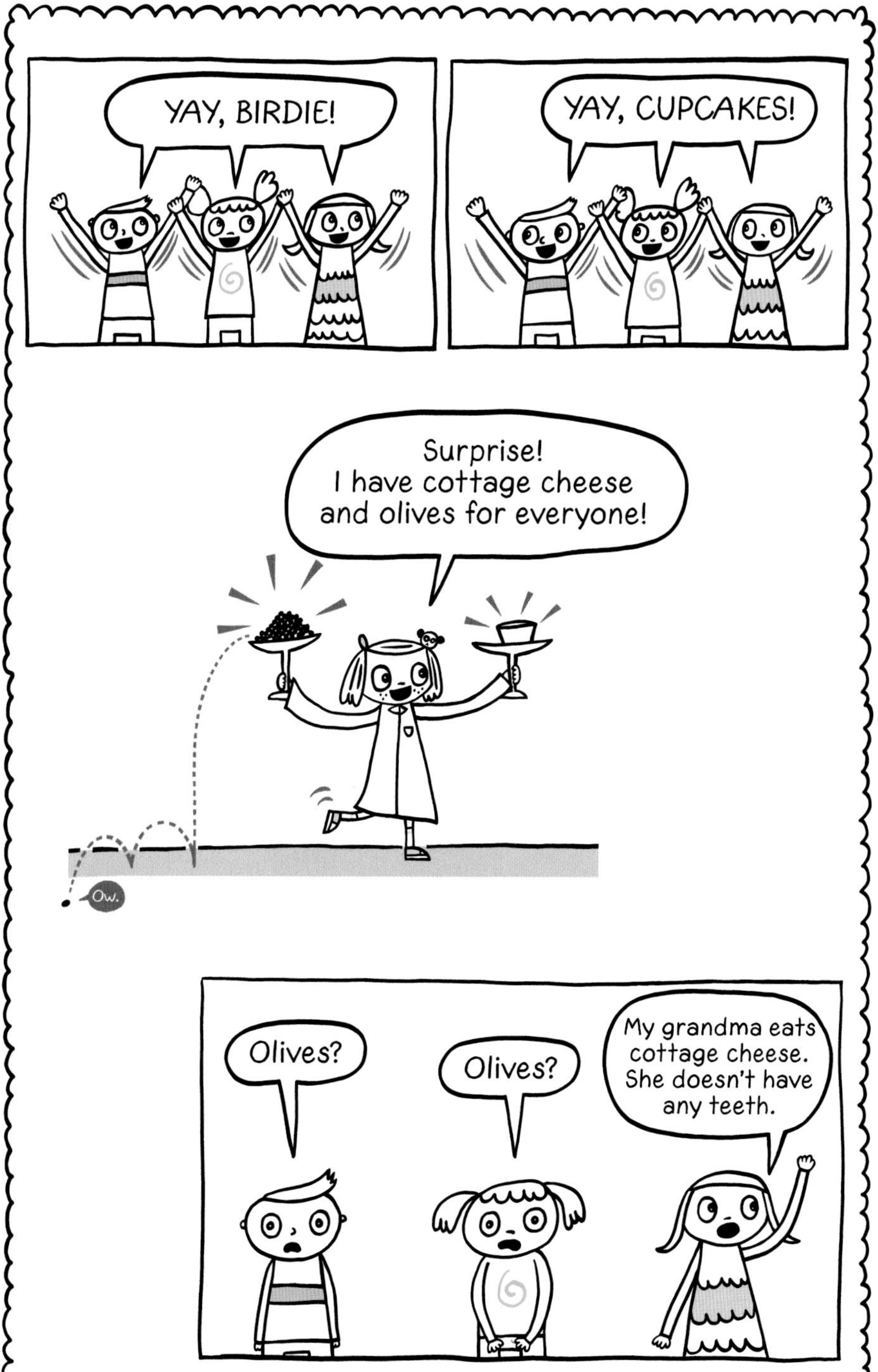
YAY, BIRDIE!
YAY, CUPCAKES!
Surprise! I have cottage cheese and olives for everyone!
Ow.
Olives?
Olives?
My grandma eats cottage cheese. She doesn't have any teeth.

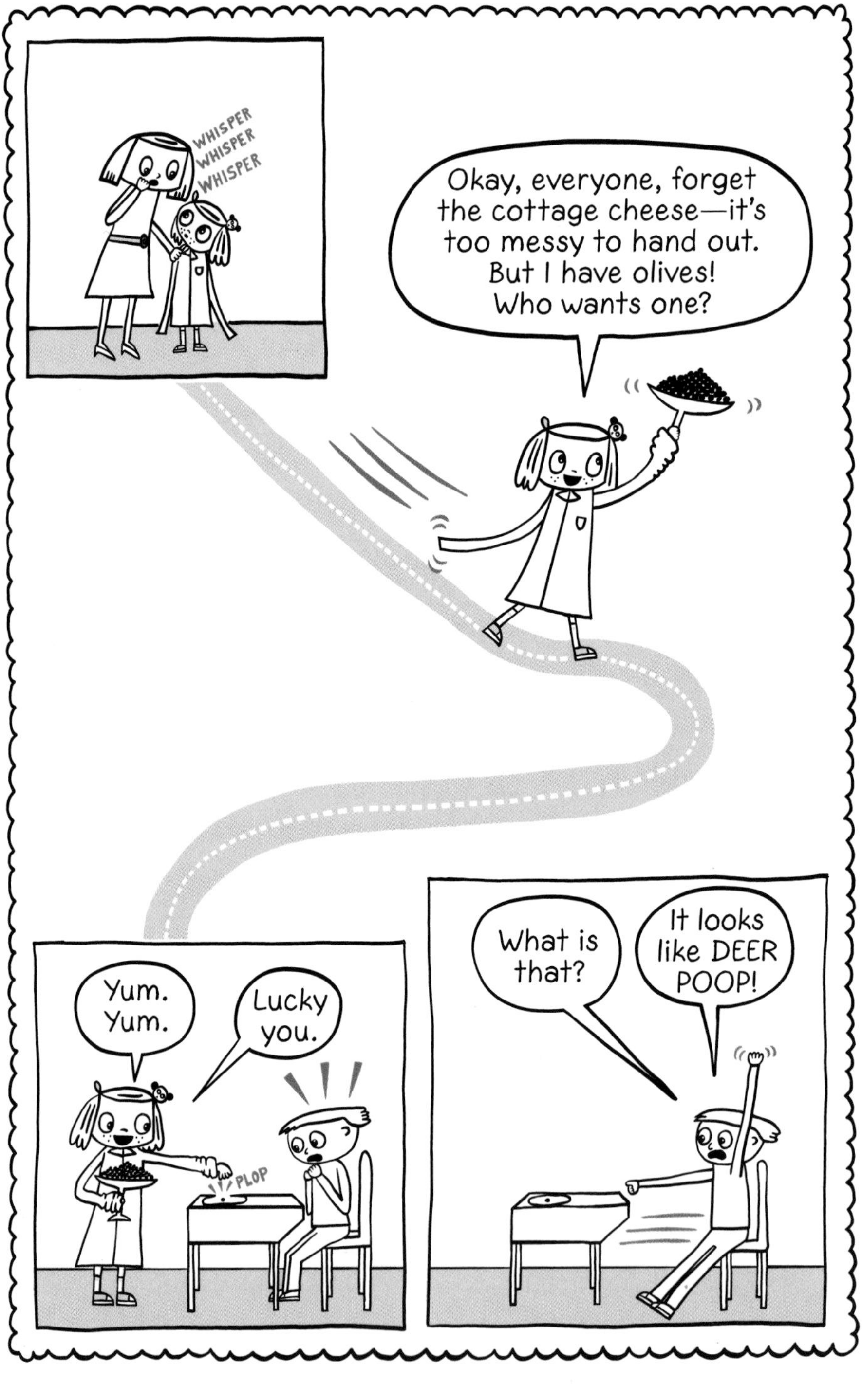
WHISPER
WHISPER
WHISPER
Okay, everyone, forget the cottage cheese—it's too messy to hand out. But I have olives! Who wants one?
Yum. Yum.
Lucky you.
PLOP
What is that?
It looks like DEER POOP!

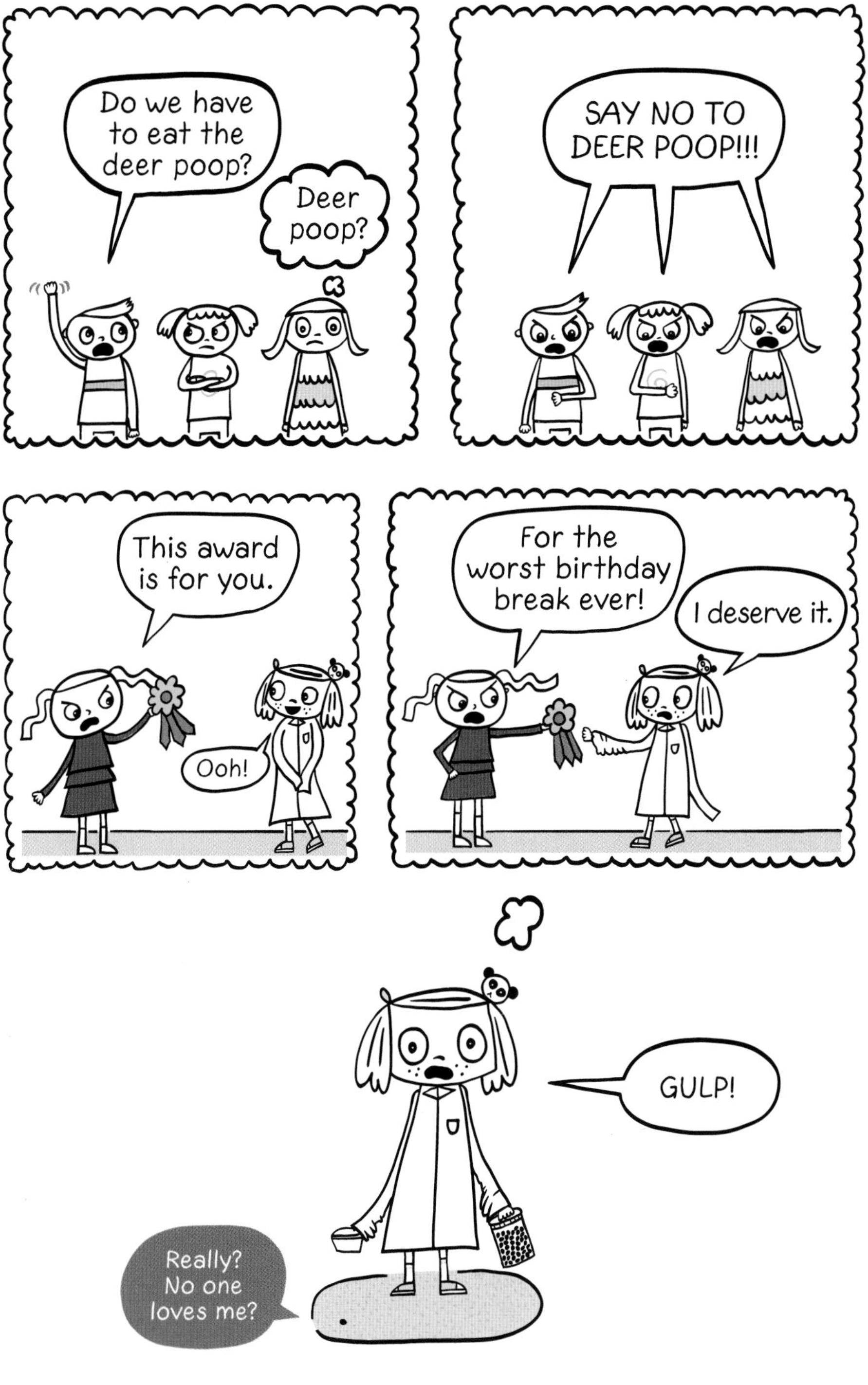
Do we have to eat the deer poop?
Deer poop?
SAY NO TO DEER POOP!!!
This award is for you.
Ooh!
For the worst birthday break ever!
I deserve it.
GULP!
Really? No one loves me?

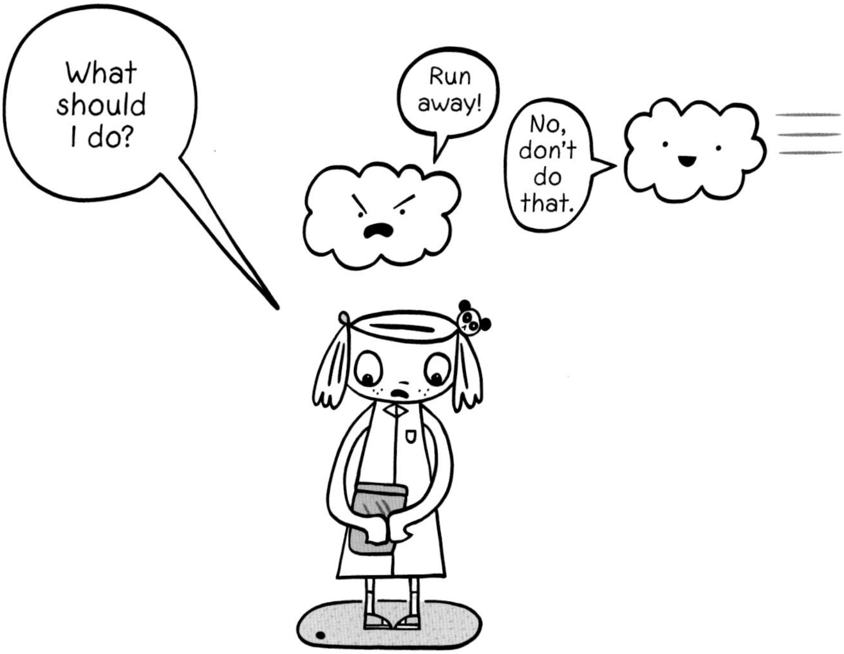
What should I do?
Run away!
No, don't do that.

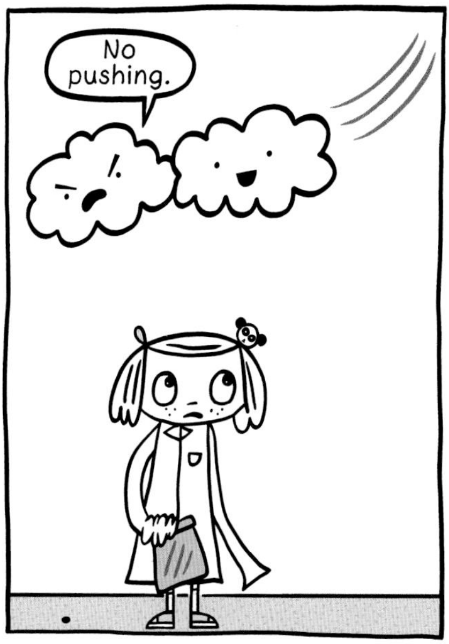
No pushing.

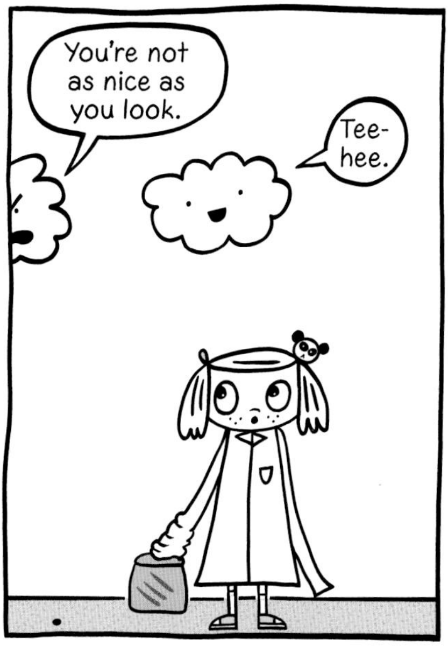
You're not as nice as you look.
Tee-hee.

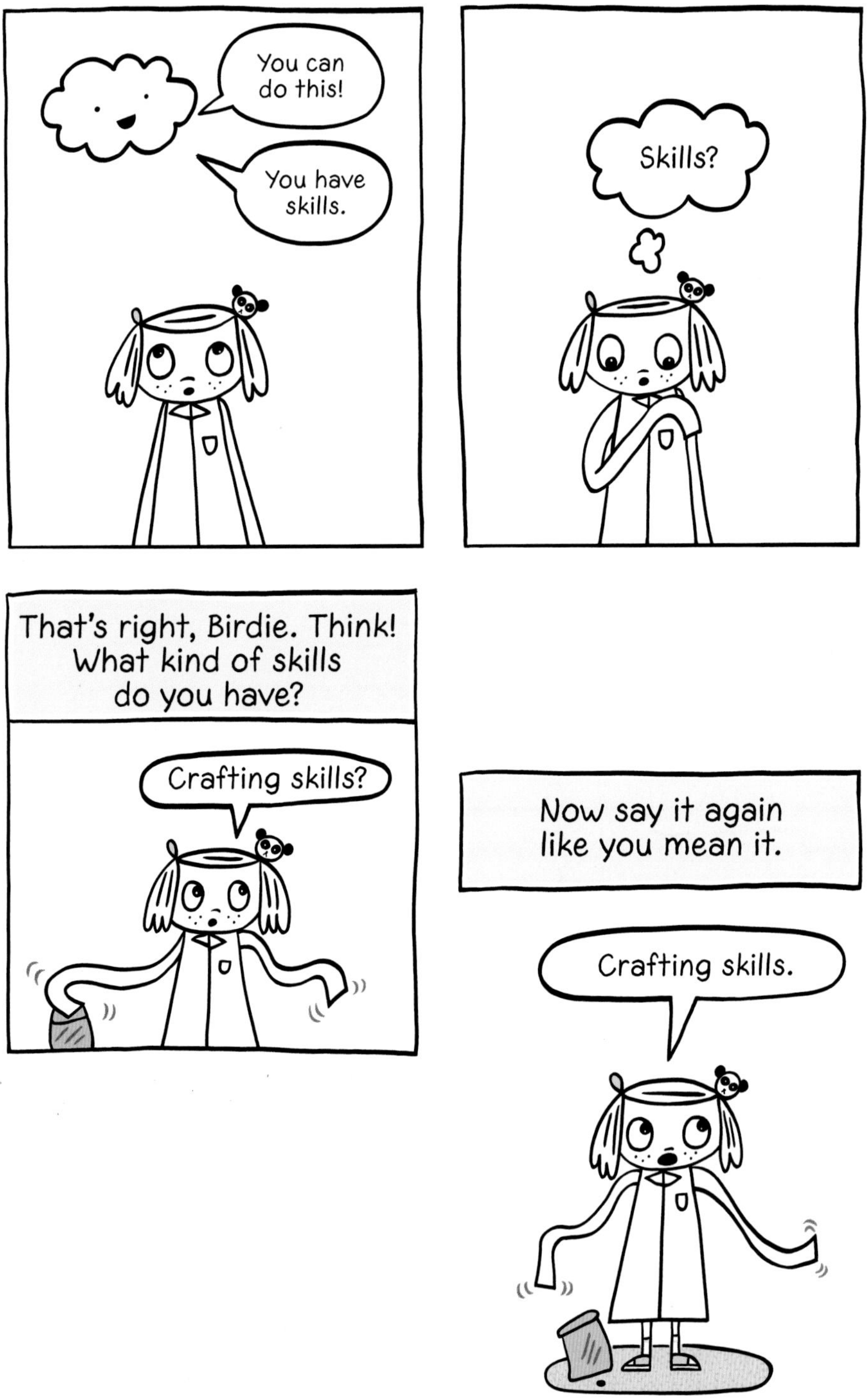
You can do this!
You have skills.
Skills?
That's right, Birdie. Think! What kind of skills do you have?
Crafting skills?
Now say it again like you mean it.
Crafting skills.

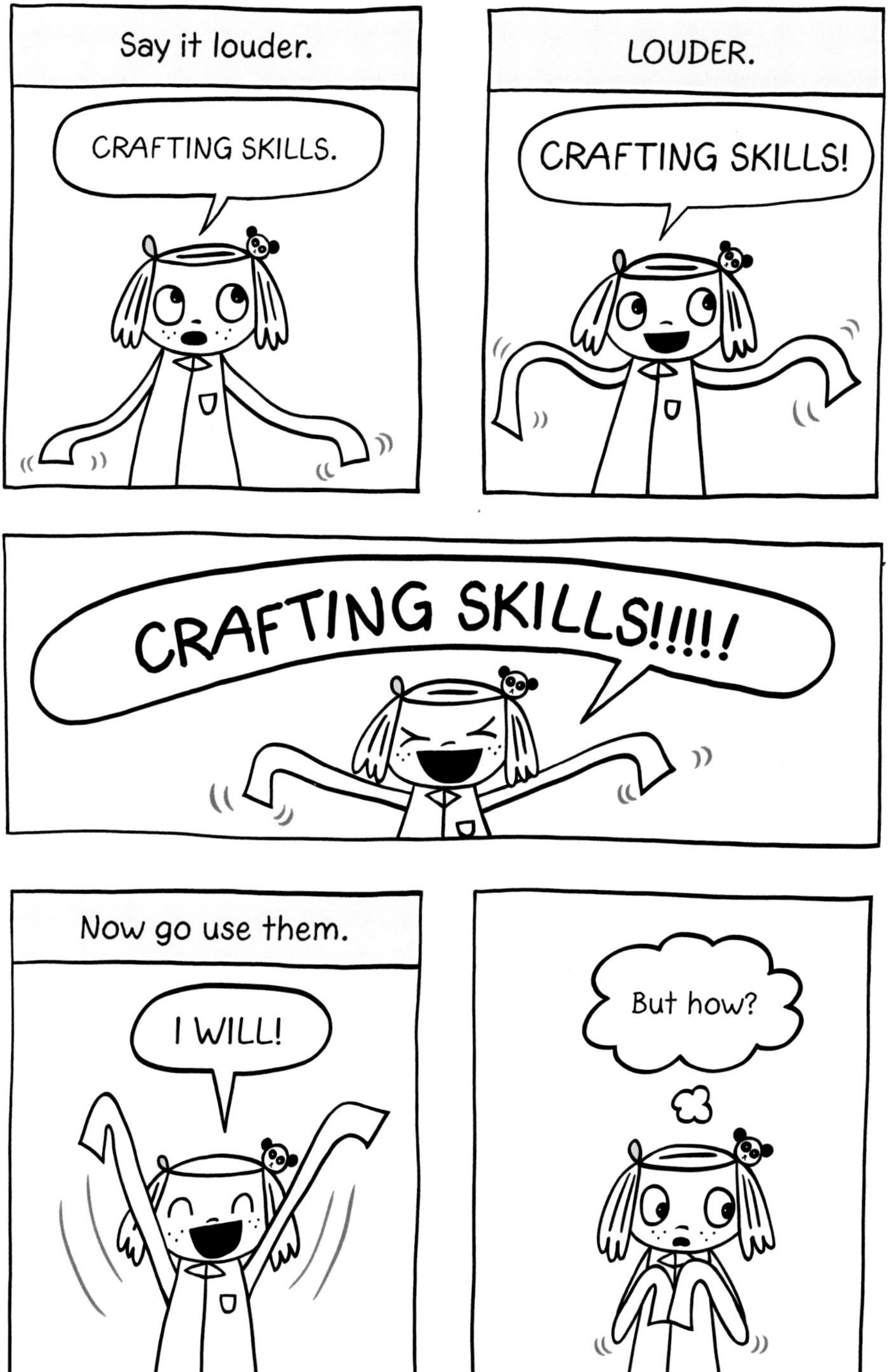
Say it louder.
CRAFTING SKILLS.
LOUDER.
CRAFTING SKILLS!
CRAFTING SKILLS!!!!!
Now go use them.
I WILL!
But how?

Sometimes lessons are learned very quickly.

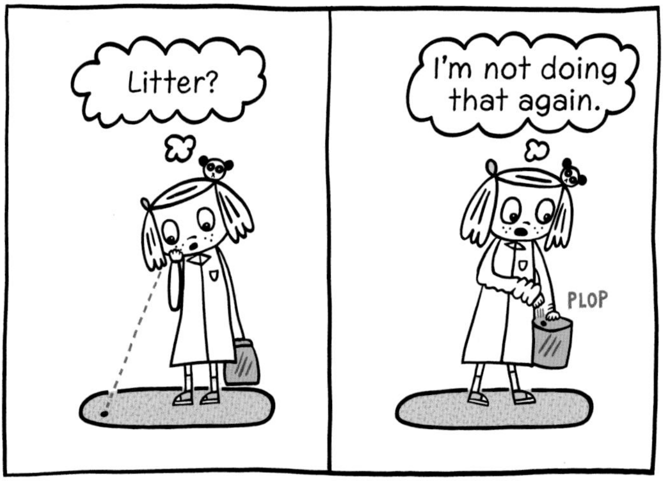
Litter?
I'm not doing that again.
PLOP

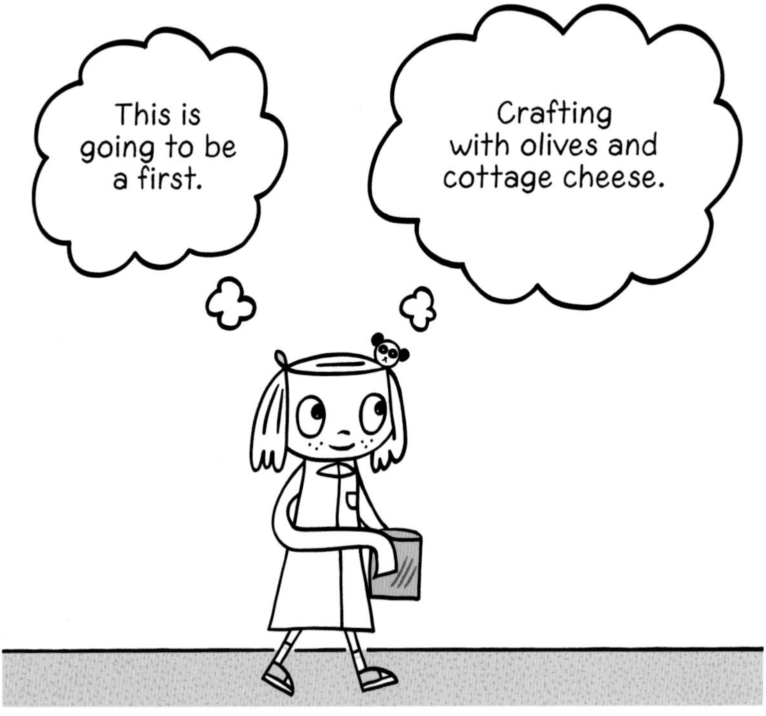
This is going to be a first.
Crafting with olives and cottage cheese.

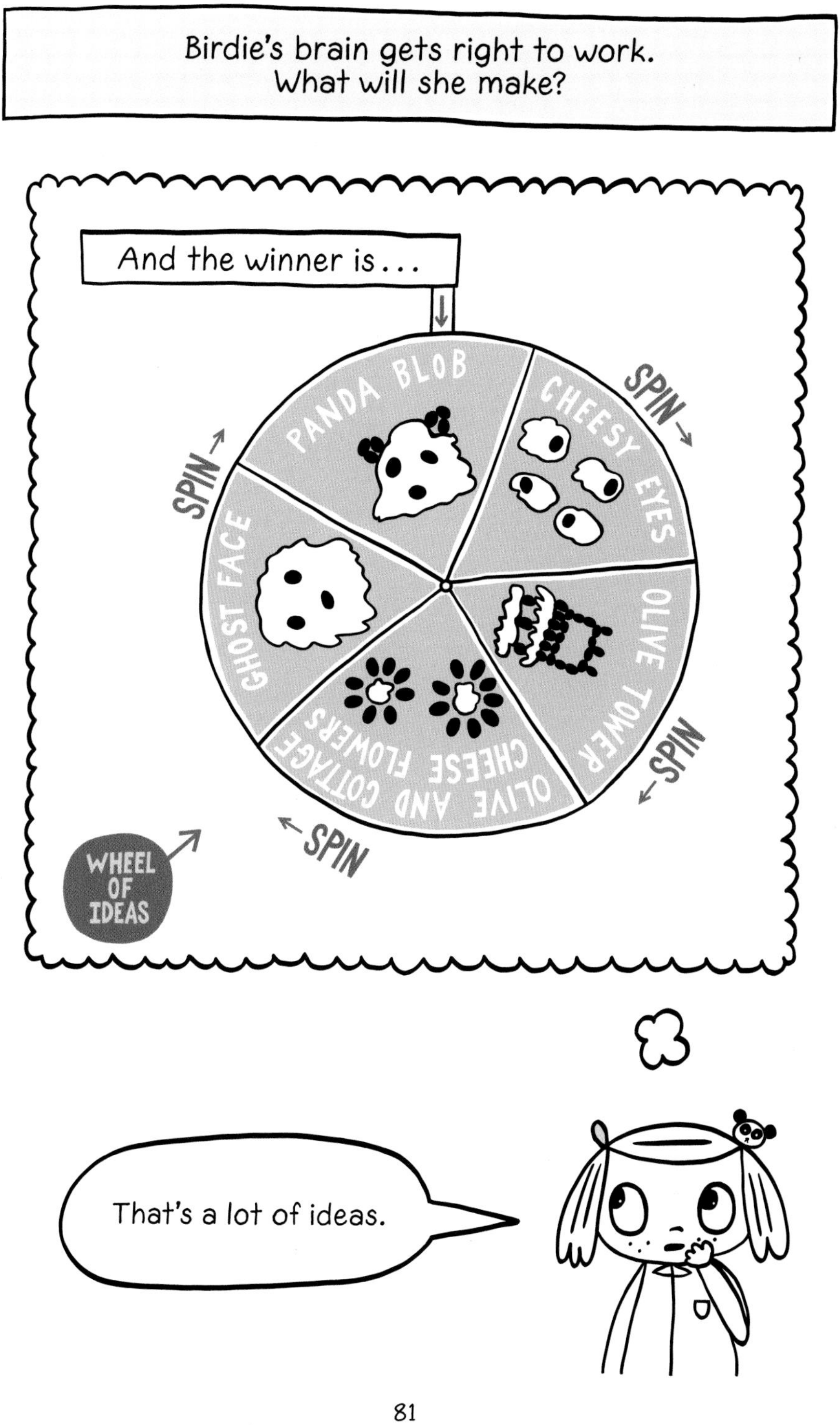
Birdie's brain gets right to work.
What will she make?
And the winner is . . .
PANDA BLOB
CHEESY EYES
OLIVE TOWER
OLIVE AND COTTAGE CHEESE FLOWERS
GHOST FACE
SPIN
SPIN
SPIN
SPIN
WHEEL OF IDEAS
That's a lot of ideas.

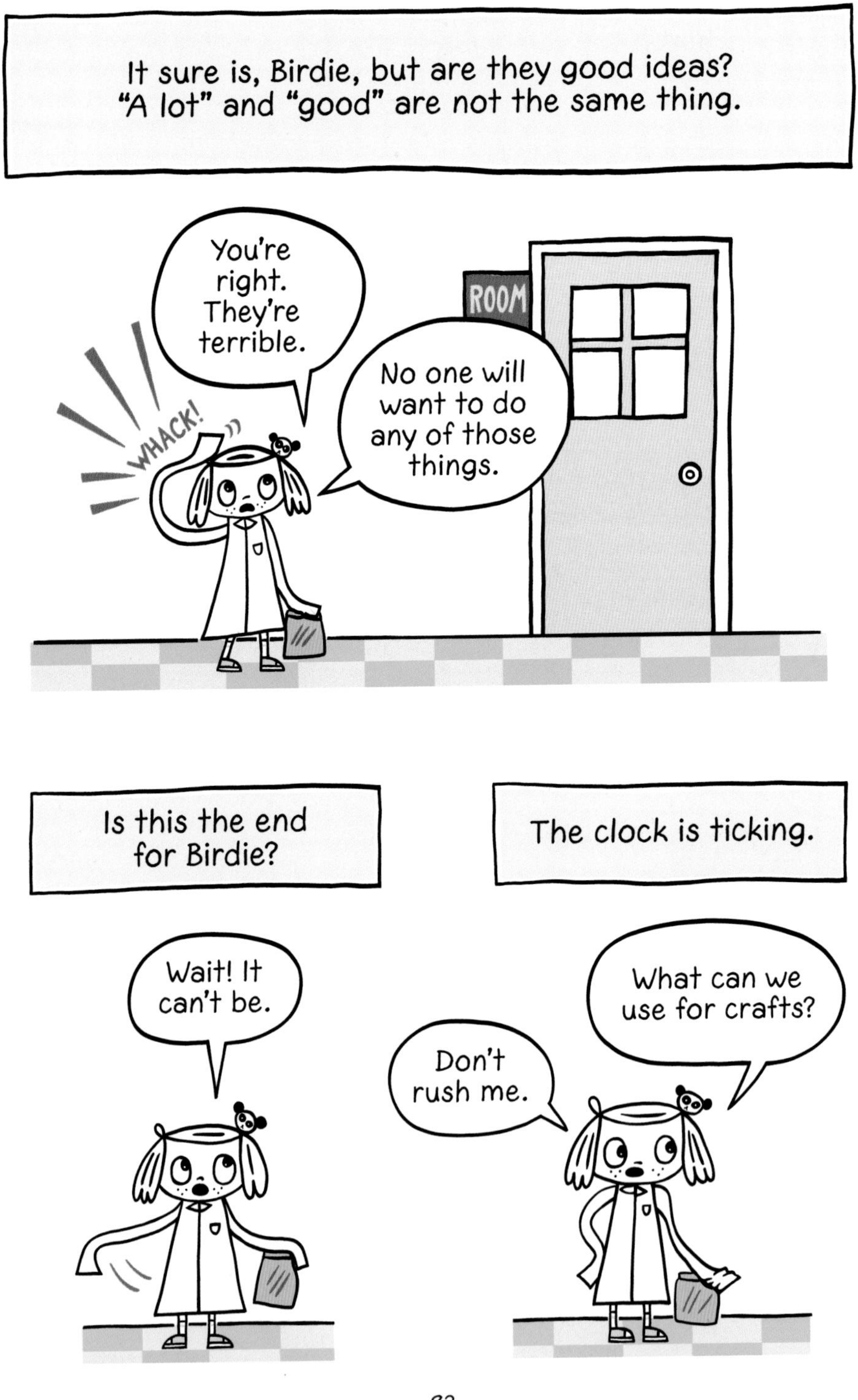
It sure is, Birdie, but are they good ideas? "A lot" and "good" are not the same thing.
You're right. They're terrible.
No one will want to do any of those things.
WHACK!
ROOM
Is this the end for Birdie?
The clock is ticking.
Wait! It can't be.
What can we use for crafts?
Don't rush me.

Think, Birdie. Think.

I am.

TAP
TAP

What does school have a lot of?

Text books.

Work sheets.

Tests.

Pencils.

Lockers.

Paper.

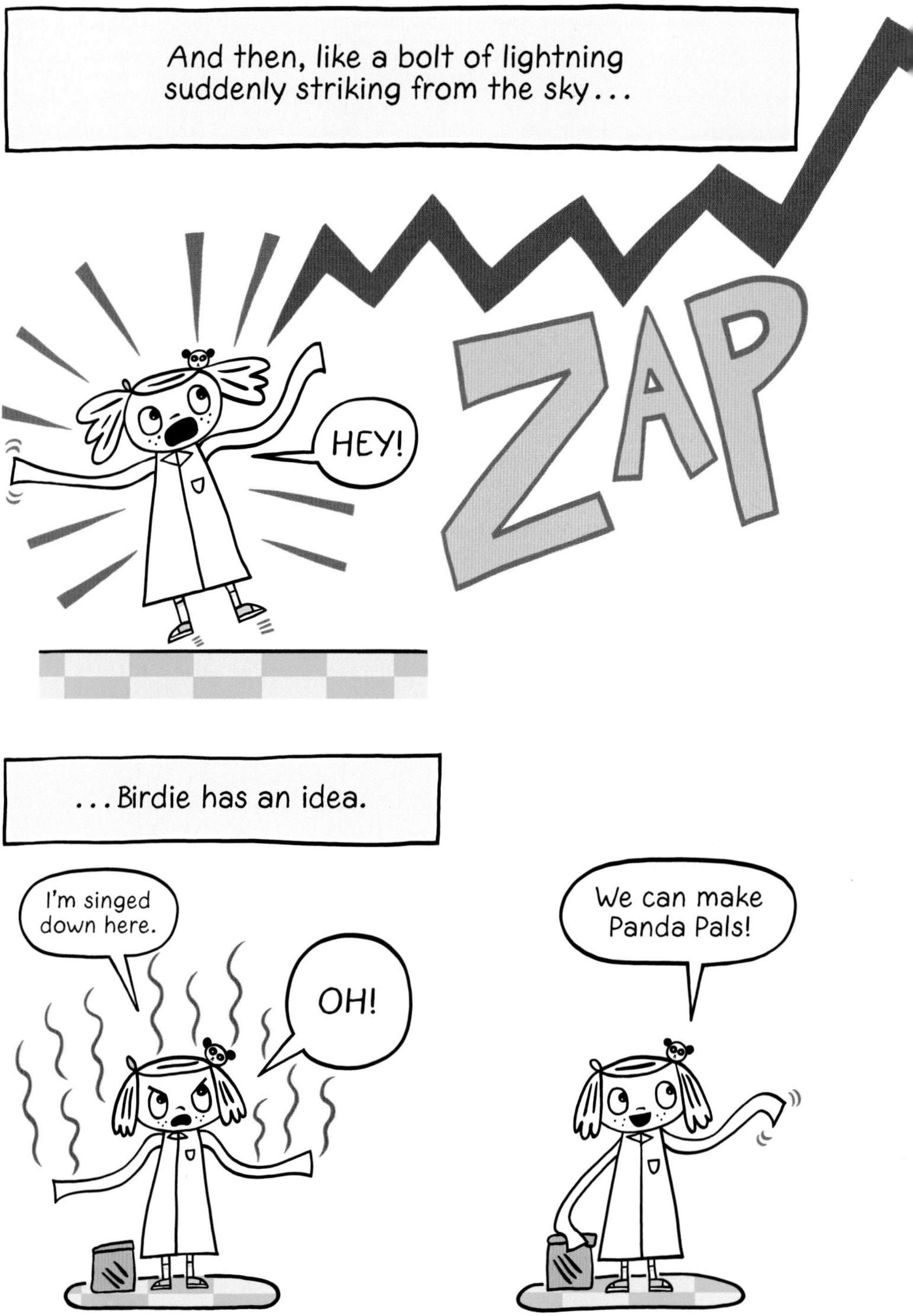
And then, like a bolt of lightning suddenly striking from the sky...
HEY!
ZAP
...Birdie has an idea.
I'm singed down here.
OH!
We can make Panda Pals!

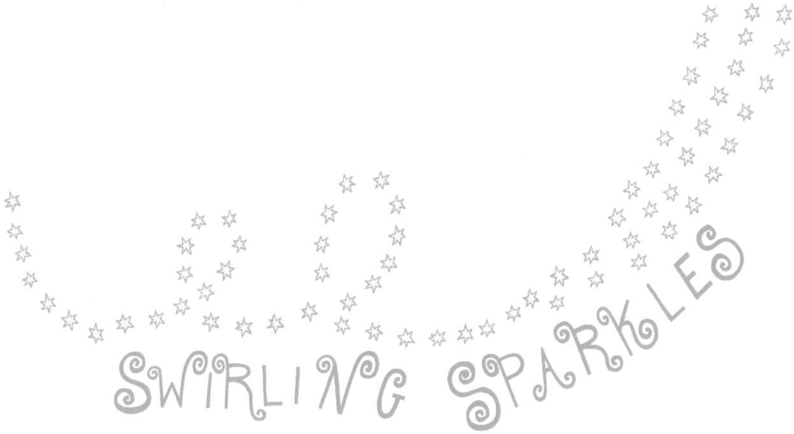
SWIRLING SPARKLES

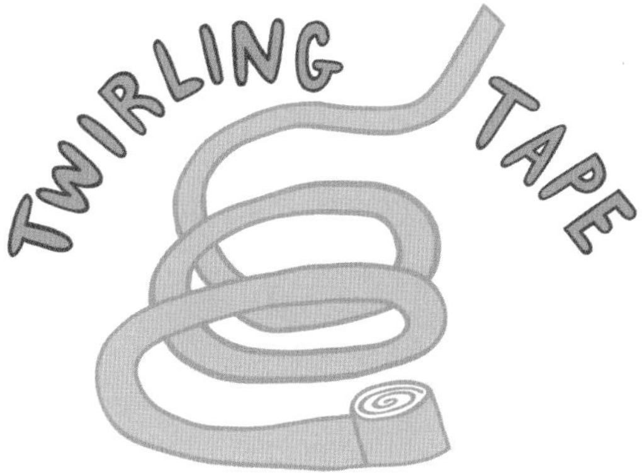
TWIRLING TAPE

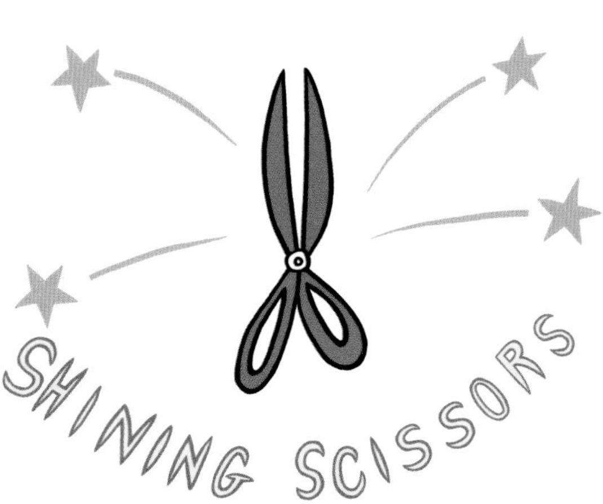
SHINING SCISSORS

Birdie is gone, and in her place stands a confident crafting genius.

It's the Amazing Crafty Cat.

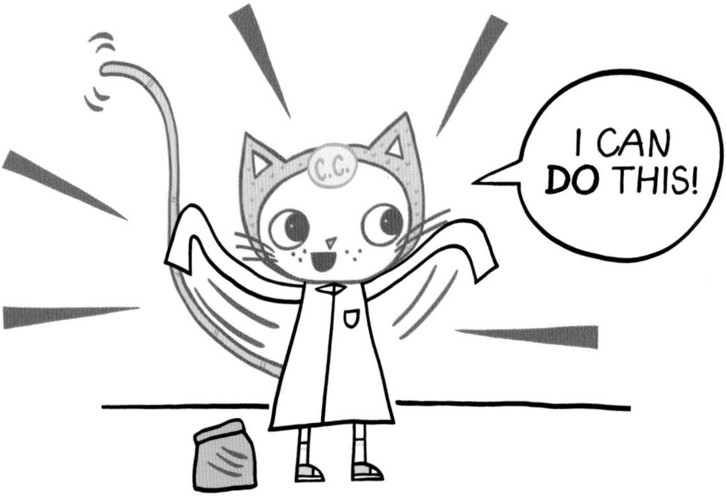
C.C.
I CAN **DO** THIS!

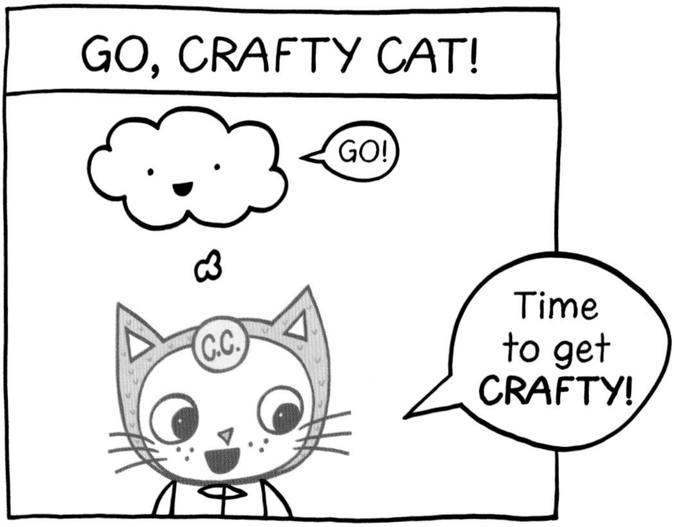
GO, CRAFTY CAT!
GO!
C.C.
Time to get **CRAFTY!**

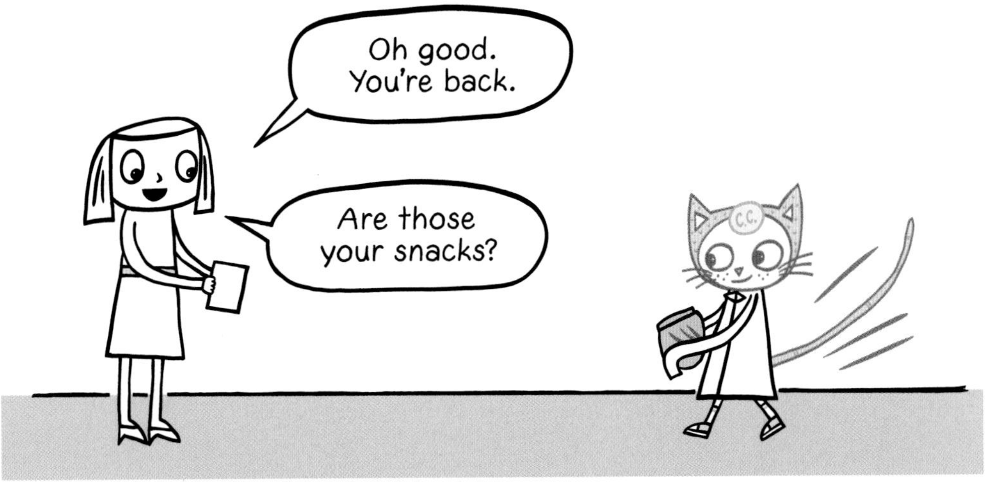
Oh good.
You're back.
Are those
your snacks?

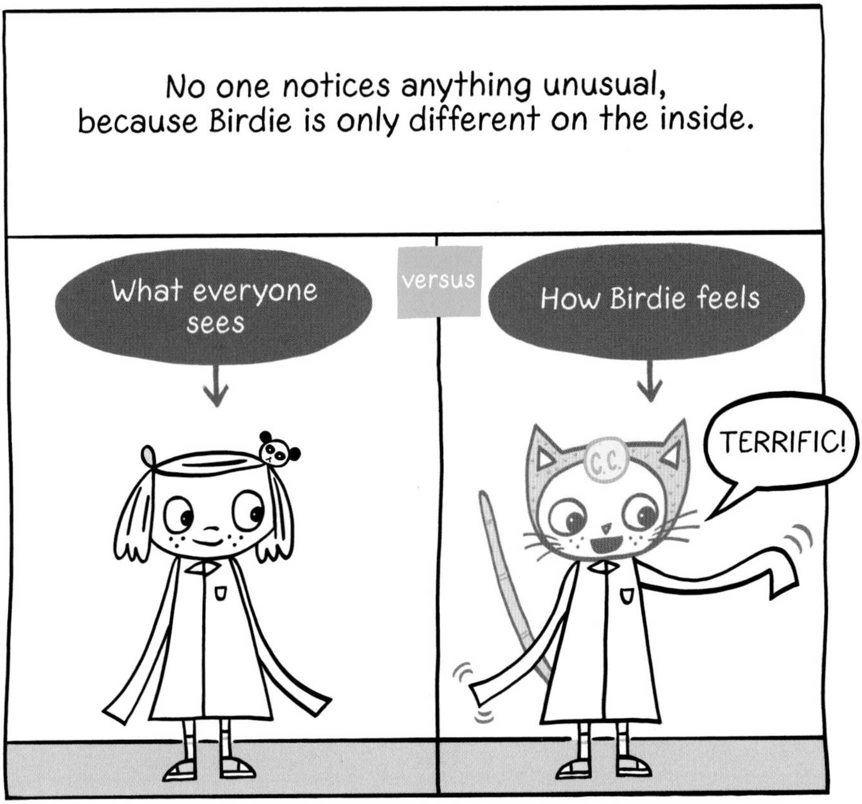
No one notices anything unusual,
because Birdie is only different on the inside.
What everyone sees
versus
How Birdie feels
TERRIFIC!

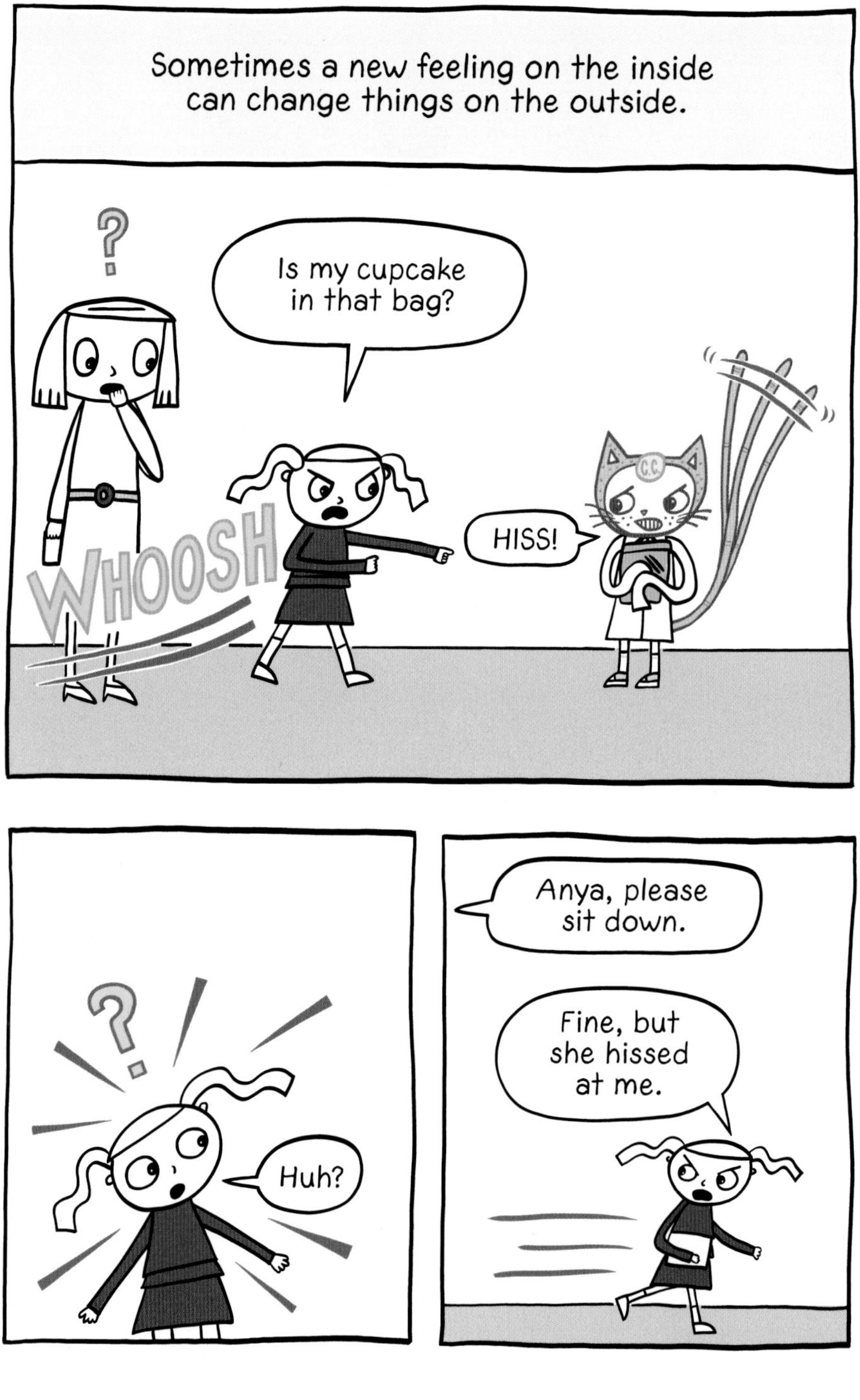
Sometimes a new feeling on the inside can change things on the outside.
Is my cupcake in that bag?
WHOOSH
HISS!
C.C.
Huh?
Anya, please sit down.
Fine, but she hissed at me.

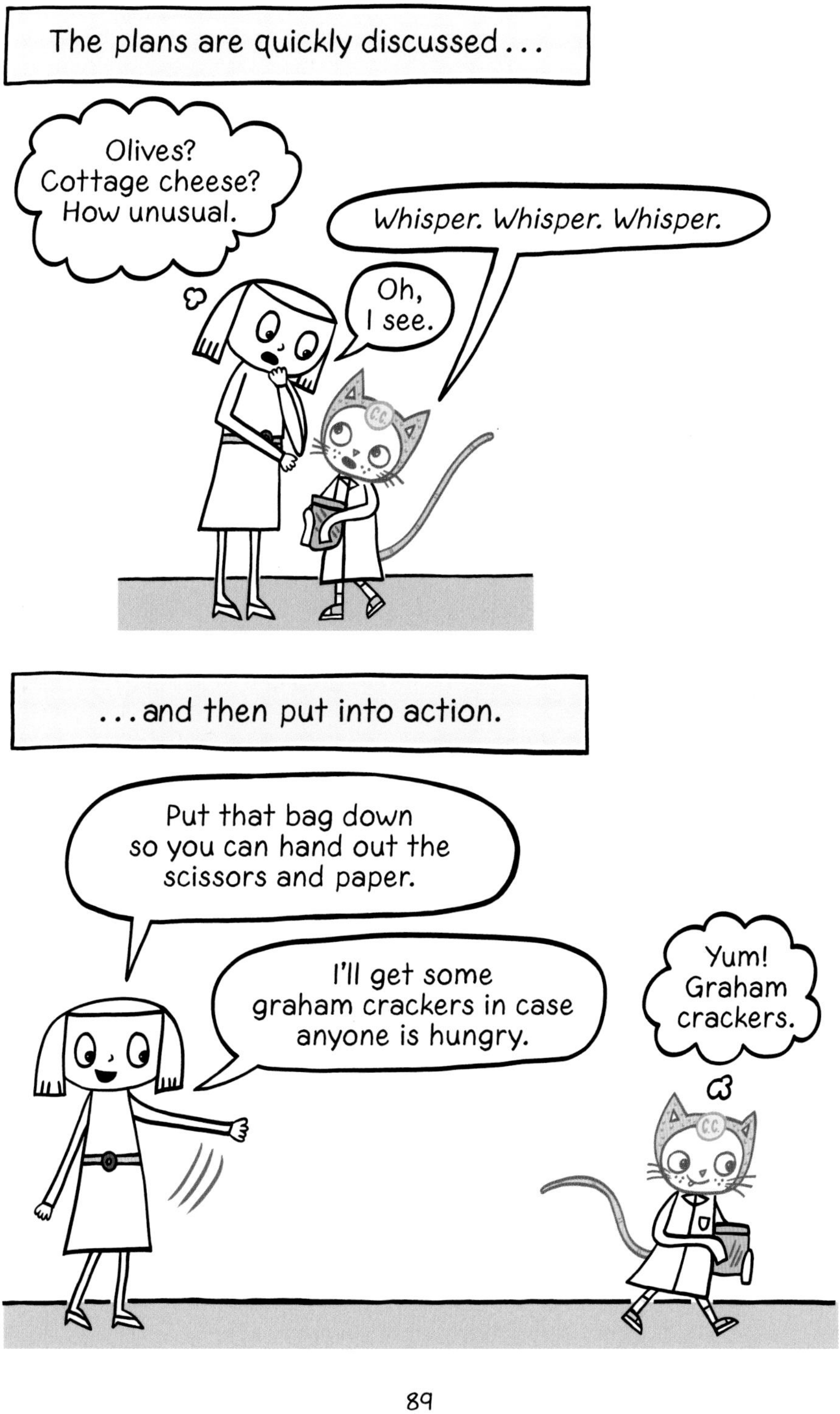
The plans are quickly discussed...
Olives? Cottage cheese? How unusual.
Whisper. Whisper. Whisper.
Oh, I see.
...and then put into action.
Put that bag down so you can hand out the scissors and paper.
I'll get some graham crackers in case anyone is hungry.
Yum! Graham crackers.

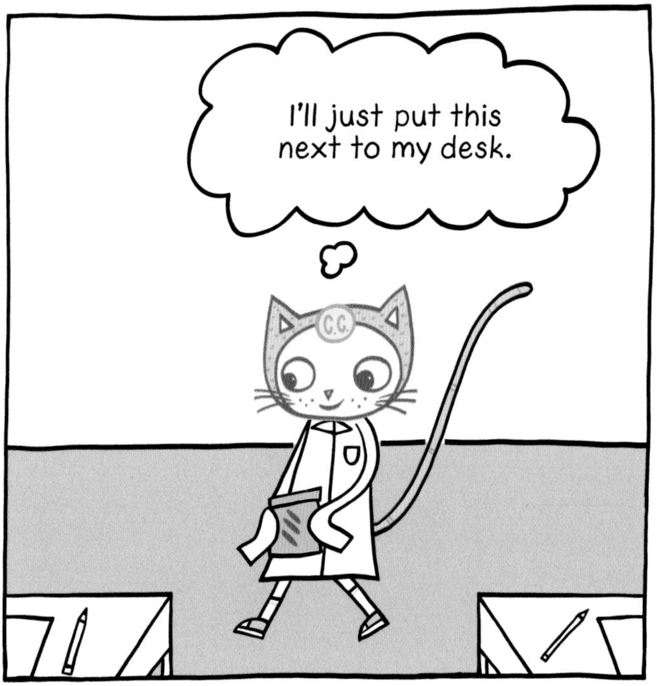
I'll just put this next to my desk.

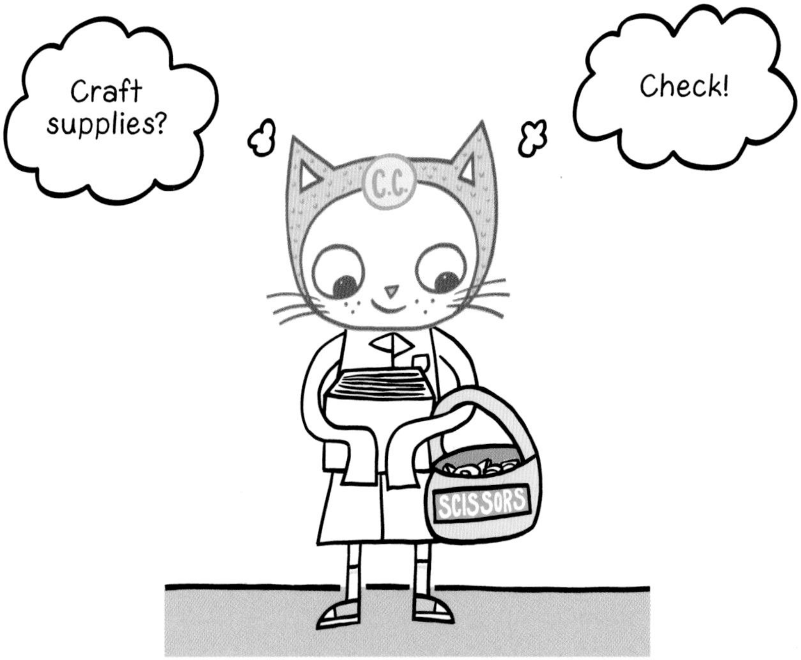
Craft supplies?
Check!
SCISSORS

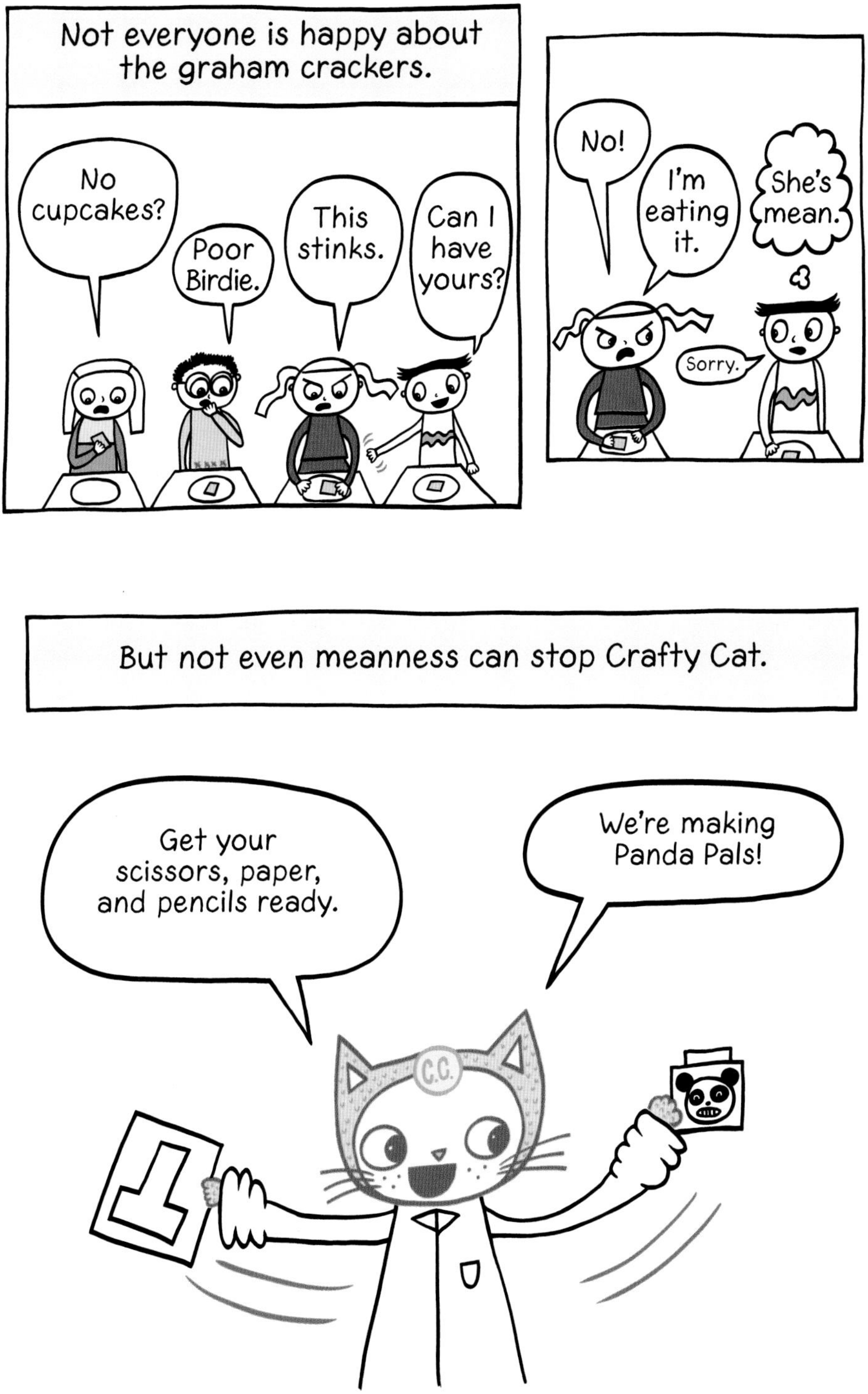
Not everyone is happy about the graham crackers.
No cupcakes?
Poor Birdie.
This stinks.
Can I have yours?
No!
I'm eating it.
Sorry.
She's mean.
But not even meanness can stop Crafty Cat.
Get your scissors, paper, and pencils ready.
We're making Panda Pals!

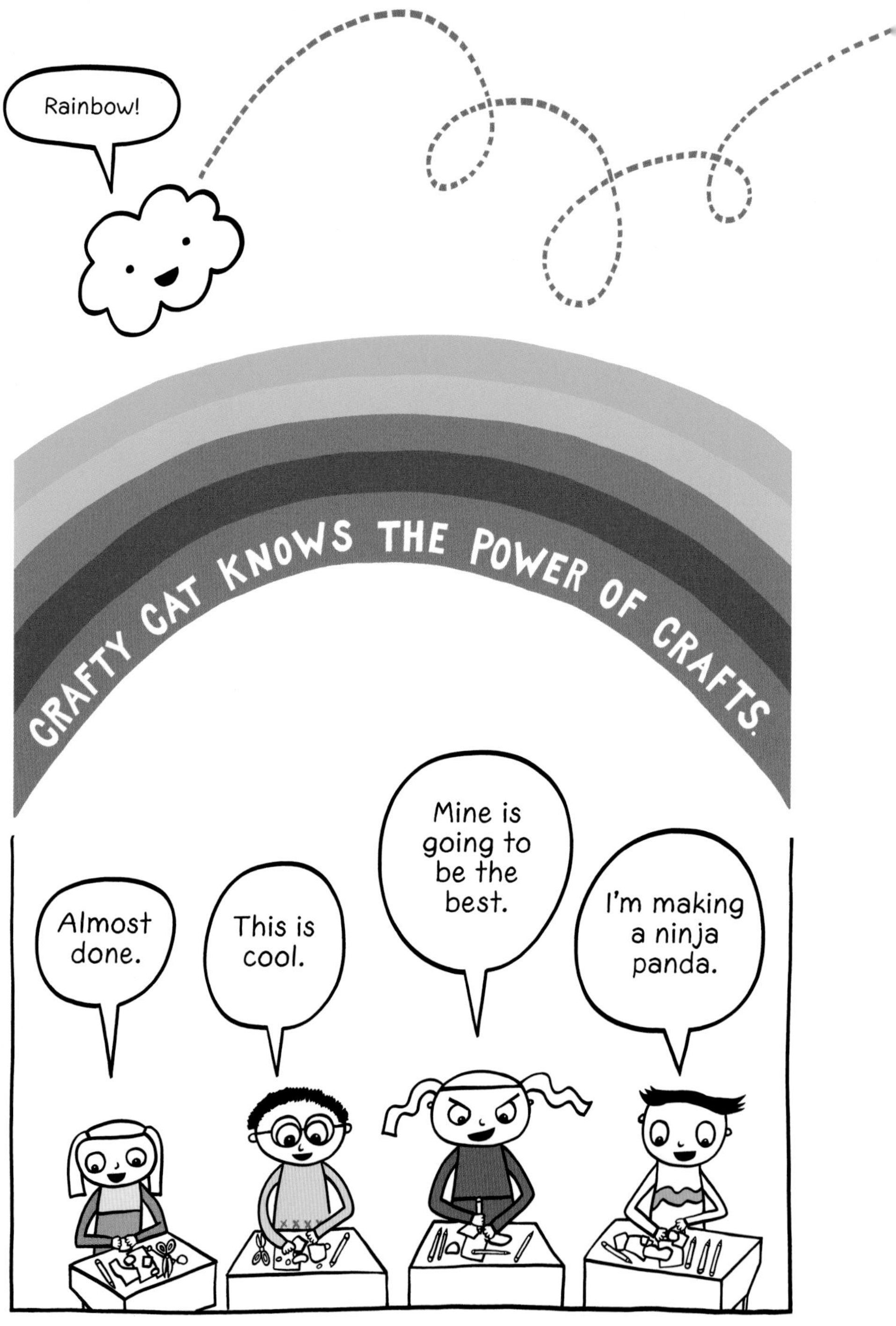
Rainbow!
CRAFTY CAT KNOWS THE POWER OF CRAFTS.
Almost done.
This is cool.
Mine is going to be the best.
I'm making a ninja panda.

The Panda Pals are fun to make.

PANDA PAL TEMPLATE

HOWDY.

FOLLOW INSTRUCTIONS IN THE BACK OF THE BOOK.

PANDA SAYS

CARDSTOCK

Soon everyone is busy cutting, drawing, and folding.

PANDA SAYS

PUSH DOWN TO SEE WHAT PANDA SAYS.

① ②

HOWDY

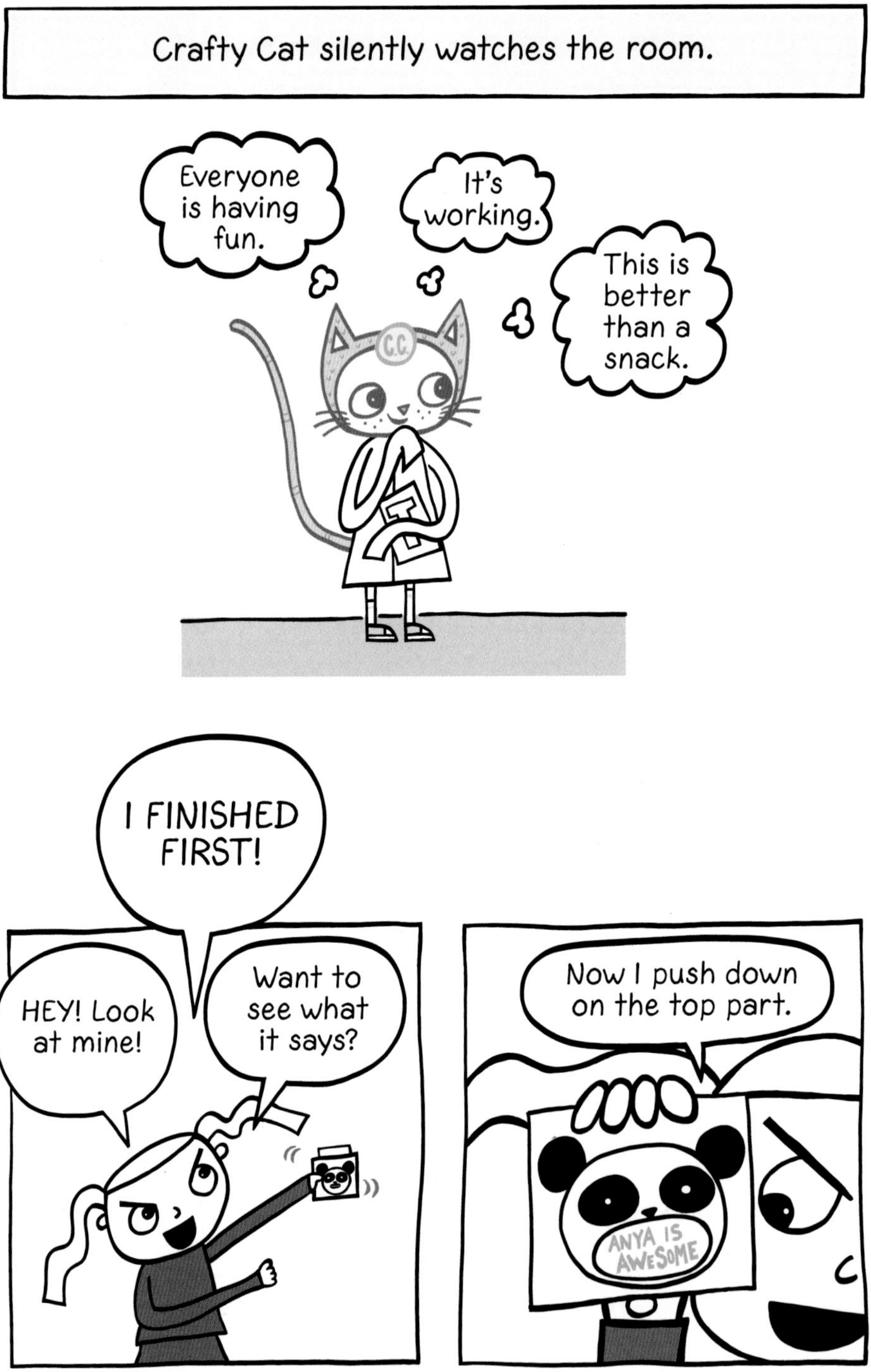
Crafty Cat silently watches the room.
Everyone is having fun.
It's working.
This is better than a snack.
C.C.
HEY! Look at mine!
I FINISHED FIRST!
Want to see what it says?
Now I push down on the top part.
ANYA IS AWESOME

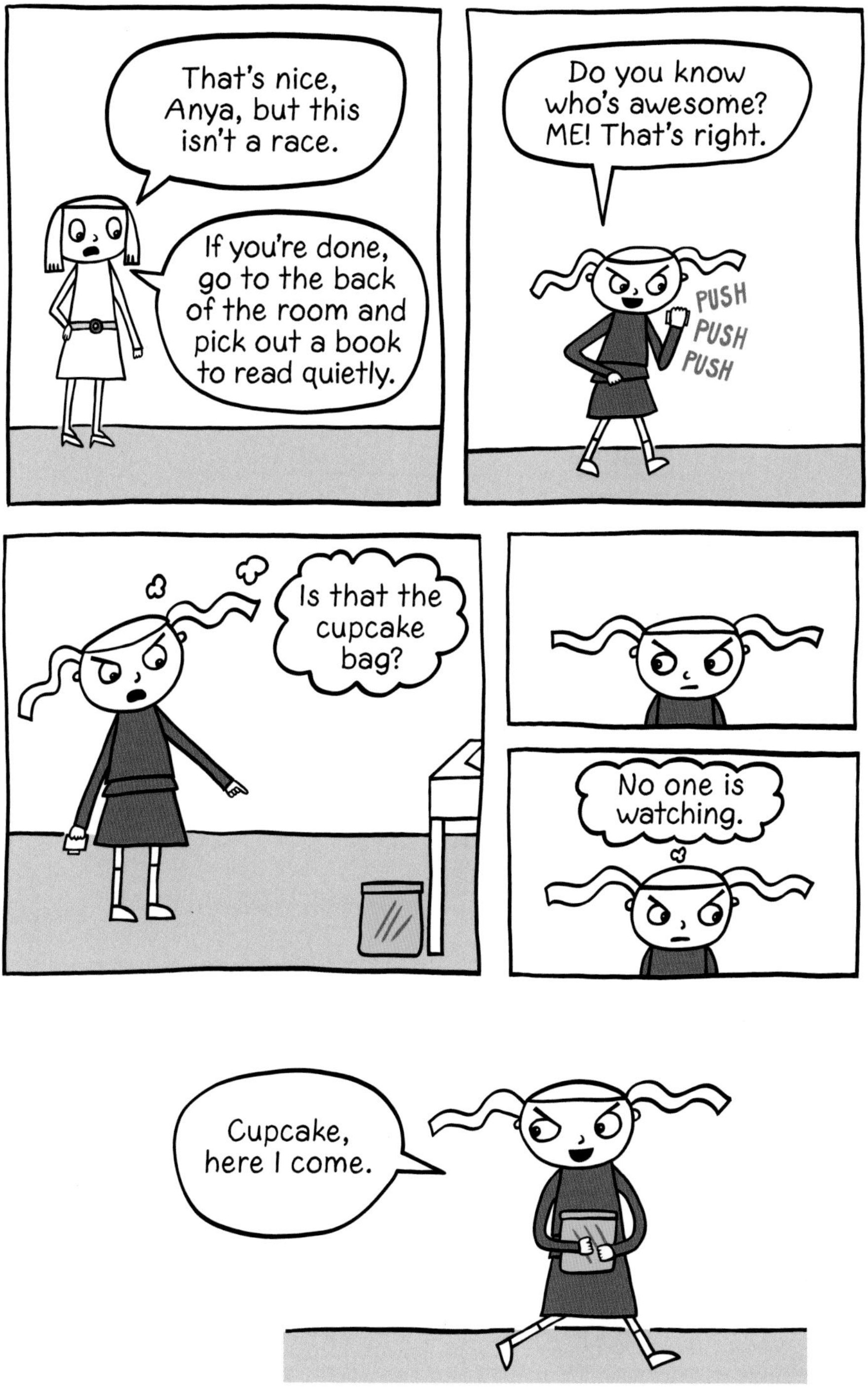
That's nice, Anya, but this isn't a race.
If you're done, go to the back of the room and pick out a book to read quietly.
Do you know who's awesome? ME! That's right.
PUSH
PUSH
PUSH
Is that the cupcake bag?
No one is watching.
Cupcake, here I come.

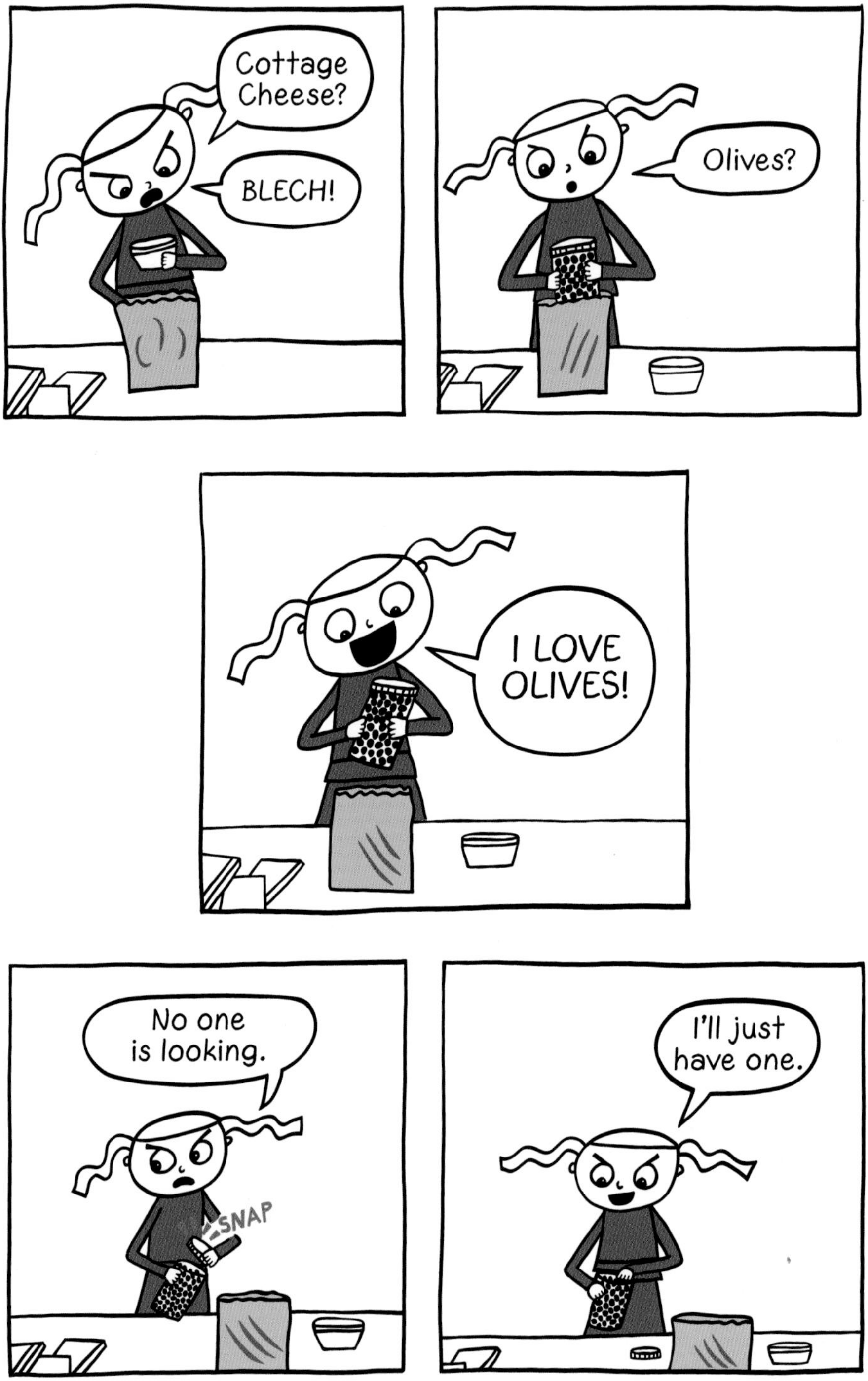
Cottage Cheese?
BLECH!
Olives?
I LOVE OLIVES!
No one is looking.
SNAP
I'll just have one.

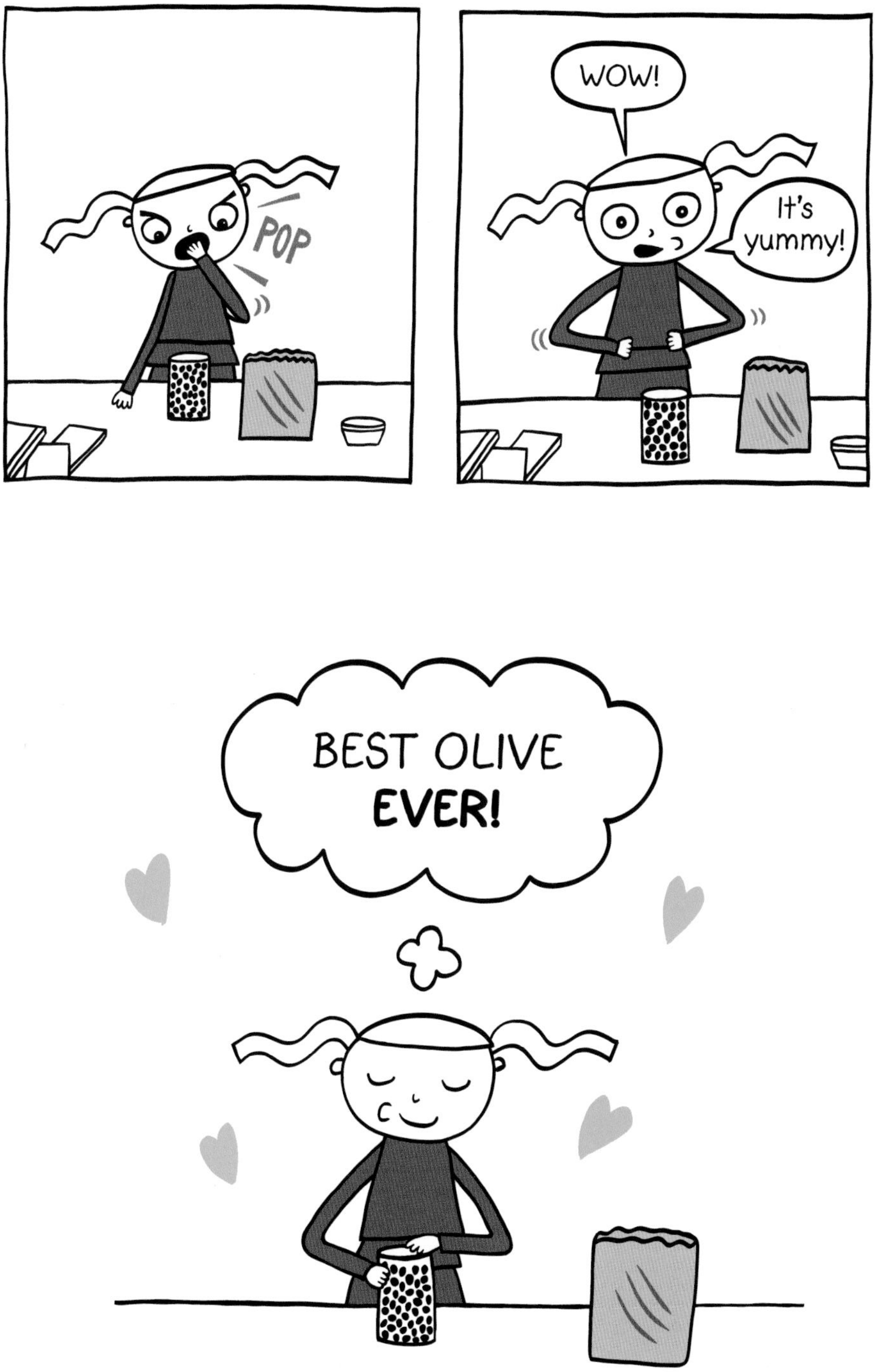
POP
WOW!
It's yummy!
BEST OLIVE EVER!

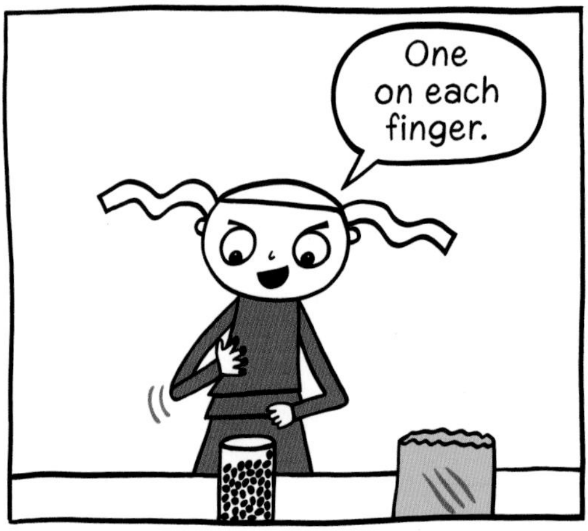
One on each finger.

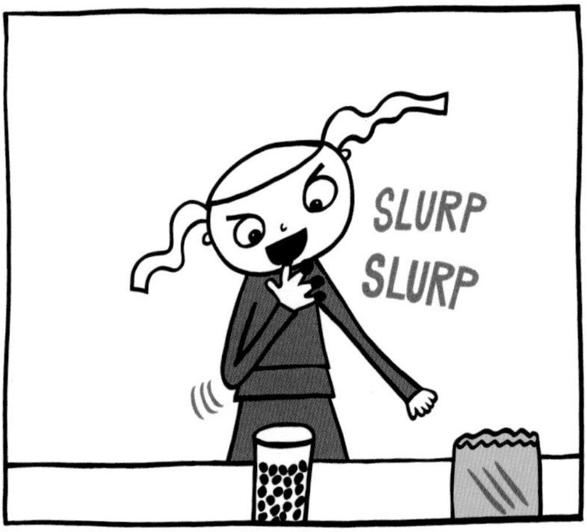
SLURP
SLURP

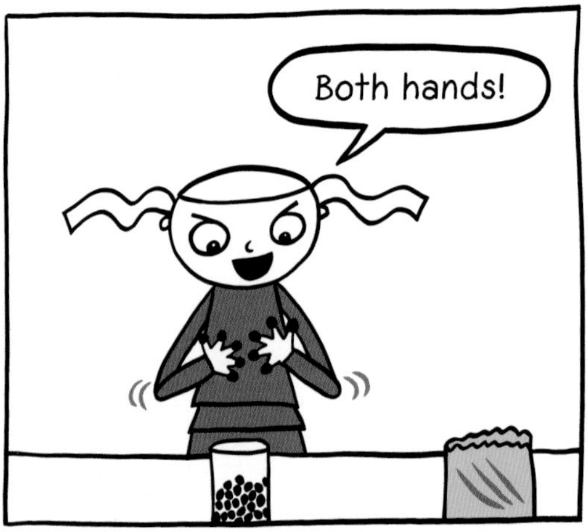
Both hands!

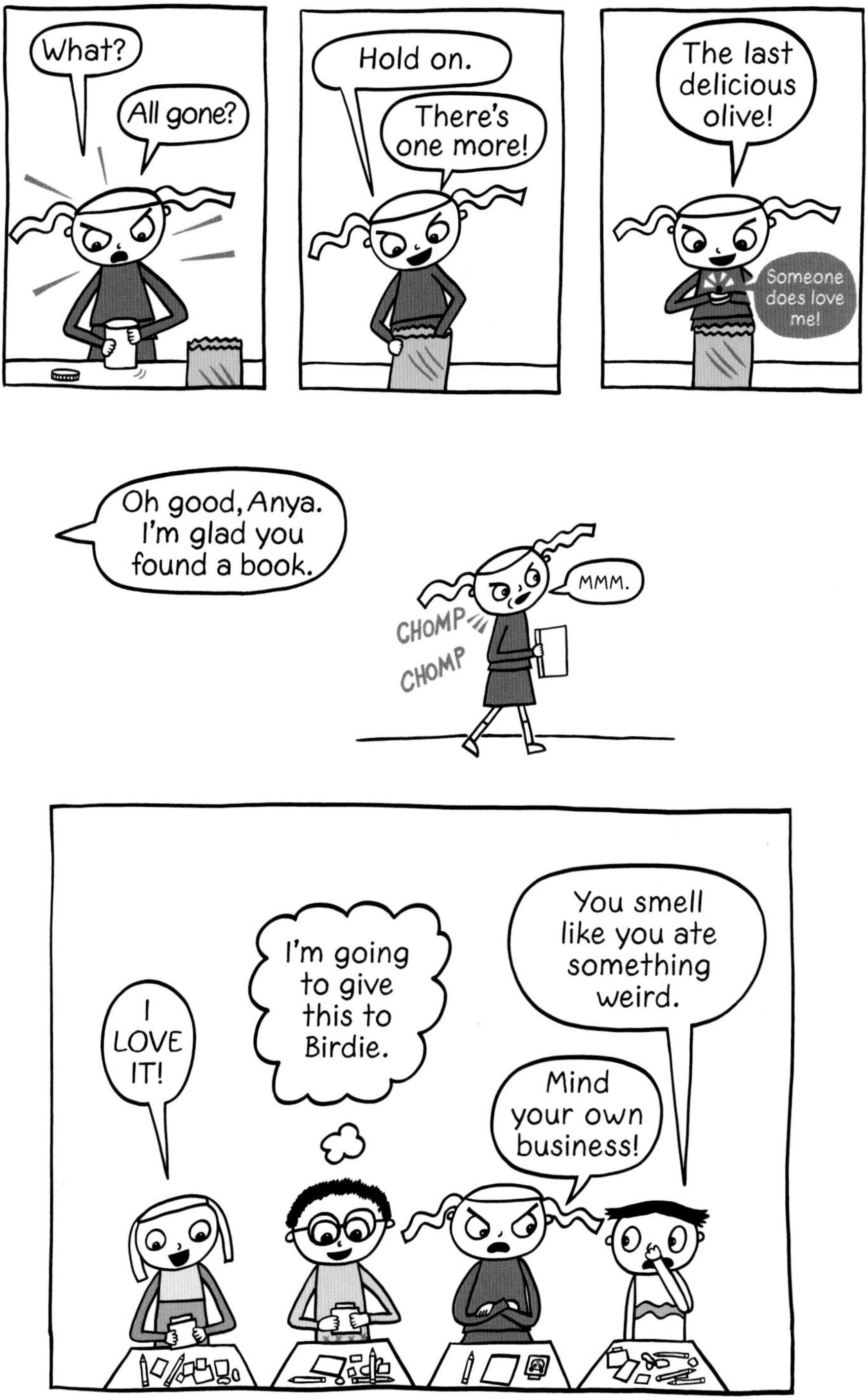
What?
All gone?
Hold on.
There's one more!
The last delicious olive!
Someone does love me!
Oh good, Anya. I'm glad you found a book.
MMM.
CHOMP
CHOMP
I LOVE IT!
I'm going to give this to Birdie.
You smell like you ate something weird.
Mind your own business!

Success sometimes sounds like this...

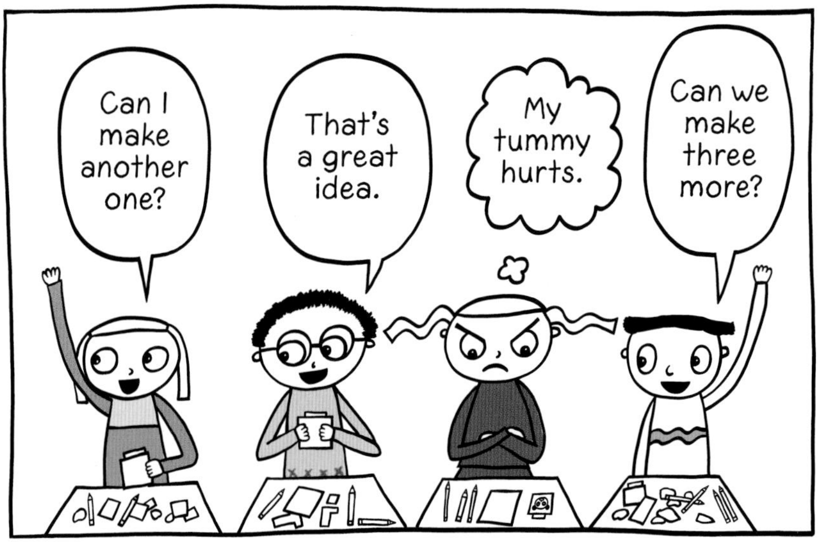
Can I make another one?
That's a great idea.
My tummy hurts.
Can we make three more?

I'm sorry, class. It's almost time for lunch.

Let's thank Birdie for sharing her Panda Pals with us.

Well done, Crafty Cat.

CLAP CLAP CLAP CLAP

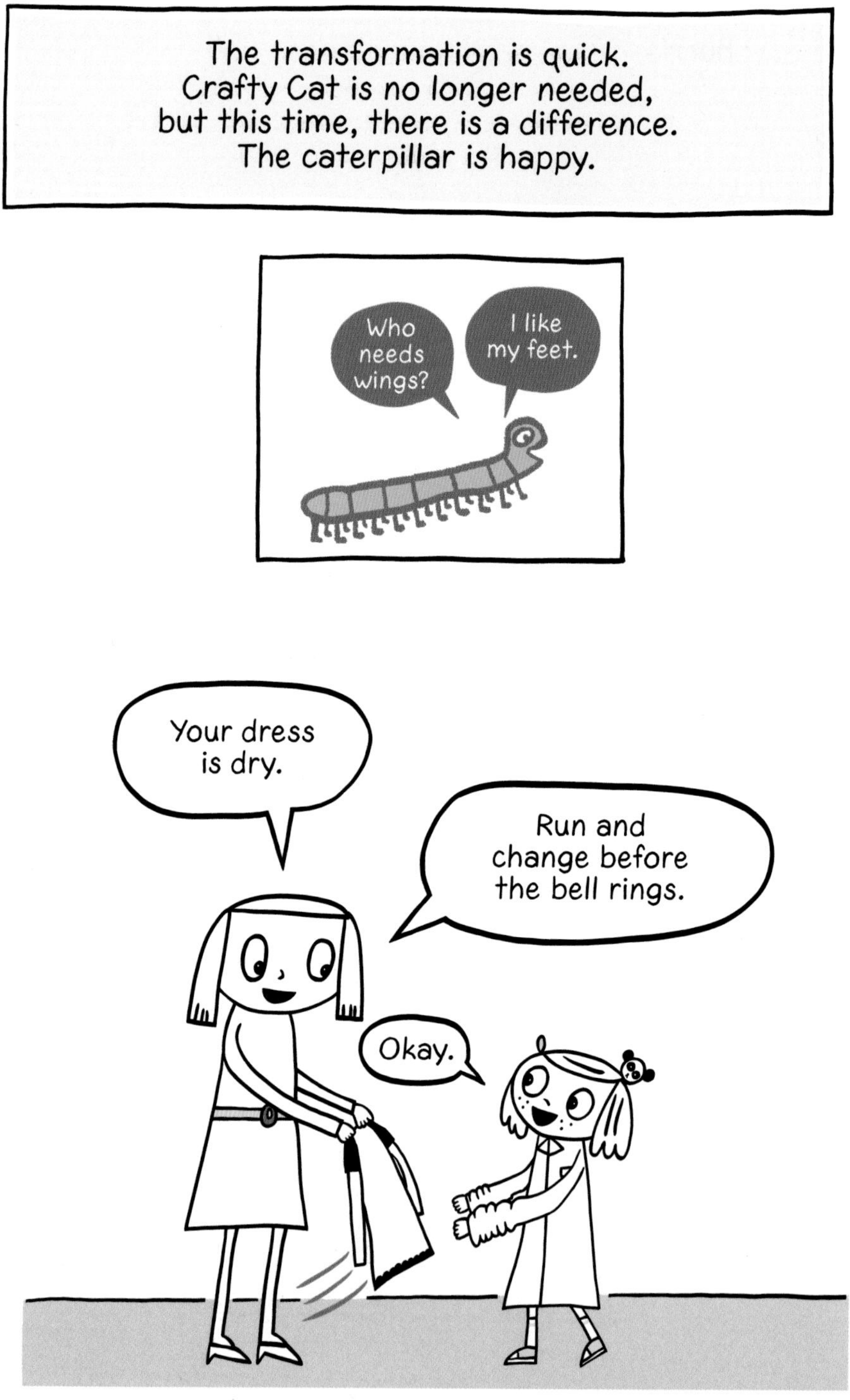
The transformation is quick.
Crafty Cat is no longer needed,
but this time, there is a difference.
The caterpillar is happy.
Who needs wings?
I like my feet.
Your dress is dry.
Run and change before the bell rings.
Okay.

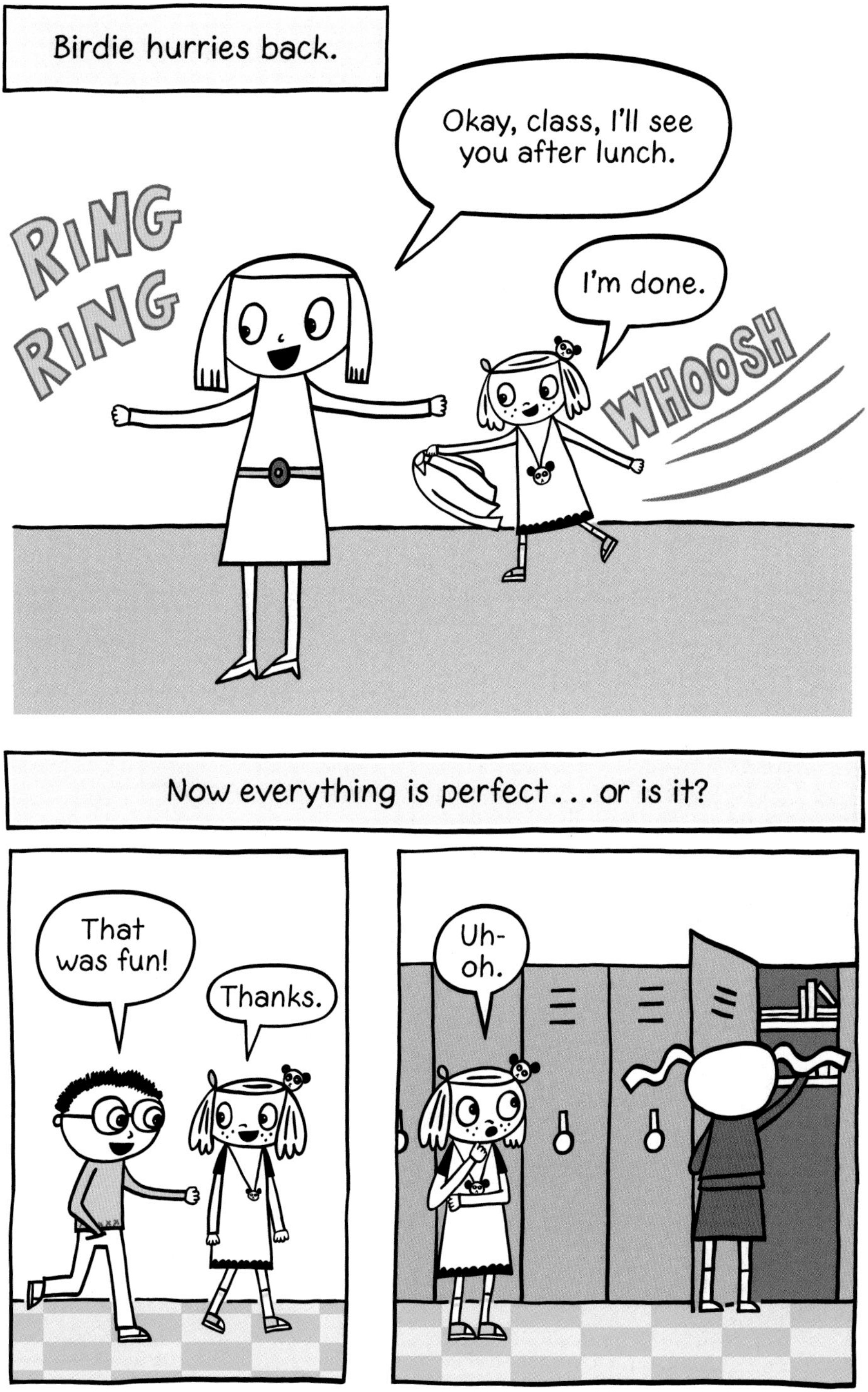
Birdie hurries back.
Okay, class, I'll see you after lunch.
RING RING
I'm done.
WHOOSH
Now everything is perfect . . . or is it?
That was fun!
Thanks.
Uh-oh.

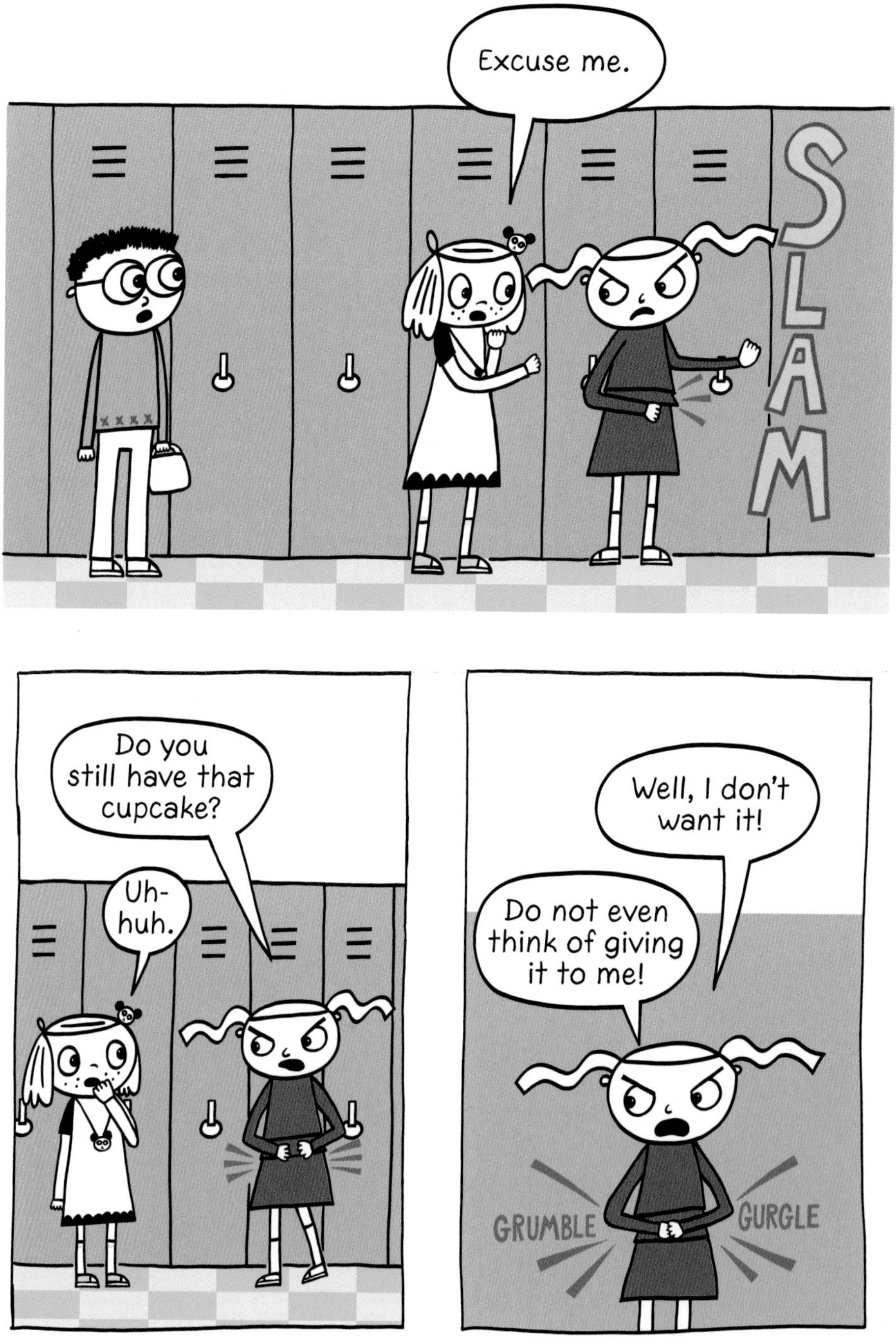
Excuse me.
SLAM
Do you still have that cupcake?
Uh-huh.
Well, I don't want it!
Do not even think of giving it to me!
GRUMBLE
GURGLE

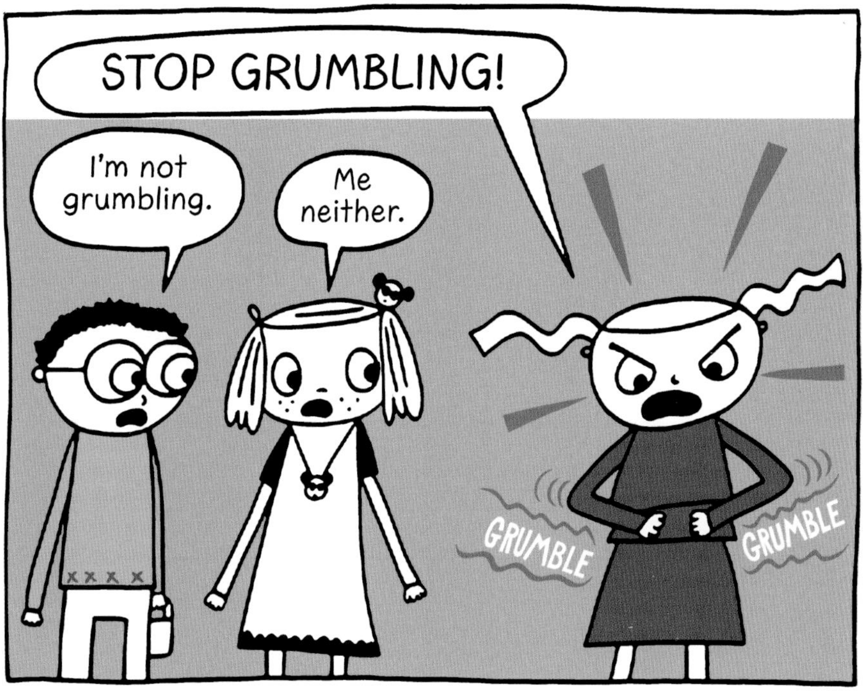
STOP GRUMBLING!
I'm not grumbling.
Me neither.
GRUMBLE
GRUMBLE

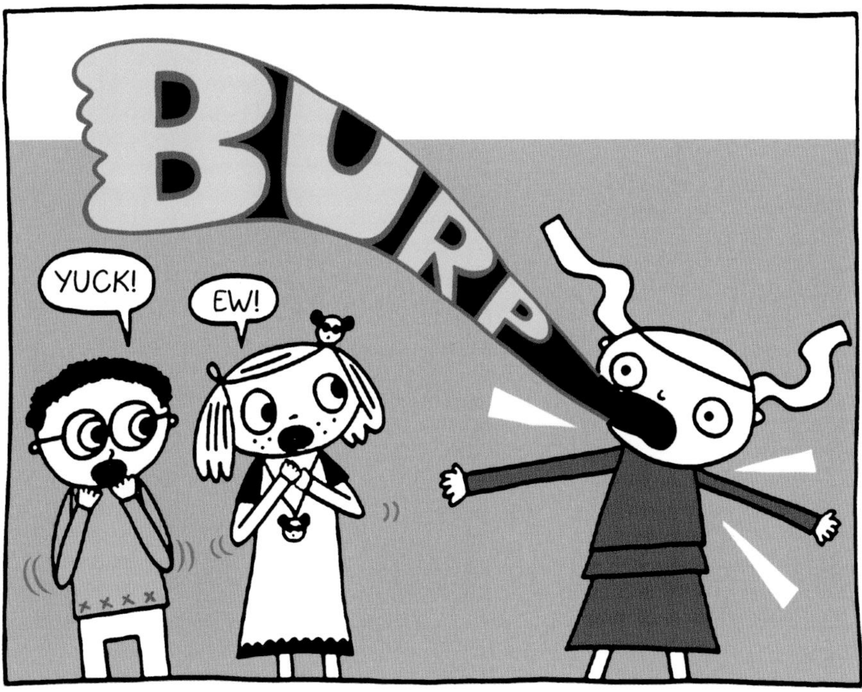
BURP
YUCK!
EW!

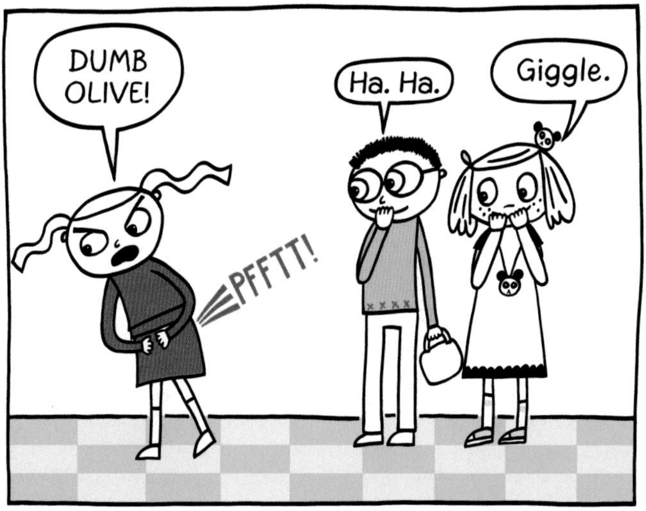
DUMB OLIVE!
PFFTT!
Ha. Ha.
Giggle.

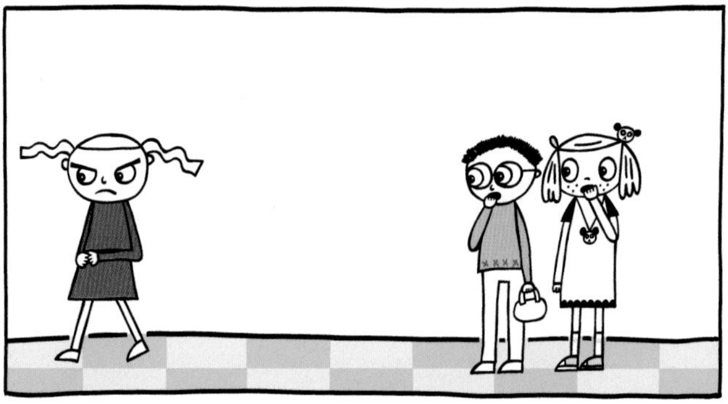

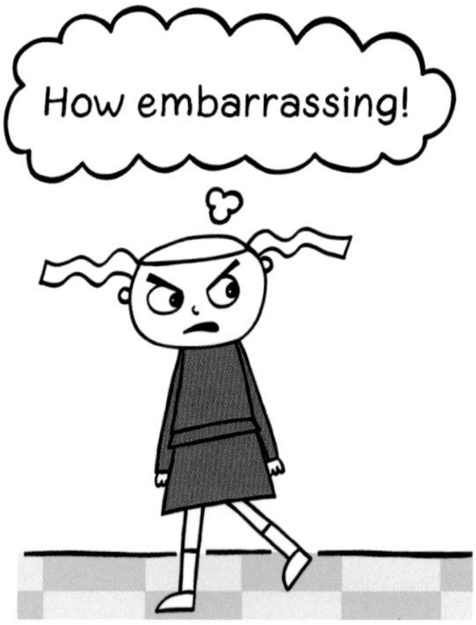
How embarrassing!

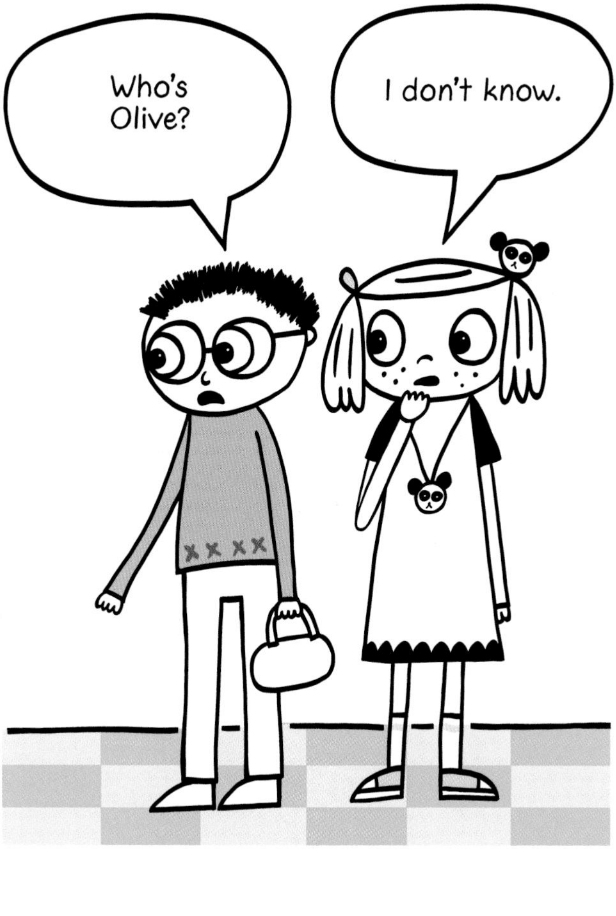
Who's Olive?
I don't know.

Are you hungry?
I'm hungry.
Let's get out of here before she comes back.
Good idea.

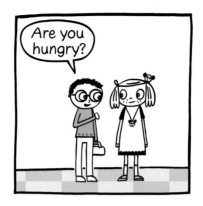

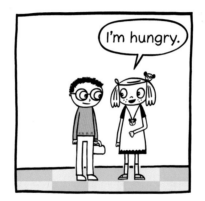

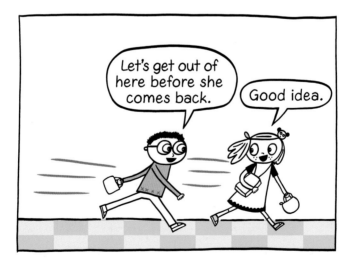

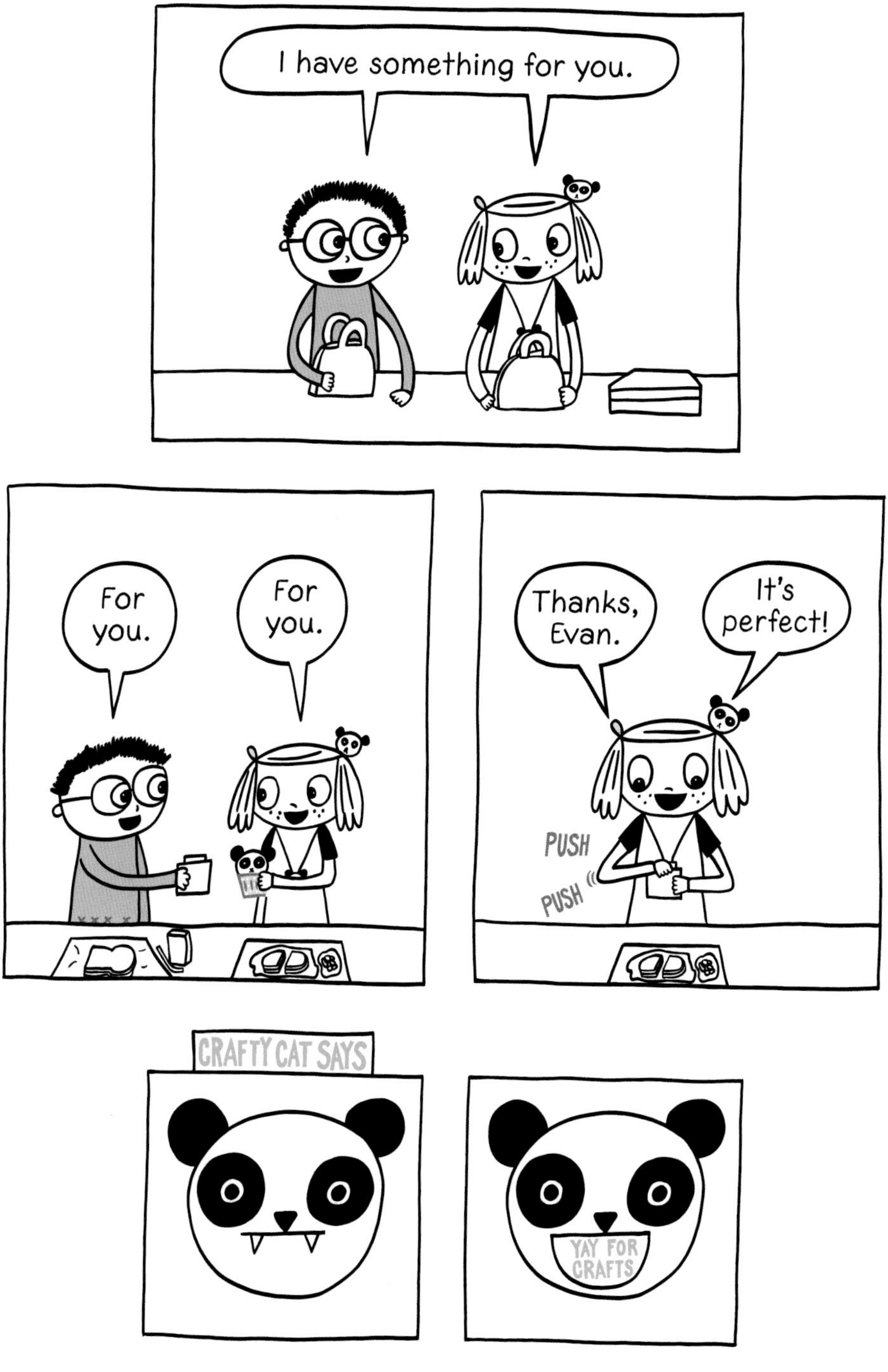
I have something for you.
For you.
For you.
Thanks, Evan.
It's perfect!
PUSH
PUSH
CRAFTY CAT SAYS
YAY FOR CRAFTS

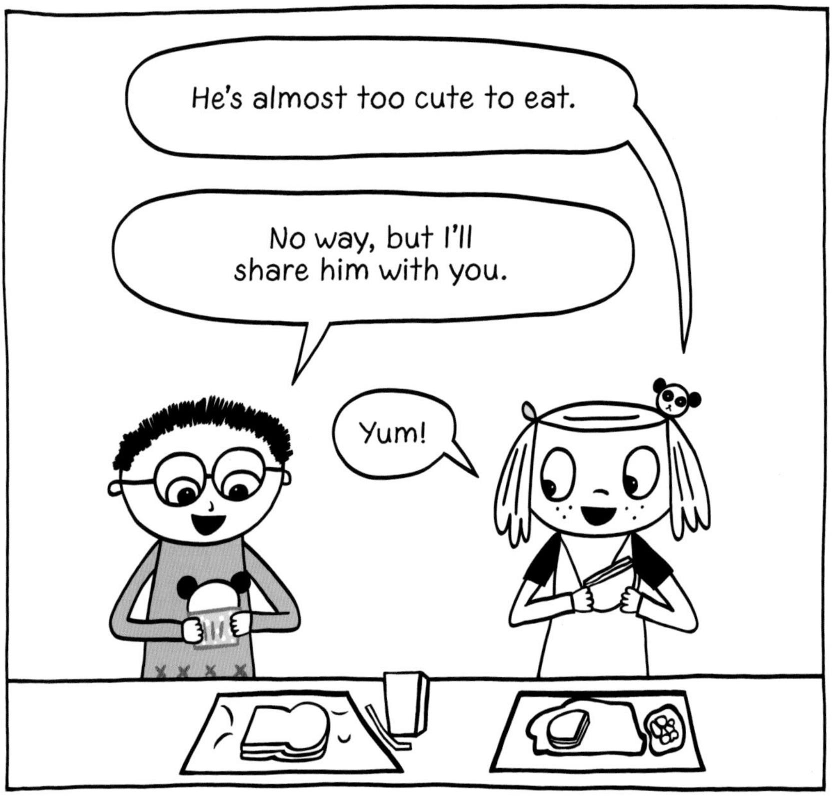
He's almost too cute to eat.
No way, but I'll share him with you.
Yum!

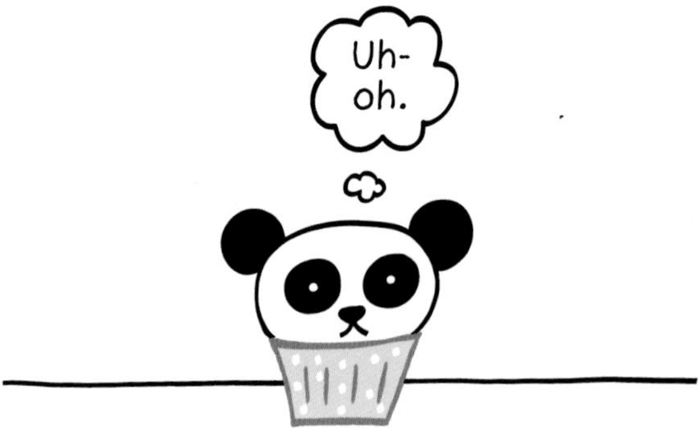
Uh-oh.

So, Birdie, was everything perfect?

NO! Not even close.

But it was still a great birthday.

She is happy.

PUSH
PUSH

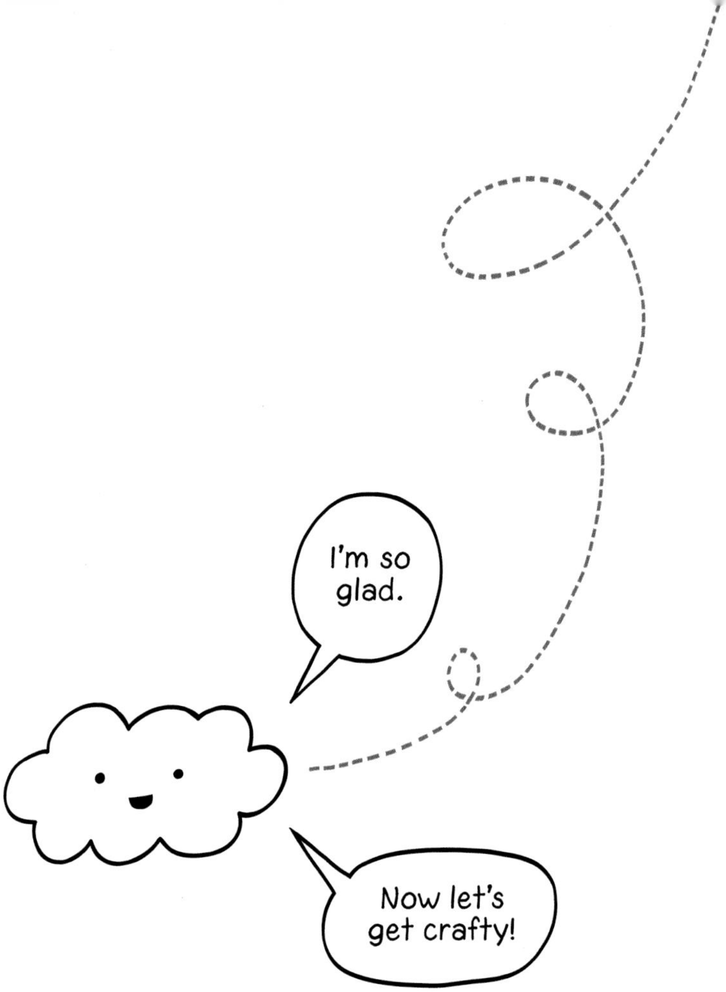
I'm so glad.
Now let's get crafty!

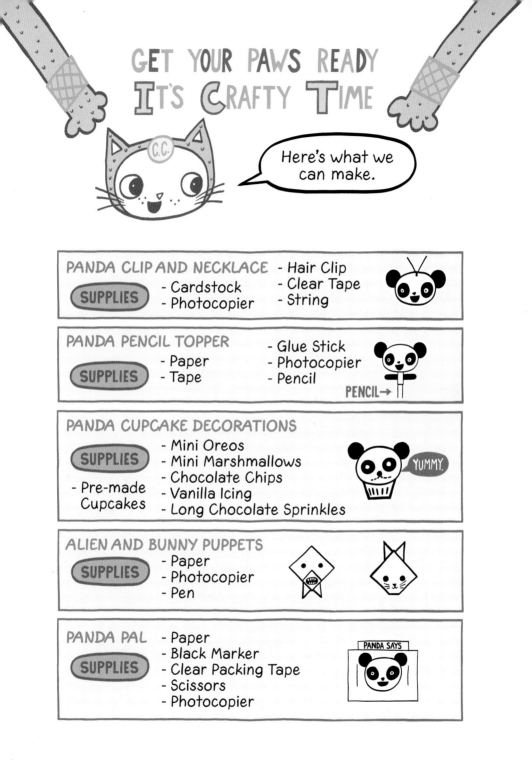

GET YOUR PAWS READY
IT'S CRAFTY TIME

C.C.

Here's what we can make.

PANDA CLIP AND NECKLACE
SUPPLIES
- Cardstock
- Photocopier
- Hair Clip
- Clear Tape
- String

PANDA PENCIL TOPPER
SUPPLIES
- Paper
- Tape
- Glue Stick
- Photocopier
- Pencil

PENCIL →

PANDA CUPCAKE DECORATIONS
SUPPLIES
- Pre-made Cupcakes
- Mini Oreos
- Mini Marshmallows
- Chocolate Chips
- Vanilla Icing
- Long Chocolate Sprinkles

YUMMY

ALIEN AND BUNNY PUPPETS
SUPPLIES
- Paper
- Photocopier
- Pen

PANDA PAL
SUPPLIES
- Paper
- Black Marker
- Clear Packing Tape
- Scissors
- Photocopier

PANDA SAYS

PANDA HAIR CLIP

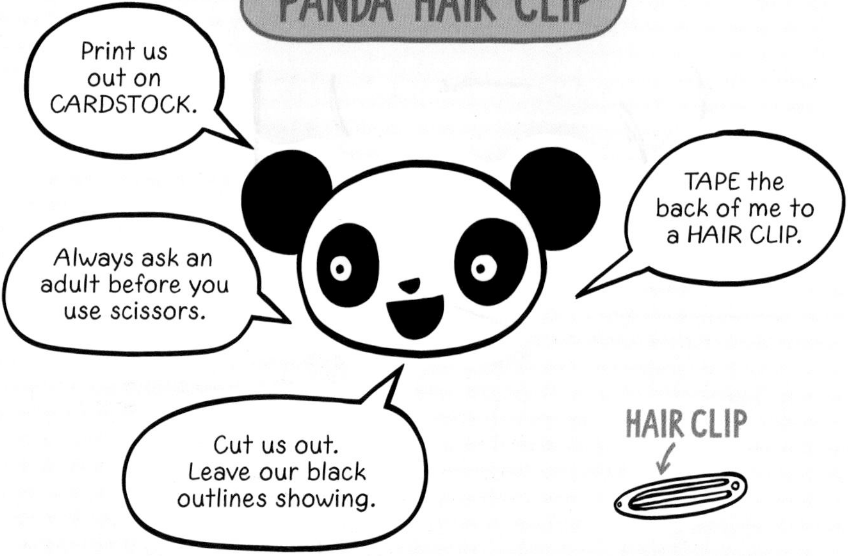
Print us out on CARDSTOCK.
TAPE the back of me to a HAIR CLIP.
Always ask an adult before you use scissors.
Cut us out. Leave our black outlines showing.
HAIR CLIP

PANDA NECKLACE

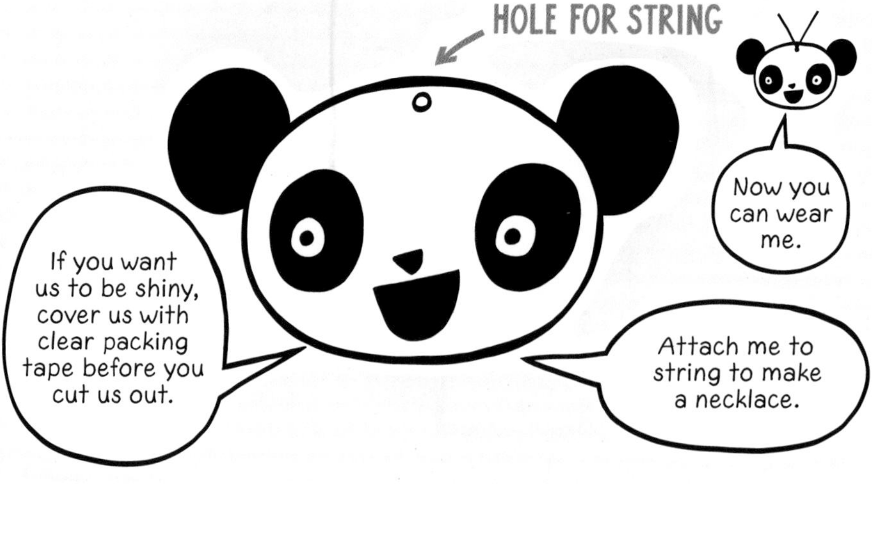
HOLE FOR STRING
Now you can wear me.
If you want us to be shiny, cover us with clear packing tape before you cut us out.
Attach me to string to make a necklace.

PANDA PENCIL TOPPER

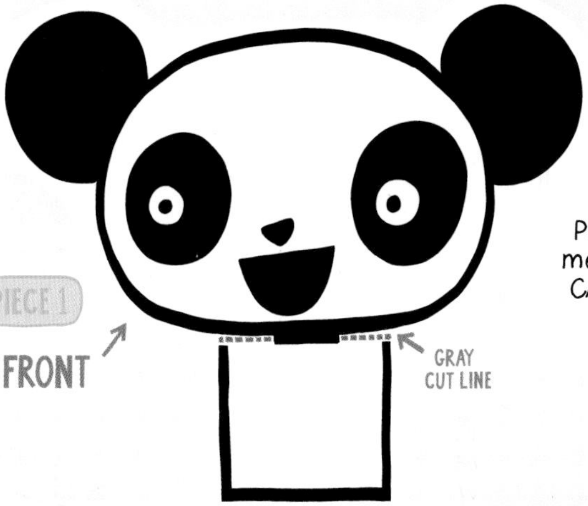

STEP 1

PHOTOCOPY me onto white CARDSTOCK.

PIECE 1

THE FRONT

GRAY CUT LINE

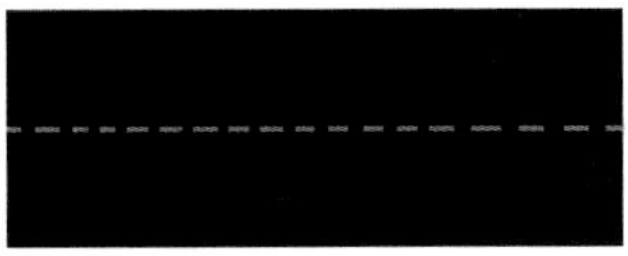

GRAY FOLD LINE

PIECE 3

THE ARMS

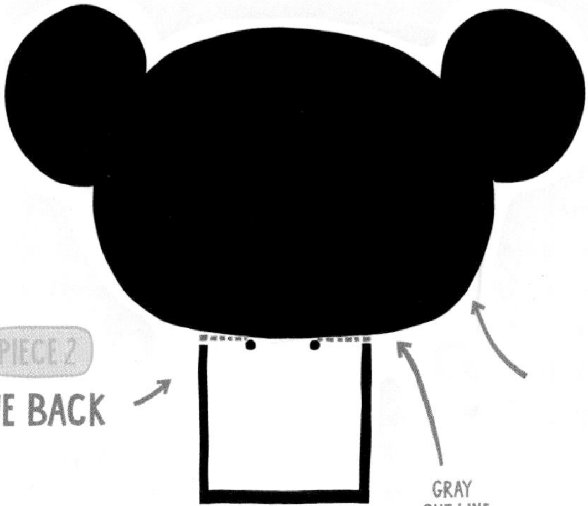

STEP 2

CUT out pieces **1, 2,** and **3.** Leave the black line showing.

PIECE 2

THE BACK

GRAY CUT LINE

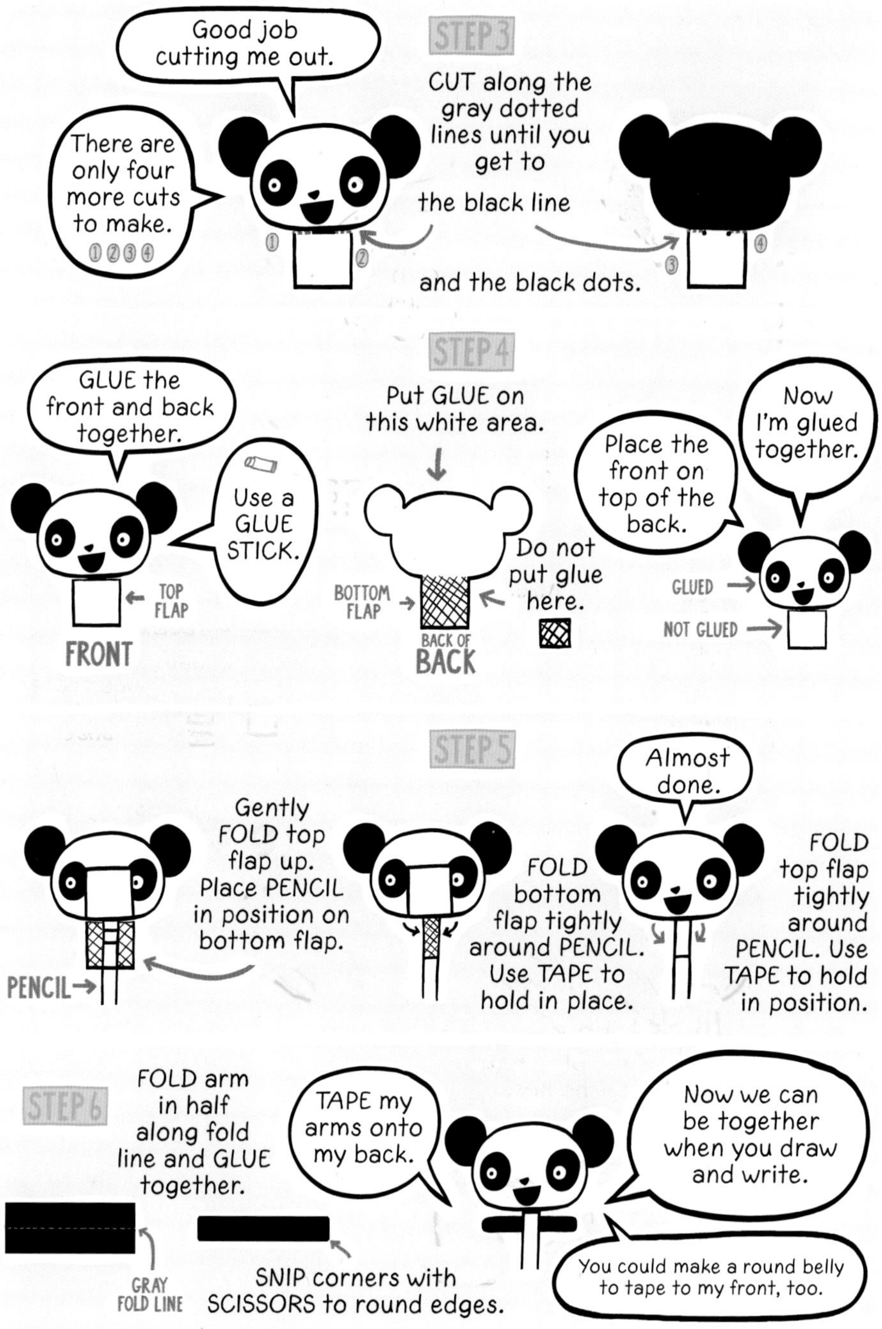
STEP 3
Good job cutting me out.
There are only four more cuts to make. ① ② ③ ④
CUT along the gray dotted lines until you get to the black line
and the black dots.
① ② ③ ④
STEP 4
GLUE the front and back together.
Use a GLUE STICK.
TOP FLAP
FRONT
Put GLUE on this white area.
BOTTOM FLAP
BACK OF BACK
Do not put glue here.
Place the front on top of the back.
Now I'm glued together.
GLUED
NOT GLUED
STEP 5
Gently FOLD top flap up. Place PENCIL in position on bottom flap.
PENCIL
FOLD bottom flap tightly around PENCIL. Use TAPE to hold in place.
Almost done.
FOLD top flap tightly around PENCIL. Use TAPE to hold in position.
STEP 6
FOLD arm in half along fold line and GLUE together.
GRAY FOLD LINE
SNIP corners with SCISSORS to round edges.
TAPE my arms onto my back.
Now we can be together when you draw and write.
You could make a round belly to tape to my front, too.

PANDA CUPCAKE DECORATIONS

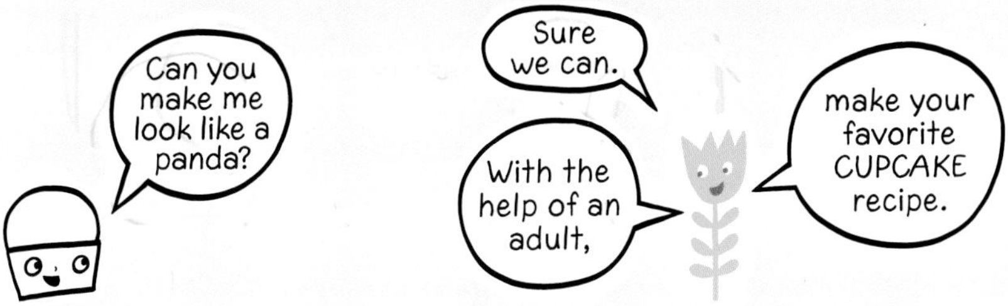

Can you make me look like a panda?
Sure we can.
With the help of an adult,
make your favorite CUPCAKE recipe.

1. ICE your cupcake with VANILLA ICING.

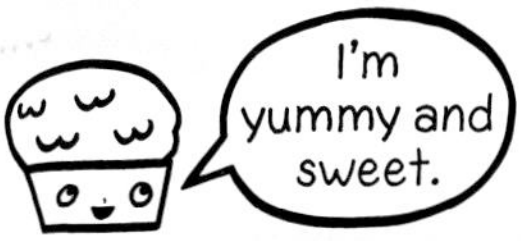

I'm yummy and sweet.

2. Break apart **2** MINI OREO COOKIES. Use them for

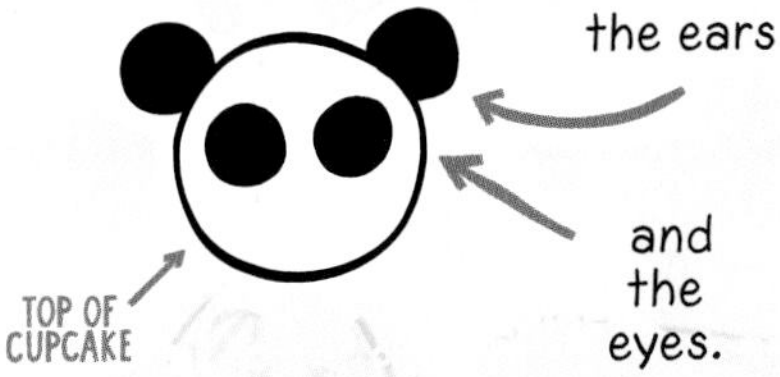

the ears
and the eyes.
TOP OF CUPCAKE

3. Slice **1** MINI MARSHMALLOW in half.

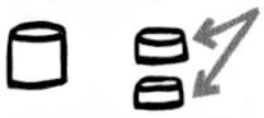

Use these for the eyes.

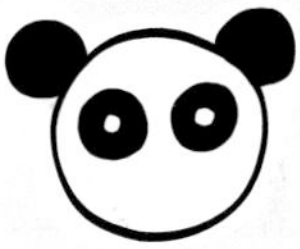

Stick them on with a little drop of ICING.

4. Use an upside-down CHOCOLATE CHIP for the nose.

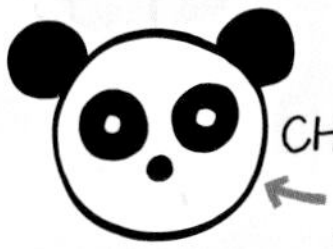

5. Use LONG CHOCOLATE SPRINKLES to make the mouth.

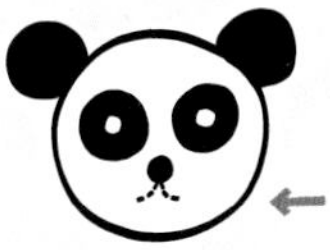

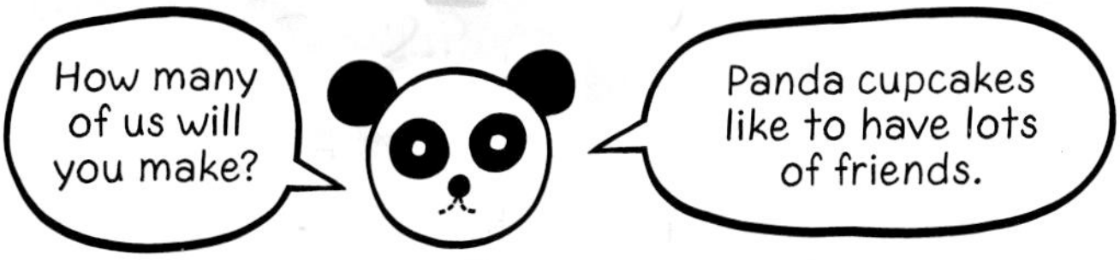

How many of us will you make?
Panda cupcakes like to have lots of friends.

ALIEN PUPPET AND BUNNY PUPPET

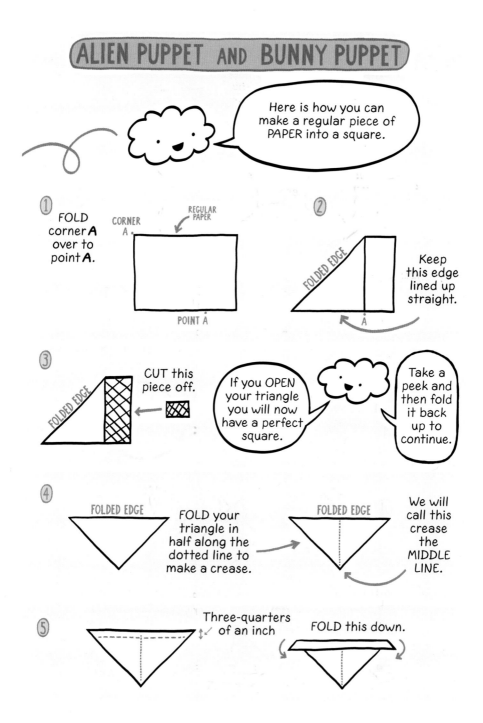

Here is how you can make a regular piece of PAPER into a square.

① FOLD corner **A** over to point **A**.

CORNER A

REGULAR PAPER

POINT A

② Keep this edge lined up straight.

FOLDED EDGE

A

③ CUT this piece off.

FOLDED EDGE

If you OPEN your triangle you will now have a perfect square.

Take a peek and then fold it back up to continue.

④ FOLDED EDGE

FOLD your triangle in half along the dotted line to make a crease.

FOLDED EDGE

We will call this crease the MIDDLE LINE.

⑤ Three-quarters of an inch

FOLD this down.

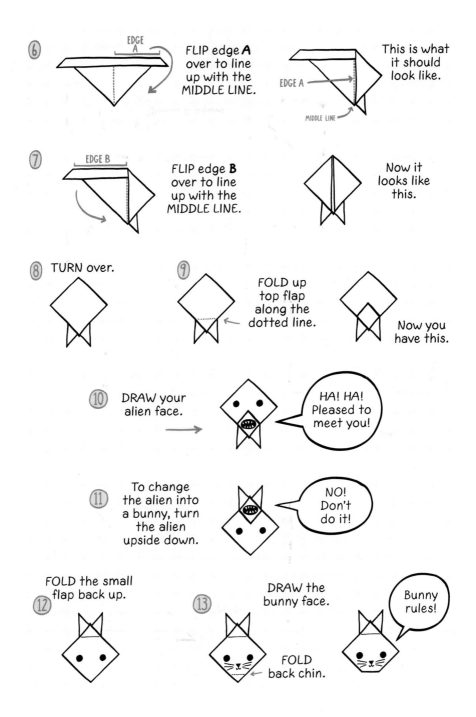

6. FLIP edge **A** over to line up with the MIDDLE LINE.

EDGE A

This is what it should look like.

EDGE A

MIDDLE LINE

7. FLIP edge **B** over to line up with the MIDDLE LINE.

EDGE B

Now it looks like this.

8. TURN over.

9. FOLD up top flap along the dotted line.

Now you have this.

10. DRAW your alien face.

HA! HA! Pleased to meet you!

11. To change the alien into a bunny, turn the alien upside down.

NO! Don't do it!

12. FOLD the small flap back up.

13. DRAW the bunny face.

FOLD back chin.

Bunny rules!

PANDA PAL

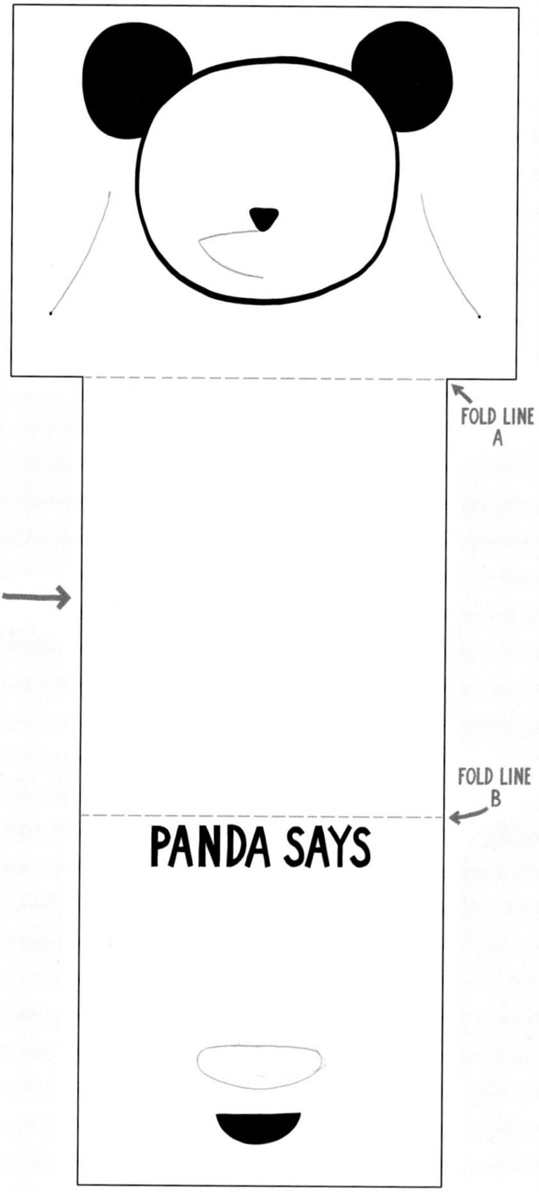
FOLD LINE
A
FOLD LINE
B
PANDA SAYS

1. PHOTOCOPY this template at 115% onto CARDSTOCK.

2. CUT out your Panda Pal along the black line.

3. FOLD on fold line **A** and fold line **B**.

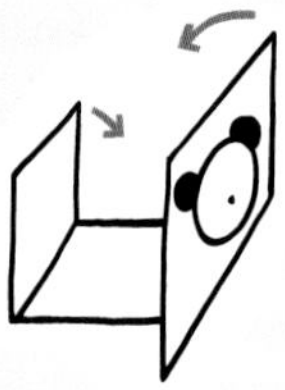

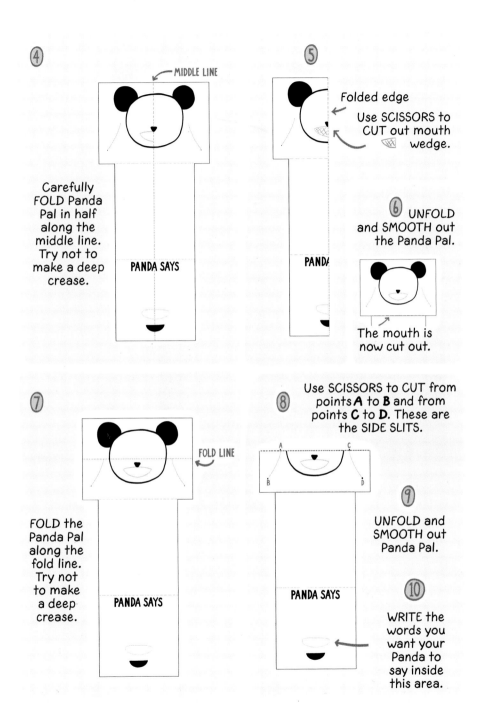

④

MIDDLE LINE

Carefully FOLD Panda Pal in half along the middle line. Try not to make a deep crease.

PANDA SAYS

⑤

Folded edge

Use SCISSORS to CUT out mouth wedge.

⑥ UNFOLD and SMOOTH out the Panda Pal.

PANDA

The mouth is now cut out.

⑦

FOLD LINE

FOLD the Panda Pal along the fold line. Try not to make a deep crease.

PANDA SAYS

⑧ Use SCISSORS to CUT from points **A** to **B** and from points **C** to **D**. These are the SIDE SLITS.

A   C

B   D

⑨ UNFOLD and SMOOTH out Panda Pal.

PANDA SAYS

⑩ WRITE the words you want your Panda to say inside this area.

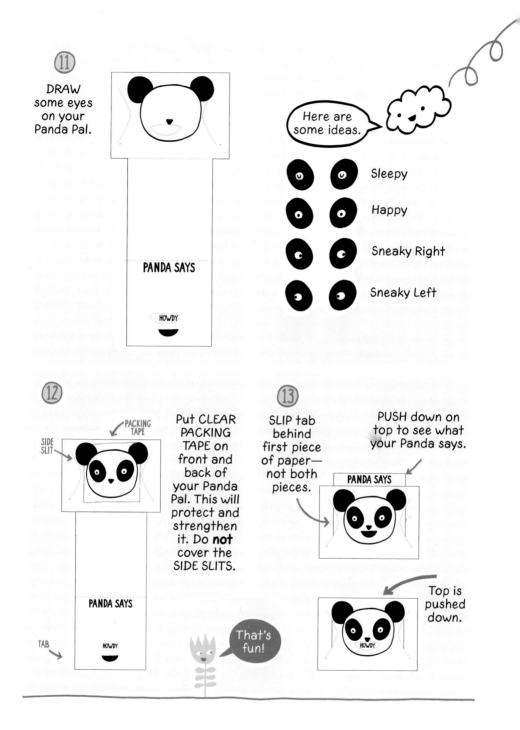

11 DRAW some eyes on your Panda Pal.

PANDA SAYS

HOWDY

Here are some ideas.

Sleepy

Happy

Sneaky Right

Sneaky Left

12 Put CLEAR PACKING TAPE on front and back of your Panda Pal. This will protect and strengthen it. Do **not** cover the SIDE SLITS.

PACKING TAPE

SIDE SLIT

PANDA SAYS

HOWDY

TAB

That's fun!

13 SLIP tab behind first piece of paper— not both pieces.

PUSH down on top to see what your Panda says.

PANDA SAYS

Top is pushed down.

HOWDY

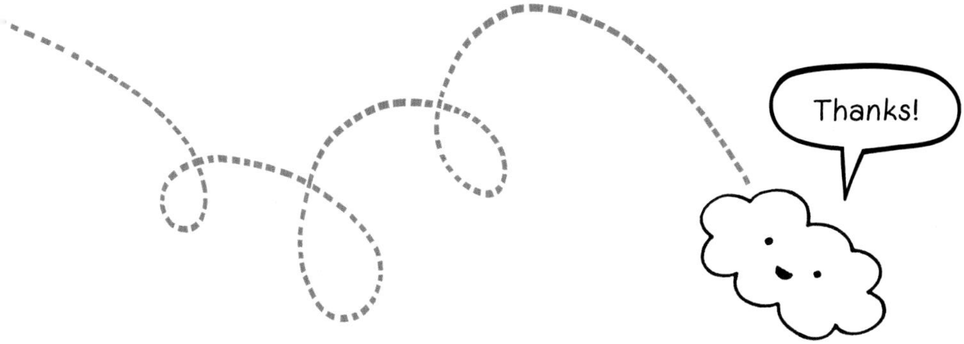
Thanks!

Charise would like to thank
the amazing people who made
this book possible.

Her mom, for teaching her hands to be crafty.
Her parents, for buying her French comic books.
Her brother, for being an imagination buddy.
Her editor, for championing this vision.

High-five crafty paw for all of you!

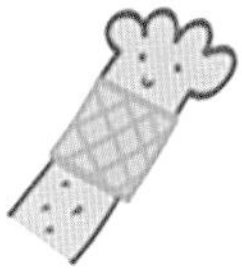

Be sure to join Birdie in her next adventure!

CRAFTY CAT

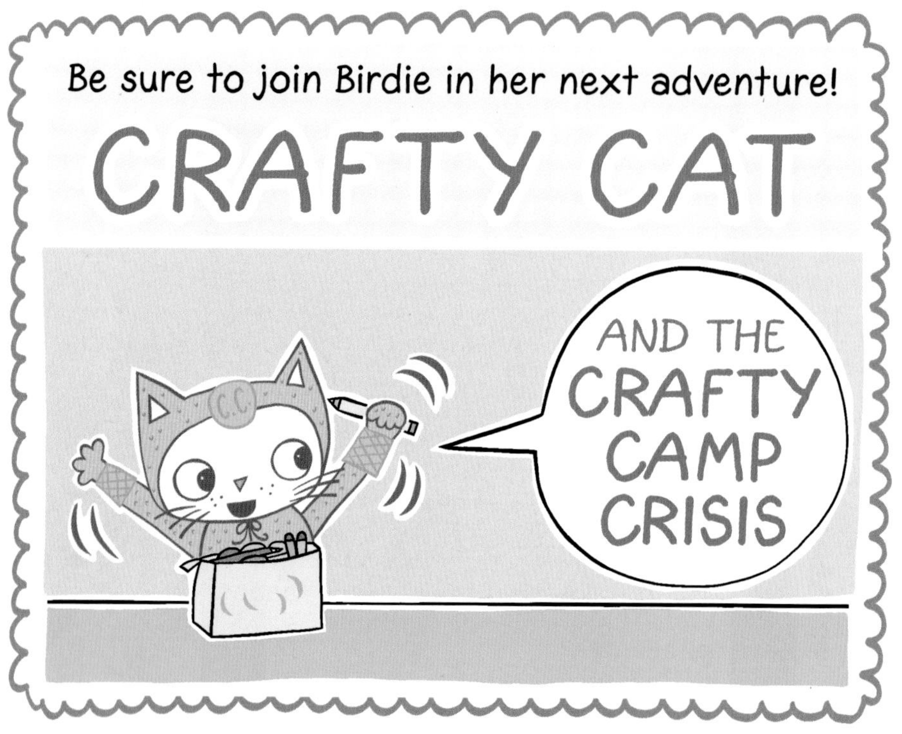
AND THE CRAFTY CAMP CRISIS